Jean Aicard

King of Camargue

Jean Aicard

King of Camargue

1st Edition | ISBN: 978-3-73407-618-3

Place of Publication: Frankfurt am Main, Germany

Year of Publication: 2019

Outlook Verlag GmbH, Germany.

Reproduction of the original.

KING OF CAMARGUE

JEAN AICARD

PRINTED FOR SUBSCRIBERS ONLY BY
GEORGE BARRIE & SONS, PHILADELPHIA

THIS EDITION OF

KING OF CAMARGUE

HAS BEEN COMPLETELY TRANSLATED

BY

GEORGE B. IVES

THE ETCHINGS ARE BY

LOUIS V. RUET

AND DRAWINGS BY

GEORGE ROUX

CHEFS-D'ŒUVRE
DU
ROMAN CONTEMPORAIN

———

ROMANCISTS

THIS EDITION

DEDICATED TO THE HONOR OF THE

ACADÉMIE FRANÇAISE

IS LIMITED TO ONE THOUSAND NUMBERED AND REGISTERED
SETS, OF WHICH THIS IS

NUMBER 358

THE ROMANCISTS

JEAN AICARD

KING OF CAMARGUE

Chapter VI

This woman had a way of looking at people that disconcerted them. You would say that a sharp, threatening flame shot from her eyes. It penetrated your being, searched your heart, and you were powerless against it.

TO ÉMILE TRÉLAT

My Very Dear Friend:

Permit me to dedicate this book to you, whose incomparable friendship has been to the poet, obstinate in his idealism, of hourly assistance, a constant proof of the reality of true generosity and kindness of heart.

3

JEAN AICARD.

La Garde, near Toulon, April 1 , 1890.

KING OF CAMARGUE

I

LIVETTE AND ZINZARA

A shadow suddenly darkened the narrow window. Livette, who was running hither and thither, setting the table for supper, in the lower room of the farmhouse of the Château d'Avignon, gave a little shriek of terror, and looked up.

The girl had an instinctive feeling that it was neither father nor grandmother, nor any of her dear ones, but some stranger, who sought amusement by thus taking her by surprise.

Nor a stranger, either, for that matter,—it was hardly possible!—But how was it that the dogs did not yelp? Ah! this Camargue is frequented by bad people, especially at this season, toward the end of May, on account of the festival of Saintes-Maries-de-la-Mer, which attracts, like a fair, such a crowd of people, thieves and gulls, and so many mischievous gipsies!

The figure that was leaning on the outside of the window-sill, shutting out the light, looked to Livette like a black mass, sharply outlined against the blue sky; but by the thick, curly hair, surmounted by a tinsel crown, by the general contour of the bust, by the huge ear-rings with an amulet hanging at the ends, Livette recognized a certain gipsy woman who was universally known as the Queen, and who, for nearly two weeks, had been suddenly appearing to people at widely distant points on the island, always unexpectedly, as if she rose out of the ditches or clumps of thorn-broom or the water of the swamps, to say to the laborers, preferably the women: "Give me this or that;" for the Queen, as a general rule, would not accept what people chose to offer her, but only what she chose that they should offer her.

"Give me a little oil in a bottle, Livette," said the young gipsy, darting a dark, flashing glance at the pretty girl with the fair, sun-flecked hair.

Livette, charitable as she was at every opportunity, at once felt that she must be on her guard against this vagabond, who knew her name. Her father and grandmother had gone to Arles, to see the notary, who would soon have to be drawing up the papers for her marriage to Renaud, the handsomest drover in all Camargue. She was alone in the house. Distrust gave her strength to refuse.

"Our Camargue isn't an olive country," said she curtly, "oil is scarce here. I haven't any."

"But I see some in the jar at the bottom of the cupboard, beside the water-pitcher."

Livette turned hastily toward the cupboard. It was closed; but, in truth, the stock of olive oil was there in a jar beside the one in which they kept Rhône water for their daily needs.

"I don't know what you mean," said Livette.

"The lie came from your mouth like a vile black wasp from a garden-flower, little one!" said the motionless figure, still leaning heavily on the window-sill, evidently determined to remain. "The oil is where I say it is, and more than twenty-five litres too; I can see it from here. Come, come, take a clean bottle and the tin funnel and give me quickly what I want. I'll tell you, in exchange, what I see in your future."

"It's a deadly sin to seek to know what God doesn't wish us to know," said Livette, "and you can guess that oil is kept in cupboards and still be no more of a sorceress than I am. Go about your business, good-wife. I can give you some of this bread, fresh baked last night, if you wish, but I tell you I haven't any oil."

"And why do they call you Livette," said the Queen calmly, "if it isn't on account of the field of old olive-trees—the oldest and finest in the country—owned by your father, near Avignon? There you were born. There you remained until you were ten years old, and at that age—seven years ago, a mystic number—you came here, where your father was made farmer, overseer of drovers, manager of everything, by the Avignonese master of this 'Château d'Avignon,' the finest in all Camargue.—'Livettes! livettes!' that's the way you used to ask for *olivettes*, olives, when you were a baby. You were very fond of them, and the nickname clung to you. A pretty nickname, on my word, and one that suits you well, for if you're not dark like the ripe olive, you're fair as the virgin oil, a pearl of amber in the sunlight, and then you are not yet ripe. Your face is oval, and not stupidly round like a Norman apple. You have the pallor of the olive-leaves seen from below.—And that you may soon see them so, little one, is the blessing I ask for you, as the curés of your chapels say, where they take us in for pity. Be compassionate as they are, in the name of your Lord Jesus Christ, and give me some oil quickly, I say—in the name of extreme unction and the garden of agony!"

The gipsy had said all this without stopping to breathe, in a dull, monotonous, muffled voice, but she added abruptly in loud, piercing, incisive tones: "Do you understand what I say?" imparting to those simple words an

7

extraordinarily imperious and violent expression. Livette hastily crossed herself.

"Come, enough of this!" said she, "I have nothing here for you, and we keep the oil of extreme unction for better Christians! Begone, pagan, begone!" she added, trying to counterfeit courage.

"Of the three holy women," continued the gipsy, "who took ship, after the death of Jesus Christ, to escape the crucifying Jews, one was like myself, an Egyptian and a fortune-teller. She knew the science of the Magi, of those with whom great Moses contended for mastery in witchcraft. She could, at will, order the frogs to be more numerous than the drops of water in the swamps, and she held in her hand a rod which, at her word, would change to a viper. Before Jesus she bowed, as did Magdalen, and Jesus loved her too. In the tempest, as they were crossing the sea, her wand pointed out the course to follow, and, to do that with safety, had no need to be very long. Must you have more pledges of my power and my knowledge? What more must I tell you to induce you to give me the oil I need so much? If you were a man, I would say: 'Look! I am dark, but I am beautiful! I am a descendant of that Sara the Egyptian who, when the boat of the three holy women drew near the sands of Camargue, paid the boatman by showing him her undefiled body, stripped naked, with no thought of evil and without sin, but knowing well that true beauty is rare and that the mere sight of it is better than all the treasures of Solomon. So be it!'"

Livette was thoroughly alarmed. The gipsy's assurance, her hollow, penetrating voice, imperious by fits and starts, these strange tales filled with evil words on sacred subjects, this devilish mixture of things pagan and things mystic, the consciousness of her own loneliness, all combined to terrify her. She lost her head.

"Away with you, away with you," she cried, "queen of robbers! queen of brigands! away with you, or I will call for help!"

"Your drover won't hear you; he's tending his drove to-day beside the Vaccarès. Come, give me the oil, I say, or I'll throw this black wand on the ground, and you will see how snakes bite!"

But Livette, brave and determined, said: "No!" shuddering as she said it, and, to glean a little comfort, cast a glance at the low beam along which her father's gun was hanging. The gipsy saw the glance.

"Oh! I am not afraid of your gun," said she, "and to prove it—wait a moment!"

She left the window. The light streamed into the room, bringing a little courage to Livette's terrified heart, as she followed the gipsy with her eyes. In the bright light of that beautiful May evening, the gipsy woman stood out, a tall figure, against the distant, unbroken horizon line of the Camargue desert, which could be seen through a vista between the lofty trees of the park.

Livette felt a thrill of joy as she saw a troop of mares trotting along the horizon, followed by their driver, spear in air—Jacques Renaud, her fiancé, without doubt.—But how far away he was! the horses, from where she stood, looked smaller than a flock of little goats. And her eyes came back to the gipsy queen. A few steps from the farm-house, in front of the seigniorial château, a huge square structure, with numerous windows, long closed,—a structure of the sort that arouses thoughts of neglect and death and the grave, —the gipsy stood on tiptoe, drawing down the lowest branch of a thorn-tree. The thorns were long, as long as one's finger. With a twig of a tree of that species the crown of the Crucified One was made.

She broke off a twig thickset with thorns, bent it into a circle, twisting the two ends together like serpents, and returned to the window.

Livette noticed at that moment that the two watch-dogs were following the gipsy, with their tails between their legs, their noses close to her heels, with little affectionate whines. And she, the gipsy Queen, as slender as haughty, erect upon her legs, in a ragged skirt with ample folds through the holes in which could be seen a bright red petticoat, her bust enveloped in orange-colored rags crossed below her well-rounded breasts, her amulets tinkling at her ears, medallions jangling on her forehead, which was encircled by a gaudy fillet of copper,—she, the Queen, came forward, holding in her hand the crown of long stiff thorns, to which a few tiny green leaves clung in quivering festoons;—and in a low, very low tone, she murmured the same caressing plaint that the two great cowed dogs were murmuring, saying to them, in their own language, mysterious things they understood.

"Take this," said the gipsy, "let your kind heart be rewarded as it deserves! Misfortune, which is at work for you, will soon make itself known to you. How, may God tell you! In love, the wind that blows for you is poisoned by the swamps. The charity your God enjoins is, so they say, another form of love that brings true love good fortune. And here is my queenly gift!"

She threw the crown of thorns through the window at Livette's feet.

"Madame!" exclaimed Livette in dismay.

But the gipsy had disappeared.

Infinite distress filled the poor child's heart. With her eyes fixed on the crown, Livette recalled the legends in which the good Lord Jesus appears disguised as a beggar—and in which He rewards those who have received Him with sweet compassion.

In one of those legends, the Poor Man, welcomed with harsh words, subjected to mockery and cowardly insults, struck with staves and goblets and bottles thrown by drunken revellers—at last, standing against the wall, begins to be transformed into a Christ upon the Cross, bleeding at the holes in his hands and feet!—And, sick with terror, she asked herself if she had not received with unkindness one of the three holy women who, after the death of Jesus, crossed the sea in a boat to the shores of Camargue, using their skirts for sails, and assisted by the oars of a boatman, whom one of their number, Sara the Egyptian, paid in heathen coin, by allowing him to see, as the price of a Christian action, her undefiled body, entirely naked, upon the self-same spot on which the church stands to-day.

Slowly she picked up the crown and threw it into the fire over which the soup was stewing. Before it melted into ashes, the crown of thorns seemed for a moment to be pure gold.

II

IN CAMARGUE

Every year, at Saintes-Maries-de-la-Mer, the village that stands at the southern end of Camargue, above the marshes, on a sand beach, the line of which is constantly changed by the action of the waves and high winds, every year, the feast of Saintes-Maries is celebrated on May 24th; and at the time of that festival the gipsies flock to Camargue in large numbers, impelled by a curious sort of piety, mingled with a desire to pilfer the pilgrims.

Legends, like trees, spring from the soil,—are its expression, so to speak. They are also its essence. At every step in Camargue, you find the everlasting legend of the holy women, just as you everlastingly see there the same tamarisk-trees, confused, against the horizon, with the same mirages.

The two Marys, so runs the legend, Jacobé, Salomé, and—according to some authorities—Magdalen, and with them their bondwomen, Marcella and Sara, adrift on the sea in a boat without masts or sails, pursued by the accursed Jews, after the Saviour's death, spread to the breeze strips of their skirts and their long, thin veils, and the wind carried them to this beach at Camargue.

There a church was built. The sacred bones, found by King René, were enclosed in a reliquary, which has never ceased to perform miracles. And every year, from every corner of Provence, from the Comtat and from Languedoc, the last of the believers throng to the spot, bringing their aspirations and their prayers, dragging with them their sick friends and kindred, or their own wretchedness, their wounds and their lamentations.

Nothing more strange can be imagined than this land of desolation, traversed every year by a multitude of cripples on their way to hope!

From afar, at the end of the desert tract, can be seen the battlemented church that tells of the wars of long ago, of Saracen invasions, of the precarious life led by the poor in the Middle Ages. It stands there with its turrets and its bell-tower, which, like the stumps of gigantic masts, tower above the cluster of houses grouped about it; and the village, cut at about mid-height of the lower houses by the horizon line of the sea, seems drifting like a phantom ship among the billows of sand, like the boat of the holy women of the olden time, doomed to founder at last in the desolation of the desert.

In this Camargue everything is strange. There are ponds like the huge central pond, the Vaccarès, in the centre of which one can wade with ease; there are tracts of land where the pedestrian sinks out of sight and is drowned. Here deception is easy. Yonder green slime that you take for a level plain—beware! —men are drowned therein; those vast stretches of water which seem to you small seas—return that way to-morrow; they will have evaporated, leaving only a mirror of white salt that crackles beneath your feet. Yonder, do you see the calm, deep water? and trees on the shore? Ah! no, you can run along the surface of that water; it is dry land; the mirage alone formed those trees, just as it showed you the little child walking a league away, apparently near at hand and very tall. A land of visions, dreams, and hard work. A land of sedentary folk, who inhabit a vast space on the shore of endless waters, with an infinity of variations of mirages, sunbeams, reflections, and bright colors. A land of fever, where strong men daily bring wild bulls to earth. A land of leave-takings, for it is on the confines of an almost uninhabited land, on the shore of that great blue and white thoroughfare, the sea; just at the point where the Rhône, coming from the mountains, sets out upon its long journey to the bottomless waters, where the sun will take it up again to restore it to its source. An impressive land, which one feels to be the end of so many things; of the great city-making river, of the great expiring Faith, which flies to the sands to breathe its last, with its dying waves beating at the foundations of a poor battlemented church, amid the psalms, mingled with lamentations of a dying race.

The ceremony of May 24th, at Saintes-Maries-de-la-Mer, is unquestionably one of the most barbarous spectacles which men of modern times are permitted to witness.

Since science made the conquest of men's minds, the faith of the last believers has changed. The most bigoted know, of course, that God can manifest Himself when and how He pleases, but they also know that He never pleases, in our positive days, to modify the movements of the vast mechanism of His creation, not even for the lowly pleasure of proving His existence to His creatures. The faith of civilized men no longer expects anything from Heaven in this world.

Saintes-Maries-de-la-Mer, on the 24th of May, is the rendezvous of the last savages of the Faith.

They who come to pray to the holy women for health of body and of heart are unpolished creatures of a primitive belief. They believe, and that is the whole of it. A cry, a prayer, and, in reply, the saints can give them what they have not: eyes, legs, arms, life! And they ask them to perform a miracle as artlessly as a condemned man implores his pardon from the head of the State. That their prayers should be granted is quite as possible, almost more probable, for the saints have more pity. The few thousands of believers—it is long since

12

their numbers have been added to—who pay a visit to the saints every year, see one or two miracles on each occasion. When the priest, coming from the church, followed by a procession, stretches out toward the sea the *Silver Arm* which contains the relics, they see the sea recede! That happens every year. Imagine, then, how strenuously they importune the saints who can do so much with so little exertion! with what energy they hurry to the spot! with what sighs they pour out their hearts! with what a howling they utter their prayers! with what fervor they raise their eyes, stretch out their necks and their arms! All, all in vain. The last posturings of the great, fruitlessly imploring sorrow are to be seen there, in that desert corner of France, between the arms of that dying stream, on the shore of the sea that is eating away the island; beneath the arches of yonder church, so white without, so black within, wherein every hand holds a taper, flickering like a star of human misery, which burns for God and greases the fingers, and for which the beggar, whose heart would be made glad by a single sou, must pay five sous.

The whole region seems to be at once the highway to exile, and a wild place of refuge. Therefore, the gipsies love it. It is one of the main cross-roads of their interlacing highways which envelop the whole world; it is one of the favorite countries of the race that has no country.

And every year, the gipsies come to Camargue to enjoy their very ancient privilege of occupying a black crypt or underground chapel, under the choir of the church, consecrated to Saint Sara the Egyptian.

In that cavern they can be seen crouching at the foot of an altar whereon is a little shrine—Saint Sara's—all filthy from much kissing, while above, in the church, the great shrines of the two Marys are lowered from the vaulted roof amid vociferous prayers.

There, in the crypt, the gipsies sit upon their haunches, curly-headed, hot-lipped, sweating profusely, amid hundreds of candles, which exude tallow and overheat the stifling oven, telling their greasy beads, exhaling an odor similar to that of wild beasts in their den, emitting from time to time a hoarse appeal to Saint Sara, wearing the smile of premeditated crime upon their faces mingled with the grimace due to remorse that may be sincere; looking with envious eye at every sou, pilfering handkerchiefs, scratching their wounds, swarming in a mysterious dunghill, where one feels, in spite of everything, that some mystic flower is springing into life, the involuntary aspiration of depravity toward purity.

Early in May of this year, the band of gipsies had brought with them to the saints a young woman whom they called their "Queen."

This "Queen," pending the arrival of the approaching fête-day, passed part of her time seated on the wooden bench under the canopy of thorn-broom erected by the customs' officers between two tamarisks, on the sand-dune just in front of the village; and there she sat and gazed at the sea.

Her name was Zinzara.

Her thick, black, wavy hair was twisted carelessly into a mass on top of her head. Two locks came forward to her temples, which were sunken and filled with shadows. Her piercing black eyes gleamed from beneath her thick arching eyebrows. A copper circlet with sequins hanging from it was placed upon her forehead, slightly at one side, after the manner of a crown.

The glaringly bright materials in which she enveloped her figure revealed the outline of her powerful chest, and her hips that swayed at every step she took. And the fragment that formed her skirt fell in graceful folds, beneath which her naked foot peeped out, glistening with sand.

Evening surprised her upon her bench beneath the broom, looking out upon the sea. The sun tinged the waves and the sand with golden yellow, then with red. The night wind made the reeds and rushes quiver. Slowly the gipsy drew a bright-colored handkerchief from her girdle and arranged it on her head. She put it over her face to tie the ends together behind the mass of hair, then raised it and threw it over her head, so that it fell upon her back. Thus arranged as a head-dress, it framed the face in stiff, broad folds, falling on both sides,—and the Egyptian, her hands spread out upon her knees, her eyes fixed on the horizon, resembled some figure of Isis, while about her a flock of red flamingoes or a solitary ibis, in hieroglyphic cries, told the sands of Camargue and the rushes of the Rhône tales of the sands of Libya and the lotus-trees of the Nile.

III

THE DROVERS

Jacques Renaud, Livette's lover, was employed as drover of bulls and horses in this strange Camargue country, on the estate of the Château d'Avignon.

The *manades*, or droves, of Camargue bulls and mares live at liberty in the vast moor, leaping the ditches, splashing through the swamps, browsing on the bitter grass, drinking from the Rhône, running, jumping, wallowing, neighing and lowing at the sun or the mirage, lashing vigorously with their tails the swarms of gadflies clinging to their sides, then lying down in groups on the edge of the swamp, knees doubled under their bulky bodies, tired and sleepy, their dreamy eyes fixed vaguely on the horizon.

The mounted drovers leave them at liberty, but keep a watchful eye on their freedom; and according to the time of year and the condition of the pasturage, "round up" their herds, keep them together, and direct their movements.

In the distance, as they sit motionless, and straight as arrows, on their saddles *à la gardiane*, astride their white horses, with the spear-head resting on the closed stirrup, they resemble knights of the Middle Ages, awaiting the flourish of the herald's trumpet to enter the lists.

The Camargue horse, with his powerful hind-quarters, stout shoulders, head a little heavy,—an excellent beast withal,—is descended from Saracen mares and the palfrey of the Crusades. He still wears antique trappings. Huge closed stirrups strike against his sides; the broad strap of the martingale passes through a heart-shaped piece of leather on his chest, and the saddle is an easy-chair, wherein the rider sits between two solid walls, the one in front as high as that at his back.

At certain times, when the best pasturage is on the other bank of the Rhône, the drovers drive their *manades* toward the river. When they reach the shore, they press close upon them to force them in. The earth-colored water of the river flows bubbling by. The beasts hesitate. Some slowly put their heads down to the stream and drink, not knowing what is required of them. Others suddenly show signs of life at the "singing" of the water, stretch their necks, breathe noisily, and low and neigh. A horse, urged forward by a drover, rebels and rushes back, then rears and falls backward into the water, which splashes mightily under the weight of his great body; but he has made a start; he swims, and all the others follow. Muzzles and nostrils, manes and horns, wave wildly about above the river, which is now a swarm of heads. They blow foam and air and water all around. More than one, in jovial mood, bites at a neighboring rump. Feet rise upon backs, to be shaken off again with a quick movement of the spinal column, and thrown back into the waves. Sometimes a frightened beast, confused by the plunging and kicking, tries to return to the bank, and, being driven in once more by the drovers, loses his head, follows the current, sails swiftly seaward, feels his strength failing, drinks, struggles, turns over and over, plunges, drinks again, founders at last like a vessel and disappears.

Finally the bulk of the drove has reached the opposite bank, and there they shake themselves in the sunlight, snort with delight, and caper over the fields. Tails lash sides and buttocks. Some young horses, excited by their bath, scamper away, side by side, toward the horizon, biting at the long hairs of each other's flying manes.

Then it is the turn of the drovers. Some ride their horses into the river. Others, in the midst of the rearguard of the *manade*, guide, with the paddle, a flat-bottomed boat that a blow of the foot would shatter, and their horses, held by their bridles, swim behind.

At other times, the drovers are employed driving from the plains of Meyran or Arles, Avignon, Nîmes, Aigues-Mortes to the branding-places at Camargue the bulls that are to take part in the sports at the latter place.

These bulls sometimes travel in captivity, in a sort of high enclosure, without a floor, mounted on wheels and drawn by horses; the bulls walk along the ground, beating their horns against the resonant wooden walls.

Generally the bulls go to the games unconfined, but under the eye of mounted drovers, spear in hand.

These journeys are made at night. As they pass through the villages, the people rush to their windows. The young men are on the watch for the "cattle" and try to drive them out of the circle of drovers, who lose their temper, and swear and strike: that sport is called the *abrivade*. In Arles, if the bulls happen to arrive by daylight, the drovers have a hard task, for all the young men in the city do their utmost to break the line of horsemen, in order to cut out one bull, or several, if possible, and then drive them through the city. The city assumes a posture of defence. Overturned carts barricade the ends of the streets. Shops are closed. The bull, in a frenzy, rushes here and there, stands musing for a moment at the corners, decides to take a certain direction, rushes at a passer-by, knocks him down, and generally selects the shop of a dealer in crockery and glassware in which to make merry, amid the shouts of an excited populace.

The drovers are a free, fearless, savage race, a little contemptuous of cities, devoted to their desert.

A drover is at home alike in sun and rain, in the wind from the land, and the wind from the sea.

A drover knows how to deal blows and to receive them; he pursues a bull at the gallop, and with a blow of the spear upon his flank, judiciously selecting his time, "fells" him unerringly.

He knows the trick of pursuing a wild bull making for the open country. His well-trained horse bites the furious beast on the hind-quarters, and he turns. The drover, spear in rest, pricks the bull in the nose as he rushes upon him, and checks him.

Sometimes a drover, on foot and alone, pursued by a cow with calf, and apparently in imminent danger from the furious beast, will suddenly turn about, and—with arm outstretched, as if he held his spear—point his three fingers at the animal, separated so as to represent the three points of the trident. In face of the motionless man, the cow, seized with terror, recoils, pawing up the earth, with lowered head and threatening horns; and, as soon as she thinks she is well out of the man's reach, she turns and flies.

A common performance of the drover, when he is in good spirits, is this: pursuing the bull, he passes beyond him some twenty or thirty yards, then stops short and leaps down from his horse; the bull, taken by surprise, rushes at the man, who has one knee on the ground. The bull comes rushing on with lowered horns. Three sharp hand-claps: the bull has stopped! His hot breath strikes the face of his subduer, who has already seized him with both hands by the horns. The man, springing instantly to his feet, struggles to throw the beast over to the right. The bull, resisting, throws himself in the opposite direction. The two forces neutralize each other for an instant, almost equal, the result uncertain; then the man suddenly yields, and the beast, unexpectedly impelled in the direction of his own efforts, falls upon his side. Skill is seconded by the creature's whole strength in its struggle for victory.

This is the method adopted at the *ferrades*, or brandings, where the sport consists in branding the young animals with a red-hot iron.

For a drover, to seize a colt by the nose, and mount him bareback; to roll with his steed at the bottom of a ditch and emerge firmly seated in the saddle; to subdue stallions by fatigue, and, if dismounted and wounded by a kick, to dress the wound as tranquilly as the cork-cutter dresses the scratch made by his knife,—all this is mere child's-play.

A drover, caught between two horns—luckily well separated—and tossed into

17

the air, has but one thought when he picks himself up after falling to the ground—a thought so surprising as not to be ridiculous: to rearrange his breeches and readjust his belt.

A unique race it is, rough and brutal, which would be esteemed heroic, like the Corsican race, if it had great affairs in which to display its great qualities.

IV

THE SÉDEN

Jacques Renaud, Livette's betrothed, was, as we have said, one of the most fearless drovers in Camargue.

He could pursue and catch and subdue a wild horse, attack a rebellious bull and master it, as no other could; he was the king of the moor.

For occasions of public rejoicing, at Nîmes or Arles, he was always sent for when they desired a really fine performance in the arena. And he had so often called forth the exclamation, in all the arenas throughout Provence: "Oh! that fellow is *the king* of them all!" that the name had clung to him. And he himself had given to his finest stallion the name of "Prince."

Whatever feats of address and strength were performed by others, he performed better than they.

And with it all he was a handsome fellow, not too tall or too short, with a well-shaped head, clear, dark complexion, short, thick, matted black hair, a well-defined moustache of the same devil's black as the hair, and cheeks and chin always closely shaven, for this savage always carried in the leather saddle-bags hanging at the bow of his saddle a razor-edged knife, a stone to sharpen it upon, and a little round mirror in a sheep-skin case.

And when, with his stout and shapely legs encased in heavy boots, his feet in the closed stirrups, his long spear resting on his boot, he sat erect and motionless in his high-backed saddle, his size heightened by the refraction of the desert, amid his little tribe of mares and wild bulls, wearing upon his head the round narrow-brimmed hat that made for him a crown of gleaming golden straw, indeed the drover did resemble the king of some outlandish race!

And yet it was not on the day of a *ferrade*, nor because of his great deeds as tamer of wild beasts, that the gentle, fair-haired girl had come to love him.

In the first place, she was accustomed to seeing many of these drovers; and then, being the daughter of a rich intendant, she might have been inclined rather to look down upon them a little, as mere herdsmen. Indeed her father and grandmother did not readily agree to give her hand to Renaud, who was poor and had no kindred; but Livette was an only child, and had wept and prayed so hard, the darling, that at last they had said *yes*.

And this is how it came to pass that the drover Renaud, who was used to being run after by pretty girls, had taken Livette's trembling little heart in his great hand.

It was one morning when he was making a new *séden* for his horse, who had lost his the night before, while bathing in the Rhône.

The *séden*, as it is called in Camargue, is a halter, but a halter made of mares' hair braided, it being customary always to allow the manes and tails of stallions to grow as long as they will, as a mark of strength and pride. The *séden* is generally black and white. It is, in a word, a long rope, which hangs in a coil about the horse's neck, and may serve, as occasion arises, many purposes, being generally used as a halter, sometimes as a lasso.

But the *séden*, being a thing essentially Camarguese, should never go from the province. Many a one does so, no doubt, but it is on account of the contemptible greed of this or that drover, who snaps his fingers at the old customs that were good enough for his ancestors.

Renaud, then, was making a *séden*. It was in front of one of the farm-houses appertaining to the Château d'Avignon, a long, low structure, rather a drover's cottage than a farm-house, lost in the moor, and so squat that it had the appearance of not wanting to be seen, like an animal burrowing in the ground.

It was October. The larks were singing merrily. Mounted upon Blanquet (or Blanchet), her favorite horse, the little one, in obedience to her father's orders, was out in search of Renaud, and she spied him at a distance, walking backward, playing the rope-maker. From a piece of canvas tied around his waist and swelling out in front of him, like an apron turned up to make a great pocket, he was taking little bunches of white and black hair alternately, braiding them together and twisting them into a rope, which grew visibly longer. A child was turning the thick wooden wheel upon which the *séden*, already of considerable length, was wound; and Renaud—keeping time to the wheel, which struck a dull blow against something or other at every revolution—was singing a ballad which floated to Livette's ears on the gentle breeze that was blowing, like a sweet, strong call from the love of which she as yet knew nothing.

"N'use pas sur les routes
   Tes souliers;
Descends plutôt le Rhône
   En bateau.

"Laisse Lyon, Valence,
   De côté;
Salue-les de la tête
   Sous les ponts."

He had a fine voice, smooth and clear, powerful without effort, and of wide range.

"Avignon est la reine——
   Passe encor;
Tu ne verras qu'en Arles
   Tes amours——

"La plaine est belle et grande,
   Compagnon——
Prends tes amours en croupe,
   En avant!"[1]

Livette had stopped her horse, to hear better. It was in the morning. In the light there was the reflection that tells that the day is young, that makes hope dance in hearts of sixteen, and sows hope anew even in the hearts of the old.

A vague hope that is naught but the desire to love; but its loss, bitterer than death, makes the thought of death a consolation!

"Prends tes amours en croupe——
   En avant!"

the singer repeated, and the little one involuntarily urged her horse toward the song that called to her to come.

"Aha!" said Renaud, pausing in his work, "aha! young lady! you are astir early!—with a white horse that will soon be all red!"

"Yes," she said, laughing, "with gnats and gadflies; there are swarms of them! too many, by my faith in God!"

"You are covered with them, young lady, as a bit of honey is covered with bees, or a tuft of flowering genesta! But what brings you here?"

"I come from my father. You must come with me at once."

"But comrade Rampal borrowed my horse just now to go to Saintes. They went off one upon the other."

"Take mine, then," said Livette.

"And what will you do, young lady?"

She was ashamed of her thoughtlessness, and blushed scarlet.

"I?" said she, and the words of the ballad rang in her heart:

> "Prends tes amours en croupe,
> En avant!"

"Unless," said he, laughing in his turn, "you care to take me *en croupe?*"

"People would never stop talking about it all over our Camargue," said she, with laughter in her voice. "A drover like you, the terror of riders, *en croupe* like a girl? No, no; no false shame, that is my place. We will take off my saddle, and you can bring it to me to-morrow."

"Very luckily," said Renaud, "Rampal didn't take mine, which I never lend."

Livette jumped down from her horse; and at the breeze made by her skirt a cloud of great flies and enormous mosquitoes rose and flew buzzing about her. Blanchet's snow-white rump looked as if it were covered with a net of purple silk, there was such a labyrinth of little streams of blood crossing and recrossing one another. Another instant, and gadflies and mosquitoes settled down again upon the bleeding surface and dotted it with a myriad of black spots; but Blanchet, albeit somewhat cross, was used to that annoyance.

Livette fastened him to one of the rings in the wall, and sat down upon the stone bench, waiting until Renaud had finished his *séden*.

The wheel turned and turned, striking its dull blow with perfect regularity at every turn.

"That was a pretty song, Renaud," said Livette suddenly, answering her thoughts without intention; "that was a pretty song you were singing just now."

"I learned it," said Renaud, "from a boatman, a friend of my father, with whom I went up the Rhône as far as Lyon—and then came down again——"

"And is all that country very beautiful up there?" said she.

"Yes," he answered, "it is beautiful."

And he said nothing more.

"You don't look as if you meant what you say, Renaud. Pray, didn't you like the city of Lyon we hear so much about?"

There was a long silence, broken only by the monotonous rhythm of the wheel.

"No sun!" said Renaud abruptly. "It's a city in a cold cloud!—The Rhône isn't fine till you come down again," he added.

Livette looked at him, and her wide-open eyes seemed to say:

"Why is that?"

He answered her look.

"When one of us goes up yonder, young lady, you understand, he leaves everything to go nowhere, and when he gets there, all he asks is to start back again!—When he comes from there here, on the contrary, he leaves nothing at all, and knows that, at the end of the journey, he will have arrived somewhere! You see, young lady, the best horse must, of necessity, stop at the sea—and that is the only place where I am willing to consent to go no farther. Where the sea is not, you have all the rest of the journey still to do.—Enough, my boy!" he added, raising his voice.

The wheel stopped. He examined the *séden*. The rope, of black and white strands in regular alternation, was finished.

"That's a good piece of work," said he; "look, young lady."

He leaned over, almost against her, to look at a point in the rope which seemed to him defective; he leaned over, and a short black curl touched lightly the disordered, almost invisible, locks that formed a sort of fleecy golden cloud over Livette's forehead. And thereupon it seemed to both of them—young as they were!—that their hair blazed up and shrivelled softly, like the fine grass that takes fire in summer, under the hot sun. Ah! holy youth!

Then, for the first time, Renaud thought of the girl. Hitherto he had seen in Livette only the "young lady." They remained bending forward, she over the rope which she seemed to be examining attentively, he over Livette's hair. Livette wore her "morning head-dress," consisting of a little white handkerchief which covered the *chignon*, and was tied in such fashion that the two ends stood up like little hollow, pointed ears on top of her head. When they are in full-dress, the women of Camargue surround the high *chignon*, covered by a fine white linen cap, with a broad velvet ribbon, almost always black, whose long, unequal ends fall behind the head, a little at one side.

Renaud, then, was looking at Livette's clear flaxen hair,—in which there was, here and there, a lock of a darker golden hue,—symmetrically massed on top of her head, advancing in little waves toward her temples, coquettishly arranged, but so short and fluffy that some few locks escaped, here, there, and everywhere, enough to form the faint golden mist above her head.

He looked at the pretty, round neck, whence the fair hair seemed to spring, like a vigorous plant, so slender and so fine! so long, and full of life! And the temptation to press his lips upon it drew him on, as, after a long day's journey among dry, stony hills, the sight of the water draws on the horses of Camargue, accustomed to moist pasturage.

She felt that she was being stared at too long.

"Let us go!" she said, suddenly. "My father's orders were that you should come as soon as possible."

Renaud felt as if he were waking from a long sleep and from a dream. He jumped to his feet. Without a word, he went to Blanchet, took off the woman's saddle and carried it into the house, placed his own upon the beast, which the mosquitoes had at last made restive, and leaped upon his back.

Livette, assisted by the drover's strong hand, leaped to the croup behind him with one spring; highly amused she was as she threw one arm around Renaud's waist. It is the fashion among the Camarguese young women, all of whom, on fête-days, ride to the plains of Meyran, or to Saintes-Maries, "fitted" to the horses of their promised husbands.

The drover started Blanchet off at a gallop, gave him his head, and let him take his own course. Blanchet left the travelled road, headed straight for the château across the moor, through the sand thickly sown with stiff, rounded clumps of saltwort at irregular intervals. The good horse flew over these clumps, scarcely touching the tops, landing always between them in the damp sand, from which, however, by force of long habit, he withdrew his feet without effort, calculating in advance the distance between the obstacles, galloping freely and evenly, changing feet as he chose, making sport of his heavy burden, happy at being left to himself.

And Livette must needs hold tight to the drover's waist; he was a lithe, supple fellow, and swayed with the horse. And the swift motion, the free air, youth and love, all combined to intoxicate the two young people; and without meaning it, without thinking of it, the horseman repeated his song of a few moments before, between his teeth, but loud enough to be overheard by the girl:

> "Prends tes amours en croupe!
> En avant!"

And it seemed to them as if the whole horizon were theirs.

When they dismounted, in front of the farm-house of the château, they had not spoken a word, but they had exchanged in silence the subtlest and strongest part of themselves.

From that day, Renaud, being sincerely in love, exerted himself to please. He was careful about his dress, paid more attention to the adjustment of his neckerchief, shaved more closely, and had not a single glance to spare for the other girls, even the prettiest of them.

At last, he said to Livette one day:

"Your father will never be willing!"

Those were his first words of love.

"If I am willing, my father will be. And when my father is willing, grandmother always is!"

"The good God grant it!" replied Jacques.

And it had happened as she said. For almost five months now they had been betrothed.

The fascinating thing about Livette was that she was just the opposite of Renaud, so slender and delicate, so fair and such a child,—and, furthermore, that she loved him with all her might, the sweetheart,—there was no mistake about that.

V

THE LOVERS

Livette was so fresh and sweet that people often repeated, in speaking of her, the Provençal expression: "You could drink her in a glass of water!"

In loving Livette, Renaud experienced the pleasant feeling, so dear to the heart of strong men, of having some one to protect, a little wife, who was no more than a child. Because of Livette's fragility and slender stature, the rough drover, made for violent passions, the horseman of the Camargue desert, the hard-fisted herdsman, the subduer of mares and bulls, felt the love that is based upon sweet compassion, upon respect for charming weakness; in a word, he learned the secret of true tenderness which he could not have felt, perhaps, for one of his own class.

It would never have occurred to him to tell her any of the vulgar jests with a double meaning, with which he regaled the more robust fair ones of his acquaintance on branding-days or on race-days. To do that would have seemed to him to be a villainous misuse of his power and his experience as a man. Still less did Livette cause him to feel the fierce desire, well known to him, which sometimes, with other girls, went to his brain like a rush of blood, —the desire to touch with his hands, to take in his arms, to throw down into the ditch, laughing at the gentle resistance, at the consent which repels a little, at the equal struggle between the youth and the maiden, who have, in reality, a tacit understanding to be robber and robbed. No: in Livette's presence, Renaud felt that he was a new man. There came to him, in regard to the little damsel with the golden hair, a tranquillity of heart that surprised him greatly. Love has a thousand forms. That which Renaud felt for Livette was a soothing emotion. He "wished her well." That was what he kept repeating to himself as he thought of her. And, as he desired all the others something after the fashion of the bulls of his *manade*, in the season when the germs are at work, it so happened that he seemed not to desire the only woman he really loved.

There was a sweet fascination in the thought, which he relished like a draught of pure water after a long day's walk through the dust in the hot sun. He rejoiced inwardly in his love as in a halt for rest in the shade of a great tree, beside a clear, cool spring, while the birds sang their greeting to the morning. Sometimes, in the blazing heat of midday, when he was riding across the mirror-like waste of sand and salt and water, his horse plodding wearily along with hanging head, the thought of Livette would steal softly into his mind, and it would seem as if a cool breeze were blowing on his forehead, washing away, in a sense, the dust and fatigue, like a bath. He would feel refreshed, and a smile would come unbidden to his lips. His whole being would thrill with pleasure, and, with renewed life, he would imperceptibly, with hand and knee alike, order his horse to raise his head. And the lover's steed would raise his head without further bidding, and snort and toss his mane, scatter, with a sudden lash of his tail, the gadflies that were streaking his sides with blood, and, with quickened step, reach the shelter of the hawthorns and the poplars on the Rhône bank—whose leaves forever quiver and rustle like the water, like the heart of man, like everything that lives and hopes and suffers and then dies!

Not only by her grace and weakness did she win his heart, strong and rough as he was; but also by the care expended on her dress, by the splendor of her surroundings, she, the wealthy farmer's daughter, enchanted him, the poor drover; and she seemed to him a strange, unfamiliar creature from another world. And so she was in fact. Of a different quality, he said to himself: a being outside his sphere, far, far above it.

That he might one day unloose the latchets of her little shoes had not occurred to him, and, lo! she was his! Livette, the daughter of the intendant of the Château d'Avignon! she was his fiancée, his betrothed, his future wife!

He seemed to himself the heir to a throne. In face of the mere thought of his future, he felt something like the embarrassment a beggar feels on the threshold of a palace, before the carpets over which he must pass to enter, with shoes heavy with mud.

She had in his eyes something of the sanctity of the blessed Madonna, carved from wood, painted blue and gold, and overladen with pearls and flowers, that he used to see when a child in the church of Saint-Trophime at Arles.

So it was that he felt a secret amazement at finding himself beloved.

It did not seem to him that it could really be true; and as he must needs be convinced of the fact every time he spoke to her, his love constantly appealed to him with all the force of novelty.

He was a little embarrassed, too, in her presence, could not find his words, contented himself with smiling at her, with yielding submission to her like a child, with running to fetch this or that for her, divining her desires from her glance; mistaking now and then, but rarely; feeling the same pleasure in being the maiden's footman that is felt by the misshapen court dwarf in love with the king's fair daughter.

His sobriquet of *The King* seemed to him a mockery beside her. She embarrassed him; in her presence he was meek and lowly.

He was surprised, indignant even, in his heart, at the familiar tone assumed by others with Livette. It seemed strange to him that her companions should treat her as an equal; that her father and her grandmother should not have the same respect and consideration for his fiancée that he himself had.

Frequently, when the grandmother cried to Livette: "Do this or that; run! be quick!" he would be angry, and would long to say to her: "Why do you order her about? She was not made to obey! You're a bad grandmother! Don't you see that she is too delicate and pretty for such tasks?"

But this was a feeling kept hidden in his heart; he would not have dared to avow it, for women are made, according to our ancestors, to be the slaves of man. So he said no word of what he felt. He even deemed himself a little ridiculous to feel it. He contented himself by doing in a twinkling, in Livette's stead, the thing she was bidden to do, if it was something within his power.

Ah! but if any man had ventured to indulge in any ill-sounding pleasantry with Livette, to take any liberty with her—oh! then, be sure that he would without reflection have felled him on the spot with his stout fist!

Why, if any one, man or woman, in the crowd on a fête-day, happened to make a coarse remark in her hearing,—one of the sort that he himself knew how to make with great effect upon occasion,—he would be overcome with rage against that person; it seemed to him that every one should take notice of Livette's presence, should feel that she was near, and understand that, before her, they should show some self-respect.

All this he would have been incapable of explaining, but he felt it all, confusedly and vaguely, in his heart.

Livette, for her part, was keenly conscious of the drover's adoration. She revelled in it, without unduly seeming to do so. She saw very plainly that she had, without effort, tamed a wild beast. She laughed sometimes, as she looked at him—a frank, ringing laugh, in which there was, however, a touch of the triumph of the mysterious feminine witchery, the marvellous invention of nature, which decrees that the strong man shall be vanquished, rolled in the dust, at the pleasure of fascinating weakness. This miracle, performed by life, by nature, by love, she believed to be her own work,—hers, Livette's,—and the little woman was a bit swollen with pride! More than frequently she would say to herself: "What have I done? I don't deserve this good fortune; no, indeed, I don't deserve it!" She saw very clearly that, in his eyes, she was a being apart: that he did not treat her by any means as everybody else did: and, greatly astonished as she was, she was proud of it.

Thereupon, wondering in her sincere heart what she had "more" or better than another, and finding no answer to the question, it came about that she deemed her lover a little, just a very little, stupid to be so dominated by her, and he so strong! And then she would prettily make fun of him and laugh aloud at him, saying:

"Ah! great booby!"

So it was that the whole essence of Woman, profound, seductive, existed in this simple, obscure peasant-girl, who could have told nothing as to her own character.

In time, too, she came to look upon herself as pretty, beautiful, the prettiest, the loveliest of all, and to admire her own charms. When such thoughts came to her, and if the truth must be known, none were more frequent,—ah! then she felt her pride! And she no longer deemed her lover stupid in the least degree; on the contrary, he seemed to her very fortunate, too fortunate! and then it was he who hardly deserved her! At such times, she received his attentions, his humility, with the air of a princess accustomed to homage.

Then, too, she would wonder why all the others did not do for her what he did? And, thereupon, she would conceive a sort of gratitude for him. Such a constant revolution in our hearts of impressions, often irreconcilable and ever changing, around a fixed idea, is love.—Yes, in very truth he deserved to be loved simply because he had known enough to appreciate her! to choose her! The other young men were the fools, one and all!

Warm was his welcome if he arrived at the farm when that thought was in her mind. She would give the little cry of a happy bird, and run to meet her lover.

"Good-morning, Monsieur Jacques!"

"Good-morning, Demoiselle Livette!"

They would shake hands.

"Will you come to the Rhône?"

"With all my heart!"

And often they would go and sit together beside the Rhône, beneath the great hawthorn—a tree more than a hundred years old and known to everybody. The hawthorn, like the aspen and the birch, is a familiar Camarguese tree.

Sometimes, on the way, she would hold out to him a flexible green twig, broken from a poplar by the roadside, and they would walk along, united and kept apart at the same time by the short branch, followed by a swarm of gnats with their tiny iris-hued wings.

She was very fond of this sport of making him walk thus, not too near, not too far away, holding him without touching him, drawing him nearer or keeping him at a distance, as her fancy dictated, making of the leafy wand a whip if he showed signs of rebellion.

She had the feeling that thus she was indeed his mistress, remembering how she used sometimes to make her horse Blanchet follow her docilely in the same way by holding out to him a small wisp of flowering oats;—how she had sometimes, by the same means, led back behind her, quiet as an ox, a vicious bull that had escaped, wounded, from the arena, and that she had encountered by the roadside, in a thicket of thorn-broom, bathing his foaming tongue in the streams of blood that were flowing from his nostrils.

Arrived at the bank of the Rhône, beneath the great hawthorn with the gnarled black trunk and smooth white branches, that stretches its abundant rustling foliage well out over the stream, the lovers would sit down, side by side, upon the roots protruding from the ground or upon a bundle of cut reeds.

And they would watch the water flow. The earthy, yellowish water, with its whirling masses of foam, rushing toward the sea.

They would sit and gaze.

They would not speak. They would live on in silence, listening to the plashing of the Rhône, the tiny wavelets that came rippling in obliquely to the bank, to loiter there among the feet of countless reeds and poplars, while the main current in the centre of the stream flowed swiftly, hurriedly along, as if in haste to reach the sea, and there be swallowed up.—There they would sit and dream, not speaking.

They felt that they were living the same life as everything about them. From time to time, a kingfisher, sky-blue and reddish-brown, would pass before them, light on a low branch, gazing sidewise at the water with his beak ready to strike, then, suddenly, fly off across the Rhône. And, with the sky-blue bird, their thoughts would cross the river, there to light again upon a branch, bent like a bow, whose slender point trailed in the water, vibrating in the current, and surrounded with a mass of foam, dead leaves, and twigs. And suddenly the bird, like a sorcerer, had disappeared.

"How pretty!" Livette would sometimes say.

And that was all.

He would make no reply. He knew not what to say to her. He was too happy. He would not call the king his cousin!

In the evening twilight, many little rabbits, young in that month of May, would run out from the park, through the wild hedges, almost invisible in their gray coats, and play in the shadow at the foot of the bushes, their presence betrayed by the rustling of a tuft of grass or a low-hanging, horizontal branch that barred their path.

To heighten the enjoyment of the lovers, there was the nightingale's song, at the rising of the moon. Listen to it: 'tis always lovely in the darkness, is the nightingale's song. It begins with three distinct, long-drawn-out cries; you would say it was a signal, a preconcerted call; it enjoins attention. Then the modulations hesitatingly arise. You would say that it is timid, that it fears its prayer will not be granted. But soon it takes courage, self-assurance comes, and the song bursts forth and soars and fills the air with its melodious uproar. 'Tis love, 'tis youth and love that can no longer be restrained, that nothing stays, that claim their rights in life.—His song is done.

His song is done, but still the lovers listen on and on to the bird's song, echoed in the dark recesses of their own hearts.

At last, it would be time to return. They would rise and walk back toward the farm, not far away.

The grandmother would be calling from the doorway:

"Livette! Livette!"

Her voice would reach their ears, with a plaintive, caressing accent, tinged with sadness, from the edge of the vast expanse that rose in the darkness toward the stars, toward life and love,—a long, melancholy call. The voice at night upon the moor fills the air and rises tranquilly, disturbed by no echo, sad to be alone in a too great solitude.

Around the lovers as they returned to the farm, in the orchards, in the park, as the darkness increased, the deafening clamor of the frogs would soon be heard, a mighty noise, the sum total of a multitude of feeble sounds, a frightful din, composed of many minor croakings of unequal strength, which, massed together, drowning one another, mount at last into a rhythmic tumult like the ceaseless roaring of a cataract.

And amid this formidable everlasting clamor, made by the voices of myriads of amorous little frogs, accentuated by the cry of a curlew, or a heron on the watch, and accompanied by the humming of the two Rhônes and the plashing of the sea—the lovers, both deeply moved, heard nothing save the calm beating of their hearts.

As time went on, their love waxed greater, increased by the memory of all these hours lived together.

31

Renaud was no longer simple Renaud in Livette's eyes, but the being by whom she knew what life was, through whom came to her that overwhelming consciousness of everything, of the horizons of land and sea, that sentiment of *being*, that longing for the future, for growth, that inflow of vague hopes that comes of love and gives a zest to life.

And now, if any one had sought to wrest Jacques from Livette, she would have died of it, and he who should try to wrest Livette from Jacques would have died of it—he would, my friends, even more certainly.

It is a good and excellent thing that love should be always busied in making the world younger—and the nightingale, like the frogs, is never weary of repeating it.

VI

RAMPAL

Rampal, who had borrowed Jacques Renaud's horse, had not returned.

Renaud now rode no other horse than Blanchet.

Rampal was a low rascal, gambler, hanger-on of wine-shops, well-known at Arles in all the vile haunts scattered along the Rhône.

Dismissed by several masters, a drover without a drove, he passed his life in these days, riding from town to town, from Aigues-Mortes to Nîmes, from Nîmes to Arles, from Arles to Martigues, and in each of these towns plied some doubtful trade, cheated a little at cards, winning the means of living a week without doing anything, and returning, for that week, to the Camargue he loved, where there were, in two or three farm-houses, women who smiled upon his mysterious, piratical existence.

For that existence, a horse was essential. Rampal, serving as a drover on foot, had, in the first place, stolen a horse from a *manade*, but he broke his tether the second night, left his master, swam the Rhône, and rejoined his fellows. Then it was that the rascal, having, in truth, important business on hand, had said to Renaud:

"I have to go to Saintes, I'll take your horse, Cabri."

"Take my horse," Renaud replied.

It did not occur to him that Rampal would not return. Jacques relied so surely upon his own reputation for strength and courage that he did not think that any one would venture to arouse his wrath.

And then he had a sort of pity for Rampal, mingled with a little admiration. He was a bold horseman, was Rampal, and, except for women and cards, he would have been, with Renaud, or just after him, a king of the drovers! So that, if Rampal aroused Renaud's compassion, Renaud aroused Rampal's envy.

However, the vagaries of this *marrias*, this good-for-nothing knave, were the pranks of a free man. Neither married nor betrothed, fatherless and motherless, with no one to support or assist, no one whom he must please, he had a perfect right to live as he pleased! At least, that is what most people thought.

Moreover, Renaud, although an honest man, had the tastes of a vagabond. Before his heart was filled with his strange affection for Livette, by which he felt as if he were bound hand and foot, he had, in truth, borne a part with Rampal in many curious adventures.

More than once they had galloped along side by side toward the open moor, each having *en croupe* a laughing damsel, who, after the close of a bull-fight at Aigues-Mortes or Arles, had consented to accompany them for a night.

But on such occasions Renaud had always dealt frankly, never promising marriage nor any other thing, but simply giving the fair one a present, a souvenir, a brass ring, or a silk handkerchief—a *fichu* to pleat after the Arlesian fashion, or a broad velvet ribbon for a head-dress; while Rampal was treacherous, promised much and did nothing,—in short, was nothing but *féna*, a good-for-nothing.

So Rampal had borrowed Renaud's horse with the intention of bringing him back the same evening; but that evening he had heard of a fête at Martigues and had ridden away thither without worrying about Renaud.

"He'll take a horse out of his *manade*," he said to himself.

Now, Audiffret, Livette's father, had insisted that Renaud should take Blanchet.

"Take Blanchet," he said. "I don't like to have our girl ride him. He's a fine horse, but bad-tempered at times. Finish breaking him for us. I want him to run in the races at Béziers this year. Take him."

Happy to have Blanchet in the hands of "her dear," for so she already called Renaud in her heart, Livette, who was fond of Blanchet, simply said:

"Take good care of him."

That was more than six months before.

Rampal, who had caused considerable gossip meanwhile, and of whom Renaud had heard more than once, had not brought back the horse.

Renaud did not lose his patience. Several times, being informed that Rampal was in this or that place, he had tried to find him, but had not succeeded.

"I shall catch him some day!" said Renaud. "He loses nothing by waiting."

He hoped that the fête at Saintes-Maries would bring the rascal back.

"He will come back with the thieving gipsies!" he said; and he was not mistaken.

Not for an empire would Rampal have missed making the pilgrimage to

Saintes-Maries. The rascal would have thought himself everlastingly damned. It had been his habit from childhood to come and ask forgiveness of his sins from the two Marys and Sara the bondwoman, at whom he did nothing but laugh in a boastful way, unable to satisfy himself whether he believed in them or not.

This year, being affiliated with the gipsies in matters of horse-trading (every one knows that the gipsies, men and women,—*roms* and *juwas*, as they say,—have a profound acquaintance with everything connected with the horse), Rampal had been a fruitful source of information to them.

By divers methods they had led him to talk about this and that, about every one and everything. He had no idea himself that he had told so many things. They had questioned him, sometimes directly, taking him unawares; sometimes in a slow, roundabout way; when he was drunk, and when he was asleep. And his replies had been pitilessly registered in the gipsies' unfailing memory—the wherewithal to astonish all Camargue.

Rampal had not even been questioned by the gipsy queen, who did not trust his discretion; she learned the secrets of the province at second-hand.

Once only had he spoken to her. It was one evening when the beggar queen began to dance for her own amusement on the high-road, to the music of her tambourine, which she hardly ever laid aside.

"You are beautiful!" he said to her.

"You are ugly!" she replied, quickly, in a contemptuous tone.

"Give me the ring on your finger," said Rampal, "and I'll give you another."

She glanced with a gleaming eye at her fantastic ring of hammered silver, then at the insolent Christian, and said:

"A sound cudgelling about your loins is what I will give you, dog, if you don't leave me!"

And she spat fiercely at him as if in disgust.

Rampal, somewhat abashed, abandoned the game.

This woman had a way of looking at people that disconcerted them. You would say that a sharp, threatening flame shot from her eyes. It penetrated your being, searched your heart, and you were powerless against it. She fathomed your glance, but you could not fathom hers—which, on the contrary, repelled you, turned you back like a solid wall. And, at such moments, she would stand proudly erect, her head thrown slightly back, her whole body poised, at once so sinuous and so rigid, that she might have been compared to a horned viper standing on his tail, fascinating his prey and preparing to spring.

"I can't explain, Jacques, how that woman frightened me," said Livette to Renaud. "My blood is still running cold!—She threatened me! And when that crown of thorns fell at my feet—Holy Mother!—I thought I was going to faint!"

"If I meet her," Renaud replied, "she'll find she has some one to settle with!"

"Let the heathen alone, Jacques! It isn't well to have aught to do with the devil."

But the drover loved a fight, and he longed for nothing so much as to fall in with Rampal and Zinzara, the gambler and the queen of the cards; "a pair of gipsies, a pair of thieves," thought Renaud.

VII

THE MEETING

The gipsy queen was the first of the two he met.

Renaud, mounted on Blanchet, was riding along the beach toward Saintes-Maries.

The sea was at his right; at his left, the desert. He was riding through the sand, and from time to time the waves rolled up under his horse's feet, surrounding with sportive foam the rosy hoofs rapidly rising and falling.

Renaud was thinking of Livette.

He looked ahead and saw the tall, straight, battlemented walls of Saintes-Maries, and wondered whether he would lead his little queen, dressed in white, and crowned with flowers, to the altar there, or at Saint-Trophime in Arles.

He looked at the sea and wondered if nothing would come to him from that source; if his uncle, captain of a merchantman, who sailed on his last voyage so many years ago, would not come into port some day with a cargo of vague, marvellous things, a million in priceless stuffs and precious stones? In the poor, ignorant fellow's imagination, the thought of a fortune was a vision of legendary treasures, like those discovered in caverns in the Arabian tales.

For an instant, he seemed to see it with his eyes, to see his vision realized in the dazzling splendor of the boundless sea, that lay glistening in the sunlight, with sharp, fitful flashes, like a mirror broken into narrow, moving fragments of irregular shape. It was an undulating sheet of diamonds and sapphires. The sun's rays, as he sank lower and lower toward the horizon, assumed a ruddier hue as they fell obliquely upon the fast-subsiding waves, and soon the water was like a sheet of old burnished gold, moving slowly up and down; one would have said it was a vast melted treasure beneath a polished vitreous surface! At long intervals, a solitary wave greater than its fellows fell with a dull roar upon the beach, and ever and anon a cloud passed overhead; and in the mist flying from the gold-tipped wave, in the slow-moving shadow of the cloud, the water seemed a deep, dark blue. The sun sank lower, and broad bright red bands began to overshadow the bands of ochre, amethyst, light green, pale blue, that rose one above another on the horizon line. The changing sea was now like a cloak of royal purple, with fringe of azure, gold, and silver.

On the desert side, the marshes likewise were changed to vast floors carpeted with gorgeous drapery and rich embroidery. Everything was ablaze with sparkles—sea, sand, and salt. At intervals, a red flamingo rose from among the reeds, flew heavily along, seeming to carry on his side a little of the ruddy hue of sky and sea,—then lighted on the brink of the gleaming water.

The gulls were like white dream-birds in this enchanted country. They sat in lines, like brooding doves, on the crests of the waves in the offing, or on the hot sands, or on the surface of the ponds.

And, down in the northwest, Renaud was looking for the high, square terrace of the Château d'Avignon, for Livette sometimes went up there to see if she could not spy Blanchet and her dear Renaud's straight spear somewhere in the plain.

Suddenly Renaud checked his horse and gazed fixedly at a black object moving on the surface of the water, rising and falling with the motion of the waves, some two hundred feet from shore.

He thought he could descry a woman's head; a head covered with dripping black hair and surrounded by a copper circlet, from which depended glistening Oriental medallions.

The gipsy was swimming, disporting herself in the waves, which, coming from the deep sea, rose and fell slowly and at long intervals. She glided through them like a conger-eel, happy in the sensation caused by the gentle lapping of the salt water caressing her flesh. Her movements were undulating, like those of the waves themselves; she writhed and twisted like seaweed tossed about by the surf. Now and then a heavier, higher wave would come upon her. She would turn and face it, put her hands together in a point above her lowered head, as divers do, plunge into the broad wave horizontally, and cleave it through from front to rear.

From his horse, Renaud watched the dark head emerge on the other side of the swelling wave, which, as it approached the shore, curled over with whitening crest, broke upon the beach in snowy foam and spread out over the sand, beneath and all about him, in shallow, transparent, overlapping streams, all studded with sparks. He could not see the swimmer's body distinctly. Its fleeting outlines could scarcely be made out beneath the clear, transparent water, ere they were blotted out again by the undulations and reflections.

Suddenly the swimmer turned toward the shore, apparently gained a footing, and, raising one arm out of the water, motioned to Renaud to be gone, shouting:

"Go your way!"

But he, who had thus far watched her with curiosity and with no feeling of anger, was irritated by those words. Certainly he had forgotten none of Livette's grievances against the gipsy. Not a week had passed since her threatening visit to the Château d'Avignon. But, in that beautiful evening light, Renaud's heart felt at peace, and he had recognized the gipsy queen without emotion. It may be that curiosity was dominant in his heart, and urged him toward this mysterious being, surprised in her bath, in the utter solitude of the desert at evening; the curiosity of a traveller to examine a strange animal, of a Christian to investigate a heathen woman. "Go your way!" This command, hurled at him from afar by a woman's voice, wounded him in that part of his heart where the memory of the gipsy's threat against Livette was stored away.

"Ah! it's you," he cried, "you, who go about and stand in doorways to frighten young girls when they happen to be left alone! who tell lies and play monkey-tricks to make them give you what they refuse to give! Don't let it happen again, thief! or you'll find out how the pitchfork and the goad feel!"

The insulted queen was absolutely convulsed with furious rage. If she had been near the drover, she would have jumped straight at his throat, as the serpent straightens itself out like an arrow and darts at its prey. She felt that she grew pale, a shiver ran through her whole body, and swaying a little, like the adder about to spring, with her head thrown slightly back, she walked toward the horseman—but how far away he was!

"Aha!" he cried, "you are coming near to hear better! Come on, you heathen, come! I will explain it all to you!"

As he remembered how the woman had threatened Livette, his wrath rose within him. They were not Christians, these Bohemian creatures, but thieves, bandits, one and all. Why, it was said that they ate human flesh, child's flesh, when they could find nothing better. If that were not true, how would they have whole quarters of bleeding flesh in their kettles so often? Ah! a race of wolves, of accursed foxes!

"Come on!" he cried again.

She came on, but not without difficulty, having to force her way step by step through the resisting waves. Her shoulders were not yet visible, and she was accelerating her speed by using her arms under the water. She could have made the same distance more quickly by swimming, but she did not even think of that. She was thinking of something very different!

Renaud mechanically cast his eye along the shore, behind him, and saw, a few steps away, the gipsy's clothes lying in a heap out of reach of the waves,— and her tambourine on top of them; then he looked around once more at the woman coming toward him. The water was now up to her armpits, and not until then did he see that she was entirely naked.

Her bust slowly emerged from the water. At a hundred paces from the shore, the water reached only to her knees. She was beautiful. Her slender, well-knit body was very youthful. She stood very erect, and seemed as if she were going into battle without any thought of shame. She had been assailed: she was rushing at her assailant, that was the whole of it. Her fists were clenched, her arms slightly bent, her head still thrown back a little. Her whole attitude was threatening. The water was rolling down in glistening pearls from her neck to her feet, over every part of her swarthy, bronzed body. Her swelling chest seemed to be put forward, as if it were ready, like a magic buckler, to receive the blows that would be powerless to injure it.

The drover sat still in speechless amazement. He gazed at the approaching woman, who, as he saw her, springing from the water, surrounded by white foam, with her unusual coloring, appeared to him like a supernatural being.

What was she there for? She came forward, boldly aggressive; and her witch's mind was revolving many evil schemes, no doubt.

Did she not bend over a moment, as if to pick up pebbles from beneath the water, with which to stone her enemy? Was she not holding them now in her clenched fists. No: the sands of Camargue stretch very far beneath the water, sloping very gradually, and not the tiniest pebble meets the swimmer's bare foot.

What was she doing then?

And now she was close beside the horseman, whose curiosity constantly increased. But he had ceased questioning himself. He simply stared at her, stupefied and enchanted.

He followed her with his eyes, fascinated, forgetting his spear resting upon his stirrup, forgetting his horse, forgetting everything.

And now she was within three paces of him, standing perfectly straight, insolent in her whole bearing, in every undulation of her figure, looking him in the face, with eyes from which a steely flame shot forth, and which no other eye could penetrate. And as she presented her profile to him for a second, he had a swift, hardly conscious thought that the lower part of the face—from below the nostrils to the base of the chin—resembled the head of the lizard of the sand, and the turtles and snakes of the swamp. There was the same vertical line, broken by thin, slightly-receding lips, whence he expected to see a forked, vibrating tongue come forth, as in a dream of the devil.

But this impression was but momentary, and he saw naught but the woman, young, fair, unclothed, seemingly offering herself voluntarily to his savage lust, in the security of that deserted shore, amid the plashing of the waves, in the fresh breeze blowing from the sea, and the evening sunlight, which, with the salt water, coursed in streams over the whole lovely body.

Dazzled, blinded, drunken with the waves of blood, which from his heart, whither it had rushed at first, suffocating him and making him waver in his saddle,—now poured back to his brain, suffusing his face and bull-like neck with red,—he was about to leap down from his horse, or perhaps to stoop over only, snatch up the creature—a mere feather in his hands—by strength of wrist, and centaur-like carry her away *en croupe*,—when she, more prompt to act, darted forward, stretching out her arms, and with her left hand seized and pulled back with all her strength the double rein of Renaud's horse, making him rear and fall back. And with her right hand she struck the creature's face!

Chapter VII

He saw naught but the woman, young, fair, unclothed, seemingly offering herself voluntarily to his savage lust, *** when she, more prompt to act, darted forward, stretching out her arms, and with her left hand seized and pulled back with all her strength the double rein of Renaud's horse, making him rear and fall back.

"Go, dog! go and tell your people that a woman has revenged herself upon you and has struck the horseman on his horse's face! Coward! Vile neat-herd! Go and tell it to your sweetheart! Go, tell her that when I struck you, you knew not what to do or say!"

There was no wrath left in Renaud; he had no feeling but fear mingled with amazement. The woman's performance seemed to him in very truth surprising, diabolical. In coloring, bearing, expression, and audacity, she was the sorceress to the life. A strange terror took possession of him. Perhaps he would have gone astray gaily, without remorse, with any other than this ill-omened gipsy, who terrified him. He was especially alarmed for Livette. He felt that she, and he himself with her, were threatened by some mysterious, obscure disaster; and the thought of being unfaithful to her filled him with dismay, as the beginning of the end. He was afraid of himself; afraid, for Livette, of this unforeseen, inexplicable creature, who rose up before him, challenging him to contend with her, for what?—Thus, malignity and hatred brought the woman to him as love would not have done!—He was bewildered. He simply waited till his rein should be let go, ready to start off at a gallop, feeling no longer in his heart the wrath a man must feel in order to ride down any woman, though she were a witch, and trample her beneath his horse's feet, at the risk of killing her.

But why was he no longer angry? Because his eyes, against his will, followed every movement of that body with its weird beauty,—the body of an enemy.

"You would like to fly like a coward, would you?" she suddenly cried. "You shall not go until I choose!"

Profiting by the horseman's open-mouthed stupor, she had seized with her teeth a hanging end of the lasso that was coiled about the horse's neck, and with the assistance of one hand—the other still holding the rein—had swiftly passed it about the nostrils and tied it in a cruel knot. With a fierce pull upon this instrument of torture, she held the beast fast just where she wished him to be.

"You must wait until your comrades pass!" she said. "They must see a bull-tamer tamed by a woman!"

"Upon my word," thought Renaud, "that would be, as she says, a very absurd thing!" And he drew his horse back a little, thinking he might release him, but the horse stretched out his head and neck, balked, dropped his tail, and stiffened his four legs, as if he were tied to a wall. The gipsy did not stir. She laughed, showing an unbroken set of small, white, pretty, formidable teeth.

"Take care!" said Renaud at last, "I am going to ride my horse upon you!"

"I defy you to do it!" she replied tranquilly.

She saw with her unerring glance signs of confusion in the drover's eyes: the charm was working! Through a mist he now gazed upon this woman, whose captive he was, by virtue of a burning curiosity already closely akin to love. She smiled.

This lasted some time. At last, Renaud felt that his wits were leaving him. To remain faithful to Livette, whom he could not betray with the very woman upon whom he had promised to avenge her, he must not dismount from his horse, for as soon as he put his foot to the ground he would have become the stronger of the two! To remain faithful he must have courage to remain vanquished in this struggle of beauty against strength. And he waited.

She surprised the drover glancing for an instant toward the moor.

"Aha! you are afraid some one will see you, coward! but never fear! Every one shall know what has happened to you, all the same. I will take care of that! Some day you shall come and tell me what your pale-faced, white-blooded blonde had to say to it!"

Humiliated at being forced thus to obey a woman, but rendered wavering and weak by the physical delight she caused him to feel, he remained where he was! His horse, as he irritated without maddening him, tried several times to free himself, but without success. Renaud looked on. Slight, supple as a tiger's whelp, active and strong, and accustomed to contend with horses, the gipsy, still holding the cruel cord in her left hand, had seized the long mane and wound it about her right hand, and when the horse reared, she being thus made fast to him, allowed herself to be raised from the ground, standing erect upon the tips of her rigid toes—or else she would twine her feet about the rider's leg, clinging to him as the polypus clings, with its tendons to the rock, and laughing always, with a wicked, obstinate, triumphant air.

"You shall never be rid of me again!"

At last, becoming more and more alarmed, he came to have a horror of her, as of a poisonous insect, seen in a dream, a spider or a dragon-fly, that follows you obstinately, or of an adder that conceives a strange, almost human hatred for you, persists in following your footsteps, with unwearying patience, and becomes an object of terror, despite his puny size, because of his supernatural tenacity.

And in very truth the fierce resolution, the malevolent perseverance, the demoniacal obstinacy of the woman, protected as she was by her beauty and her weakness, were terrifying.

But the play of the muscles, causing that gleaming flesh, now moist with perspiration, to throb and undulate, aroused the man's interest, in spite of everything, and pleased him more and more. Desire awoke in him. And instantly he refused to accept his defeat, and rebelled.

"Look out!" he cried, and he urged his horse forward, driving his spurs into his sides; but the beast, held fast by the nostrils, gave but three leaps and then stopped short, breathing fire. Poor Blanchet, who was used to his young mistress's caresses and sweetmeats! he was learning now to know woman's true nature.

At last, the gipsy released her double prey.

"Go! you have looked at me enough!" she suddenly exclaimed.

Renaud gazed at her an instant longer, without speaking or moving. The strength and chaotic character of his temptations held him fast there for another moment. So this extraordinary experience (which would never be repeated!) was ended at last!—Mad thoughts, each clear enough in itself, but confused by their great number, jostled one another in his brain. Why had he not sooner put an end to this conflict? What would people say of him when it was known? How could it be that he, the king of the moor, had not stooped to pick up this joy?—But Livette?—ah, yes! Livette!

He buried his spurs in Blanchet's flanks, and the beast flew away toward Saintes-Maries.

The gipsy stood on the shore a long while, looking after the fugitive. She smiled. She reviewed in her mind the varying fortunes of the battle, and gauged the extent of her victory. She recalled, one by one, to enjoy them to the full, the thoughts that had passed through her mind when she was wading toward the shore.

She had not premeditated her assault, as she made it—her first idea had been to pick up some stones and throw them at Renaud's head, being an adept in the art. But she could find none. So she had continued her forward movement, not knowing what she would do, but certain that she must do something to punish the insolent Christian.

But when she felt the cool air blowing upon her bare breast, she had said to herself in her mysterious language, full of cabalistic words and images, that if a saint had been able to recompense a boatman—her good friend—simply by revealing to him her beauty all unclothed, a heathen might, by similar means, chastise a brutal drover; for love is the magician's herb, the bitter-sweet, the plant with two savors, balm and poison at once; and woman is bitter as the salt sea water, frightful as death,—her hands are chains stronger than iron, and her whole being is as much to be dreaded as an army!

Could not she, brown as she was, almost black beside the white-skinned blondes, domineer over the pale-faced Livette's lover, if she chose? Indeed, what more need she do, to make him unfaithful to his fair fiancée, than show herself to him, and could she not do it without seeming to intend it? As she had, beyond question, been insulted by this Christian, she could pretend to forget her nudity in her wrath, and thus attack him with that same nudity!— No, no, there was no need of philters, magic incantations, or fires lighted at night when the moon is young, under tripods on which marsh-water, filled with snakes, is boiling—no need of such things to bewitch this fellow! She would come forth from the water, naked and lovely as she was, and the devil, at her command, would do the rest! What were the stones she might throw at a young man, compared with the power that exhaled from herself? Yes, therein lay the charm of charms. She knew it,—being a witch like every other woman! Lust for her body was what she would throw at him like an evil destiny; with that she would poison his life—and then, she would calmly watch the ravages of the poison.

And so she had come forward, small but formidable—the queen! She knew also that in former times, in the days of pagan Europe, an immortal goddess had issued from the sea, had sprung forth, fair and naked, like a marvellous flower, and, standing on the blue waves, her feet resting in a shell of mother-of-pearl, had long held sway over men—before the reign of Jesus Christ.

Renaud, turning in his saddle, saw the gipsy standing there, still naked, waving her arms in the sunlight, as if she wished still, from afar, to hold Livette's betrothed spellbound and fascinated by her beauty.

The sun disappeared below the horizon, and the naked woman's figure, even more mysterious in the gathering twilight, was outlined in black against a coppery red sky.

VIII

ON THE BENCH

From Saintes-Maries, whither he went to ask how many bulls he was expected to bring on the day of the fête, Renaud rode away at once to the Château d'Avignon.

He was in haste to see Livette once more, and sitting by her side to forget the scene of the afternoon, to which, despite his efforts, his mind constantly reverted.

A ride of four or five leagues and he reached his destination.

Livette and her father and grandmother were sitting just outside the farmhouse, enjoying the fresh air on the stone bench against the façade of the château, among the old climbing rose-bushes which frame the windows above with their bunches of green leaves interspersed with flowers.

This was also one of the favorite resorts of our lovers, who liked to have above their heads the perfumed foliage, to which one of the nightingales from the park often came to sing.

"Ah! good-evening, Jacques."

"Good-evening, all."

"What brings you so late? You have dined, of course?"

"I ate some anchovies at the Saintes——"

"They're good for nothing but to give you an appetite. Would you like something else? you have only to speak."

"Thanks, Master Audiffret. I'll just go and look after Blanchet in the stable and then come back. I won't go to the *jass* to-night. I'll sleep in the hay-loft with the horses."

Master Audiffret, with his pipe between his lips, rose and followed Renaud as far as the door of the stable, and from there watched him rub down his horse.

"Whenever you please, Master Audiffret, you can take him back for Livette. I don't find any faults in him; far from it. He is a good horse, and very gentle."

"He is quiet with you because you tire him out, you see; but she didn't use him every day, not by any means; I am always afraid for her. If she takes a fancy to ride him sometimes, you can lend him to her, and take the first horse that comes along for yourself. By the way, I hope you will soon have your Cabri again. Somebody saw Rampal yesterday in Crau. He was riding your horse, so he hasn't sold him, at all events. It's fair to suppose he means to bring him back to you."

"Oh! I will go to meet him," said Jacques, "for as to thinking he will bring him back to me—oh! no; he would have done that before now!—Can you tell me, Audiffret, where Rampal was seen yesterday?"

"Between Tibert's farm and Icard's in Crau. Right there, as you know, in the middle of a bog, is a hut you can only get to by a plank walk built on piles and covered by the water—you can only tell where it is, when you know the place, by stakes sticking up at intervals the whole length of the walk. I have an idea he means to go in hiding there, the beggar, like the deserter who went there to pass his time of service——"

"Aha! he has gone to the Conscript's Hut, has he? Very good; I will go to see him there, never fear!" said Renaud.

Blanchet, having been well rubbed down, was grinding the good lucern between his teeth. Renaud went out of the stable, and with Audiffret sat down beside Livette and the grandmother.

All four kept silence for a long moment. Nothing could be heard but the unceasing, melancholy croaking of the frogs, and beneath it, but indistinguishable, the dull murmuring of the two Rhônes and the sea.

The sky was swarming with innumerable tiny stars, which seemed to answer the various noises of the palpitating moor; and, just as the waters of the Rhône, after it rushes into the blue ocean, pursue their own course for a long while therein, unmingled, without losing their earthy color; so the Milky-Way, made of a dust of stars, pursued its course, easily distinguishable, through the ocean of starry worlds.

Renaud had a feeling of constraint.

When he joined his fiancée, he did not feel all that he ordinarily felt—a joyful impulse to run to meet her, a sort of oppression at the pit of the stomach, a sudden delicious rush of the blood to the throbbing heart!—And Livette, too, so soon, was conscious of a vague inexplicable feeling at the bottom of her heart that something was wrong. There was something between them! Indeed, he had, for the first time, something to conceal from her; and, thinking that it might, that it must be apparent, he suddenly said:

"I am not well to-night."

"Look out for the fever!" said Audiffret. "I know it is not as frequent or as dangerous as it used to be, but you must be on your guard, all the same! Be on your guard, and take the remedy. Up in the pharmacy of the château are the registers of the time the land was first exploited—the time when the Château d'Avignon people were gaining a little arable land from the swamps every day. Why, men went to the hospital, fifteen, twenty a day. And such doses of quinine, my children! It is all written down in the *Livre de Raison* up there. In those days, all the farms hereabout had the same kind of a book, called by the same name, just as sailors have a log-book. Those were the days of good order and gallantry. The peasant-women in those days didn't try to copy Parisian bourgeoises,—eh, grandmamma?—by wearing dresses that didn't suit them, instead of the old-fashioned gowns that made them attractive because they were so becoming."

"Yes," sighed the grandmother, "this is the age of pride, and my time has gone by."

That is the common remark of all our old peasants.

"People didn't read so many newspapers in those days," continued Audiffret, "they didn't worry so much about the affairs of the whole world, and every man paid much more attention to his own affairs. Things went better for it. Landowners lived on their estates and raised families, instead of going to Paris and dying there, of pride or debt or something else. The *Livre de Raison* up yonder describes our ancestors' battles with the swamps and the fever. The pharmacy is still in good order, with the scales and the jars in the pigeon-holes, under the dust. And the book tells everything, diseases and deaths. To-day, hardly any one dies of the fever in our neighborhood. It is dying out. The dikes and canals have done good service, and this Cochin China of France, as that sailor called it that I took to see the Giraud rice-fields, this Camargue of ours is as healthy to-day as Crau!—However, be on your guard, I tell you, and take the remedy! don't wait till to-morrow; Livette will give you what you need. Now, I am going to bed. Stay up a little longer, young people, if you choose. Are you coming, grandma?"

"No, I'll stay out a moment longer with the young folks," said the old woman.

Audiffret knocked the ashes out of his pipe against the corner of the bench, and having put it in his pocket, went up to bed.

Silence reigned upon the bench.

The grandmother was tired and sleepy: every little while she would raise her head as if suddenly awakened,—then it would begin to fall forward again, slowly, slowly——

"A heavy dew is falling," observed Livette, suddenly.

"Yes, demoiselle."

"See!" said she ingenuously, holding out her arm so that he could feel the dampness on the sleeve of her dress. But he did not put out his hand. He was not all Livette's that evening, as usual. Strangely enough, she did not frighten him that evening. He was not, as usual, overcome with diffidence in her presence. She no longer dominated him. And he was angry with himself. He suffered. He realized that his thoughts were more frequently busied with the memory of the day than with his sweetheart, who was sitting so near him.

"What are you thinking about?" said Livette, who had had her eyes upon him for a moment past, as if she could see his face distinctly, although they were sitting in the shadow. Beyond question, she felt that his thoughts were elsewhere. There is nothing more subtle than a lover's divination.

"I am thinking," said Renaud, a long minute after the question, "about my horse, which I propose to take back from Rampal to-morrow if he can be found in Camargue or Crau."

"And then?"

"And then?" he repeated—"I was thinking of the Conscript's Hut, where he is at this moment, perhaps,—in hiding."

"And of what else?" Livette insisted.

"Oh! how do I know! of the fever—of all we have just been saying——"

"Alas!" said the maiden, "and not at all of me, Renaud? do you not think of me any more?"

Her voice was sad.

He shuddered, and the movement did not escape the little one's notice. It seemed to him, as Livette uttered that reproach, that he saw the gipsy again as he had seen her in the afternoon, standing before him, near at hand, all naked and so brown! as if she were accustomed to pass her days naked in the sun, and were tanned from head to foot by his rays. And how lithe and sinewy the wild creature was! A genuine animal, a little Arabian mare, of much finer breed than the Camargue stock. Alas! for too long a time, through fidelity to his fiancée, he had been as virtuous as a girl, and now the hot-blooded fellow's continence was taking its revenge upon him, a cruel revenge, arousing mad, amorous longings that were not for Livette. And so his very respect for her—poor child!—turned against her!

"Jacques?" said Livette, in the hardly audible tone the sentiment of love imparts to the lover's voice, a soft, veiled tone, heard by the heart rather than by the ear.

Renaud did not hear her. He *saw.*—He saw the gipsy as plainly as if she were there before him, even more plainly. In the darkness of the night, her body, brown as before, seemed luminous, like an opaque substance giving forth a pale light. Her naked figure, obscure and bright at the same time, was standing motionless before his eyes—then it moved—and he fancied that he saw the gipsy bathing in the phosphorescent water peculiar to the summer months,—when swimmers cause a cold, liquid light to dart hither and thither through the dark water, following and marking the outlines of their forms, from which it seems to radiate.

"Have I the fever?" he said to himself.

As if in answer to the unspoken question, Livette took his hand. She felt it from wrist to finger-ends, to see if it were dry and hot.

"Yes," said she, "you must look out; father was right, you have a touch of fever. Come up and find the medicine."

"Come on," said he, glad of the diversion.

"Come," she repeated, "but move softly: grandma has fallen asleep!"

The old lady was asleep, as she said. She was leaning against the wall, perfectly motionless. The white handkerchief, tied in the Arlesian fashion, instead of covering her *chignon* only, enveloped almost her whole head, allowing two tufts of coarse, white hair, all in disorder, to protrude, like mist, on each side of her face.

She was asleep, her mouth partly open, a ray of light shining through upon her teeth, which were still beautiful.

They left her there.

IX

THE PRAYER

Livette opened the farm-house door, which creaked loudly in the resonant emptiness of the spacious stone staircase.

She lighted the lamp, which was hanging on a nail, and they went up-stairs together, she absorbed by thoughts of him, and he of her, but no longer in their accustomed condition of affectionate embarrassment.

He held the iron lamp, hanging at the end of its hooked stick; and to relieve his conscience, to do his duty as a lover, and perhaps in that way to change the current of his thoughts, perhaps to set at rest the amorous anxiety with which he was assailed,—to force himself to return, heart and soul, to Livette, and, who knows?—so hard to fathom is man with his background of devil!— perhaps, with her and unknown to her, to satisfy to some extent the passion kindled by the other—for all these reasons together, more inextricably mingled than the twigs of the climbing rose-bushes, he said to himself: "I will kiss her!" He had never done that thing,—except in the presence of the old people,—but the Renaud of that evening was not the Renaud of other days, in his feeling for Livette. The powerful leaven of his wild nature was swelling his veins to bursting. In very truth, he had the fever,—at all events, a species of fever. All his nerves were overstrained; in his eyes, even the most indifferent objects wore an unusual look. And in Livette he saw, in spite of himself, reproaching himself bitterly therefor, things which ordinarily he refused to see. And as, being always dressed in the Arlesian fashion, she wore the *fichu* of white muslin crossed upon her breast so low as to afford a glimpse, beneath the gold chain and cross, of the white throat, above the meeting of the stiff folds, laid neatly one upon another, his passionate gaze fell upon that spot, amid the modest arrangement of muslin, prettily called "the chapel."

In his left hand was the lamp, which he held shoulder-high, and as far away as possible, to avoid the drops of oil,—and he wound his right arm about Livette's waist as she placed her hand upon the iron rail.

At every step they climbed, he felt the play of the muscles of his fiancée's youthful frame, imparting to the arm about her waist a soothing languor that ran through his whole being,—and yet his heart did not rejoice thereat; and he realized that, ordinarily, if the end of the velvet ribbon in Livette's head-dress touched his face, it caused a sweeter thrill of pleasure in his blood, and more than all else, a pleasure which there was no mistaking. And, thereupon, he grew vexed with himself as for a failure of duty, he was oppressed by a presentiment of disaster, vague but inevitable. And she felt more and more keenly the rebound of his emotions. She was conscious that her peace of mind was endangered. Something certainly was against her. The arm, which had sometimes been about her waist as now, no longer seemed to be her lover's arm, but a mere ordinary man's. She suffered, and did not understand. The look she saw in his eyes was a strange look from him, without affection, without pity even. She knew him well, honest Renaud, her promised husband, and yet she was afraid of him as of a stranger!

All these thoughts passed very quickly through their minds, the more quickly because they were simply conscious of them, and did not stop to try to analyze them. The all-powerful human electricity, less known than the other variety, was playing its game, impossible to follow, in their hearts, with its vast net-work of currents and connections. In these two creatures of instinct, the ever-recurring prodigy of love, of natural affinity—of the sympathies and their opposite—was seen once more, as mysterious, as marvellous, as profound as ever. So far as nature is concerned, there are two beings: man and woman; there are no subdivisions. At the basis of humanity, all life is the same, all passion is the same. The student of the higher races labors incessantly to perfect his reasoning and his powers of expression, but there is more overflowing, complicated life in the heart of his ignorant brother than in the heads of the philosophers, who, by dint of self-analysis, have lost the faculty of emotion. They who deem themselves most skilful in discovering the real man in themselves, do not perceive that they pervert the secret impulses of their hearts by keeping too close a watch upon them. The light of their miner's lamp changes the psychological conditions, just as constant light would modify the physiological condition of human beings and plants. And, meanwhile, love and death repeat, in the eternal darkness of their simple hearts, their unwitnessed miracles.

They had reached the landing on the first floor—as large as an ordinary room. At the last step, Renaud, almost lifting Livette to the landing, tried to draw her to him, but she was seized with an impulse to resist, and he with a sudden impulse to resist himself; separately, the two impulses would have had no effect; but combined, they exerted sufficient force to place an obstacle between them, as if by mutual consent. That force was the witchery at work.

As they did not exchange a word, their embarrassment increased.

Hastily, to escape the constraint each imposed upon the other, she ran to the door at the right and entered. And he, well pleased to be able to do or say something to bring them nearer together, called out:

"Wait for the light, Livette! I am coming."

But Livette had suddenly remembered the gipsy's threat. "It is fate," she said to herself, "I see it now!" And she felt herself grow pale.

Then she had an inspiration.

"Follow me, Renaud."

They passed through rooms where furniture of the time of the Empire was sleeping beneath its covers, and the long hangings falling from the ceiling in broad, stiff folds, and withered, as it were, by time; rooms seldom visited by the master, but kept in order by Livette and her grandmother.

At last, Renaud and Livette reached an apartment with bare, whitewashed walls, once used as a chapel.

A wooden altar, entirely devoid of fittings and ornament, stood at one end of the room. Before the white and gold door of the tabernacle the sacred stone was missing, leaving a square hole in the wood-work of the altar.

But Livette opened a broad door flush with the wall. It opened into a closet in the wall. When the door was thrown wide open, they could see, below a shelf about level with their heads, chasubles and stoles hanging straight and stiff—with great crosses in heavy gold embroidery—suns from which the dove came forth; and mystic triangles, and *Agnus Deis*. Among all the others were vestments for use in mourning ceremonies,—black, with bones and executioners' ladders, hammers and nails, in heavy white embroidery; and—to Livette's amazement—there, in the centre of a stole, on silk as black as night, was worked a crown of thorns in silver, which, in the lamplight, seemed to emit bright rays.

On the shelf, above all these priestly vestments—which were arranged with the backs outward, hung in such fashion that you seemed to be looking at the priests standing at the altar—on the shelf, between the goblet and the pyx, shone the consecrated host, a radiant sun, mounted upon a pedestal like a candelabrum; and in the centre of its rays was a gleaming circle of plain glass, which also reflected, in fantastic guise, the flame of the lamp.

"Kneel, Renaud!" said Livette. "Prayer is the cure for what is happening to us. Kneel and let us pray!"

The drover obeyed. He understood that Livette's purpose was to exorcise fate.

She prayed in silence fervently. He, marvelling, unwonted to the attitude of prayer, and striving to keep himself in countenance, looked from time to time at the lamp he held in his hand, raised it to get a better view of the ecclesiastical treasures, and, diverted for the moment, by constant effort, from the perplexity that weighed upon his heart, he was the more wretched when his mind suddenly reverted to Livette.

Thereupon he said to himself that she certainly had guessed the truth; that there was, in fact, a spell upon him, and, in his heart, he implored the merciful God of the Cross, the mystic triangle, the symbolical bird and lamb, to come to his aid.

Chapter IX

In his left hand was the lamp, which he held shoulder-high, and as far away as possible, to avoid the drops of oil,—and he wound his right arm about Livette's waist as she placed her hand upon the iron rail.

"Forgive us our trespasses as we forgive those who trespass against us!" Livette suddenly exclaimed, aloud, thinking of the gipsy.—"O God," she added, "we promise Thee that on Saintes-Maries Day, which is near at hand, we will each carry three tapers to their church, and wait, until they are so far consumed, one after the other, in their honor, that our finger-tips are burned!"

Then she rose—but before they left the room, they closed the unpretentious double door upon the objects of a dead cult, left in the darkness of abandonment—the goblet without wine, the pyx without bread, and the consecrated host, whose polished metal case held naught within.

X

THE TERRACE

He was well aware that he needed no fever medicine, and that his fever did not come from the swamps.

She said no more about the drug, but as they stood on the landing and he was preparing to descend, she said:

"Suppose we go out on the terrace?"

Livette wished to prolong the tête-à-tête, to ascertain if, after her prayer, she would find *her* Renaud in him once more.

He placed his lamp on the floor at the top of the staircase, and, pushing open the door just above the last step, they both stood on the terrace that overlooks the whole château.

A square terrace, and in the centre the great bell lay upon its side in its iron cage—the great bell, three feet in diameter, that in the old days called to work as well as to prayer, and when it rang the Angelus caused the fever-haunted farm-laborers to fall upon their knees on the brink of the miasmatic bogs.

Both of them, one after the other, mechanically struck the bell with their foot, as it lay there on its side. It gave forth a short, plaintive note, quickly stifled by contact with the flag-stones. It was like the sigh of a mystery-haunted soul.

With hearts as sad as the bell, they leaned on the stone parapet in presence of the night.

Livette and Renaud loved each other, but affection was no longer enough for him. The sap of the spring-time, boiling in his veins in lustful desire, gave birth, in Livette's heart, to sweet flowers of reverie.

The swarming of the stars above their heads was beyond comprehension. They were as many as the gadflies and frogs in the desert, or the waves of the sea. They seemed to open and half close, like flowers in a meadow, waved to and fro by a light, quickly-passing breath, like eyelids making signs.

They seemed to have something to say, to move like lips speaking a living language, telling of something of great moment that must be known at once— but no sound coming from them reaches the ears of men, for human hearing is not keen enough. Nor is the human sight keen enough to see that the dust of the Milky-Way (pale as the pollen of flowers) is also made of stars. Though men have seen it with a different sight, afforded by man's inventive genius, that sight is powerless to pierce farther and deeper—to learn all there is to know.

Moreover,—and Renaud himself had heard the story from the shepherds who pass the winter in Camargue and Crau, and spend their nights in summer counting the stars upon the summits of the Alps,—there are, in space, beyond the skies visible to our eyes, fires alight so far away from us, so far away that their light, now on its way toward our earth, will not reach us for centuries to come. The men who follow us centuries hence will see twinkling stars that even in our day were lighted and making signs we could not see. And in those days ideas, which are already kindled in men's minds, and are seen to-day by none save those in whom their light is shed, will shine for all, and one of them will be, for every mortal, the love and pity of the world.

Certain it is, that neither Renaud nor Livette could fathom those infinite depths; but from the vast expanse of heaven, swarming with tiny lights, a nameless emotion stole into their hearts, made up of all their hopes to come.

Future worlds, lovelier than this of ours, were dreaming in them, with them.

In them, too, because they were young and human, there was a share in the future. In them, too, was the responsibility for future lives. In them, too, lurked the mystery of generations to be born, for whom a single couple, surviving the wreck of the demolished world, would be enough to bestow upon them the desire to live and the power.

A spark is the basis of all fire. A man and a woman are the basis of all love. Infinity is no greater than the number two. And that is why the great scholars, who figure like Barrême, know no more of life and the heart than Livette and Renaud—who knew nothing at all.

They knew naught save that they were alive and that they wished to love each other and that they sought and shunned each other at the same moment—but they did not ask each other why. They said nothing. They felt. They could not say to each other that rivalry and jealousy, that is to say grief, serve the designs of nature, whose purpose doubtless is, by arousing those emotions, to quicken desire, so that creation may be assured by outbursts of passion, and the future of mankind by the imperious need of pleasure.

What does the law care for the weak and the vanquished? the strong alone, they say, it wishes to perpetuate.

Pity and justice are human inventions, and will never triumph until they have been slowly assimilated by the human mind to the matter of which it is made.

They suffered, they longed for happiness—beneath that mystery-laden spring sky. They awaited the coming of their joy, they summoned their every hope, and they gazed at the dark horizon, at the desert, where the tracts of sand shone like mirrors among the dark reeds, and the ponds glistening with salt between the black lines of tamarisks. They gazed upon the boundless expanse in which they seemed lost, and where, nevertheless, they felt that they alone were an epitome of everything; they listened, without hearing them, to the unending noises of the island,—the murmuring of the water, the rustling of the reeds, the waving foliage, the growling of wandering beasts, the distant roaring of two rolling rivers and a restless sea;—and this combined voice of the whole island formed a fitting accompaniment, by reason of the extent and number of the sounds that composed it, to the silent twinkling of the stars, that no one hears.

There was in the park, invisible to them at that hour, a foreign tree, on which the flowers could be seen, by daylight, opening with a slight noise. They sometimes amused themselves by watching that tree, said to have come from Syria. A slight report, as if muffled, and a tiny cloud, of very powerful odor, would issue from the bursting cell. The tree continued, during the night, to send out its dust of passions in quest of prey, and its strange perfume was wafted upward to the lovers.

They trembled with joy at the slightest contact with each other. Ah! if she could but have given him, on that beautiful May evening, all the love his lusty youth demanded; if he could but have felt her clinging lips melt beneath his burning ones, upon that lofty terrace overlooking the rounded tops of the huge trees in the park, beneath that dark star-spangled sky, doubtless his little betrothed would have remained sole mistress of his heart!

But there were too many obstacles between Livette and Renaud; and as he struggled virtuously to keep away from her, his thoughts flew off to the other.

And Livette was already conscious of the heartache of the deserted lover. All the broad expanse of level country that her eyes knew so well, and that she felt about her in the darkness, suddenly seemed empty to her, a desert in very truth, and thereby to resemble her own heart. And softly, silently, she began to weep,—whereupon one of the great farm dogs, her favorite, who had been seeking her in every direction, came up to her and licked her hand as it hung at her side.

And down yonder, far down above the dark line of the sea, Renaud, meanwhile, fancied that he saw a naked woman's form emerge from the water, and await his coming, suspended in mid-air, or standing on the surface of the waves.

"Livette! Livette!"

It was the grandmother's voice calling.

They went down without exchanging a word.

"Good-night, Monsieur Jacques," said the maiden.

"Good-night, mademoiselle," Renaud replied.

So they called each other monsieur and mademoiselle that night, and, a moment after they had parted, Renaud took his horse from the stable in perfect silence, and rode away.

His heart did not tell him that Livette, at her window, watched him depart, her eyes filled with tears.

"Where is he going?"

She followed for a moment with her glance the luminous point (the reflection of a star upon the head of the drover's spear) dancing about in the darkness among the trees like a will-o'-the-wisp,—and when that spark went out, she no longer saw the stars.

XI

THE HIDING-PLACE

Whither he was going he had no idea. He rode at random under the spur of the energy that was rampant within him, demanding to be expended.

Love guided him as he himself guided his horse. He was the rider of his own steed, and at the same time the accursed steed of the passion that impelled him, spurred him on, shouted to him: "Forward!" guided this way and that, without purpose, his mad race across the moor. He, too, was mounted, harassed, bridled, whipped, bit in mouth, raging and powerless. And the horse shared the mad humor of his master, who was under the spell of love, so that Blanchet, wearied though he was by his day's labor, having had but a very brief rest, was wild with excitement none the less. Fortunately, he knew all the ditches and canals and bogs, and, in his rapid flight with the reins lying on his neck, he chose his own road. Sometimes he would slacken his pace on approaching a ditch, in order to walk down into it, head first, compelling his rider to stand in his great stirrups, with his back touching the croup: sometimes he leaped them at full speed.

Drunken, bareheaded,—his hat having blown away somewhere in the darkness,—the wind whistling through his hair, Renaud rode, for the sake of riding, because the violence of his pace corresponded to the violence of the passions that were raging within him. He tore along as a beast does in the rutting season, from its mad desire to be alone.

And he said to himself that it was abominable to think of the other, when he had for his own that flower of beauty, chastity and sweetness; but he was thirsting for something very different; and he was conscious of an intensely bitter taste in his mouth, a clinging, dry saliva, a moisture that made his thirst the more unbearable.

Powerless to devise a means of escape from all the evil impulses in his heart, he rode on confessing to two longings: either to meet Rampal and take vengeance upon him for everything, or else to fall over backward into a ditch and rise no more, thus giving a different turn to his evil destiny;—and a third longing which he did not admit even to himself: to meet the gipsy at daybreak, begging at the door of some farm.—And then?—He did not know!

Suddenly he thought that he heard a beating of hoofs behind him, the echo of his own gallop; he turned and saw—he saw in very truth!—pursuing him at full speed, the naked gipsy, sitting firmly astride her saddle, man-fashion, upon a shadowy horse whose feet did not touch the ground.

She flew through the air, laughing in mockery as she cried to him:

"Stop, coward!"

He said to himself that it was not real, but he did not say to himself that it was a vision; he thought: "It is witchcraft!" and fear seized upon him, fear as powerful as his desire, and he fled from the image of her he sought.

He turned to look no more; he fled. He heard the double gallop still: his own and the other's. He rode through the transparent mist that hovered over the damp, salt sand; and as he cut through those crawling clouds it seemed to him as if he were riding through the sky, above the higher clouds. In very truth, his brain was wandering, for love will be obeyed, and his youthful passion was like insanity.

Suddenly Blanchet's four legs, as he flew over the ground, became motionless and rigid as stakes, and his shoeless feet began to slide over an absolutely smooth surface of clay, hard as iron and as slippery as if it had been soaped. Swiftly the horse slid along, digging furrows with his hoofs upon the polished surface, and when he lost his acquired momentum, he stopped, tried to resume his former pace, raised one foot and fell heavily to the ground, exhausted, his mouth and nostrils breathing despair.

In an instant, Renaud, leaning on his spear, which he had not let go, stood at his horse's head, struggling to lift him up, and encouraging him with his voice. Blanchet, supported by the rein in his master's hand, regained his feet after two fruitless slides.

Renaud looked about: there was nothing to be seen save darkness, the desert, the stars,—tatters of pallid mist that strayed hither and thither, as if clinging to a bush, a tamarisk, a clump of rushes,—and assumed, from time to time, the shape of fantastic animals.

Renaud mounted Blanchet once more, but he was moved to pity for him. And the horse, sometimes letting himself slide upon his shoeless feet, his four legs perfectly stiff, sometimes putting one foot before the other, testing the ground, which was firm and hard beneath his weight, but soft beneath his sharp, scaly hoof, carried him at last away from the clayey tract.

Pity and remorse at once were awakened in Renaud's heart by Livette's horse.

What right had he, the drover, to ruin the favorite steed of his darling fiancée in the service of his passion for a witch?

So Renaud dismounted, removed Blanchet's saddle and bridle, and said to him: "Go! do what you will." Then he cut a bundle of reeds with which he made himself a bed, and lay upon his back, with his saddle under his head and a handkerchief over his face, waiting for dawn.

He fell into a heavy sleep, during which his trouble swelled and burst within him, forced its way out, and took on form and feature.—The same vision constantly returned.

When he awoke, two hours later, he found his cheeks wet with tears and his hands over his face. Then he took pity upon himself, and, having begun to weep in his dream, he let the tears flow freely that he would have forced back had they sought an outlet on the previous day.

He deemed himself a miserable wretch, and wept over his fate, at first madly, convulsively, and then with joy, as if, in weeping, he had poured out all his sorrow forever. He wept to think that he was caught, powerless, between two contrary, irreconcilable things: that he wished for the one, and thirsted, against his will, for the other. He beat his hands upon the ground; he tore his cravat, which strangled him; he ground the reeds with his teeth, and cried aloud like a child,—he, an orphan:

"O God! my mother!"

And he would have wept on for a long while, perhaps, and emptied the springs of bitterness in his heart, had he not suddenly felt a warm caress—two soft, warm, moist caresses upon his cheek, his forehead, his closed eyes.

He half opened his eyelids and saw Blanchet standing beside him, touching his face with his pendant lip as he used to touch Livette's hand when in search of a bit of sugar.

Another animal had imitated Blanchet; it was the *dondaïre*, Le Doux, the drover's favorite, the leader of his drove of wild bulls and cows, whose bell he had not heard, but who had recognized his master.

The compassion of these two dumb animals aggravated Renaud's bitter grief at first. Like children, who begin to howl as soon as you sympathize with them, he, when he found he was so wretched as to arouse the pity of beasts, cried aloud in his heart, but stifled the cry at his throat; then, touched at the sight of their kindly faces, and distracted thereby from his own thoughts, he became suddenly calm, sat up, put out his hand toward the muzzles of the powerful yet docile creatures, and spoke to them:

"Good fellows, good fellows! oh! yes, good fellows!"

Day began to break. And the great black bull and the white horse, both, as if in answer to the man and in answer likewise to the first gleam of returning day, which sent a thrill of delight over all the plain, stretched out their necks toward the east; and the neighing of the horse arose, loud and shrill as a flourish of trumpets, sustained by the bass of the bull's bellowing.

Instantly a chorus of neighs and bellows arose on all sides of Renaud. His free drove had passed the night in the neighborhood. He was surrounded by the familiar forms of his own beasts.

They came at the call of Blanchet and Le Doux and the drover's voice. The mares were white as salt. Some of them came trotting up, some galloping, some followed by their foals; and passed their heads between the reeds, peered curiously in, and stood there,—or else, with a cunning air, set off again, as who should say: "There's the tamer, let us be off!" And there was a great kicking and flinging of heels away from the man's side.

Some bulls, thin, nervous black fellows, whipping their sides with their long tails, also came up, took alarm, remembering that they had been punished for some shortcoming, and, turning tail, decamped in the same way, and when they were out of sight, suddenly stopped.

But as the *dondaïre* remained there, few of the horses and cattle left the spot.

Some, the oldest or the wisest, slowly assumed a kneeling posture, as if to resume their interrupted repose, then, scenting the approaching sun, wound their tongues about the tufts of salt grass, drew them into their mouths and chewed placidly, while the silvery foam fell from their muzzles.

Others, in the same posture, lazily licked their sides. A mother, nursing her calf, watched him with a calm, gentle eye.

Here a stallion drew near a mare, reached her side in two bounds, with tail in air and bristling mane, and bold, sonorous, trumpet-like call—then reared, and when the mare leaped aside, bit at her and with a sudden sidewise movement dodged the kick she aimed at him.

More than one bull, too, paid court to the other sex, rose clumsily on his hind legs, only to fall again on his four feet, with nothing beneath him.

The awakening of the drove was not complete. The animals were still dull and heavy. They were awaiting the coming of the sun.

Renaud approached a half-broken stallion he had sometimes ridden, and threw over his neck the *séden* he had just coiled for that purpose—Livette's *séden* and Blanchet's, all stained with mud from having brought so many beasts to earth.

He gave sugar to the wild creature, who allowed himself to be saddled without overmuch resistance, desirous, perhaps, to enjoy for a day the abundant supply of hay in the stables of the château, which he had not forgotten.

"Go and rest, old fellow!" said Renaud to Blanchet.

And he set off on his fresh steed, spear in hand, with the idea of seeking Rampal.

The stallion he rode was his favorite, the one he had named Prince. And he felt a thrill of honest satisfaction as he said to himself that at all events Livette's horse would not have to put up with his whims and follies as a lover any more. He felt highly pleased at that thought, being lightened of a threefold responsibility, as rider, drover, and lover.

Prince seemed disappointed when Renaud compelled him to turn his back on the Château d'Avignon.

He rode in the direction of the cabin mentioned by Audiffret. It was very possible, after all, that Rampal had taken up his quarters there, and he proposed to find out. Now, as this cabin was, as we have seen, not in Camargue, but in Crau, not far from the Icard farm, between nine and ten leagues to the eastward, it was necessary to cross the main stream of the Rhône. But, in that vast plain, men rode long distances for a *yes* or a *no*, and thirty or forty kilomètres had no terrors for Renaud.

From his present position, it seemed to him that his shortest road would be to skirt the southern shore of the Vaccarès.

The cool, fresh morning air drove away all his black thoughts, his visions and nightmares; he felt something like tranquillity. Moreover, he was so overdone with weariness that he seemed half-asleep, and the feeling was delicious. He no longer had the strength to follow his thoughts, still less to guide them, so that he was submissive as a blade of grass, as any inanimate thing, to the passing breeze, to the sun's rays.

The hour and the coloring of the earth and sky were in very truth enough to rejoice the heart, and physical gaiety took possession of him, as he had ceased to reflect.

A fresh breeze, smelling of the sea, sent a shiver over the water and the grass. The sun was rising. A moment more and he would appear to cast his net of gold horizontally over the plain. He appeared. The vague murmurs became distinct sounds; reflection changed to brilliant light, drowsiness to activity.

Renaud, who was galloping along with his spear resting in his stirrup, his head leaning heavily on the arm that held it and his eyes closed, under the influence of the rocking motion of the horse, suddenly reopened them, and looked about with the joyous glance of a king.

He paused a moment to gaze at a huge plough drawn by several horses, which was transforming a wretched stony field into cleared land ready for the vine.

The phylloxera, which has done so much harm in rich and healthy districts, affords Camargue a new opportunity to fight the fever and to gain ground on the swamp. The sand is, in fact, very favorable to the vine and very unfavorable to the parasitic insect, and this watery country will gradually become, please God, a genuine land of the vine!

Renaud watched the ploughman with a feeling of delight at the thought of his native country being enriched by honest toil; and with a confused feeling of regret, too, for he preferred that the moor should remain uncultivated and wild and free. The idea of a flat plain, tilled from end to end, where no room was left for the straying feet of horses as God made them—that idea saddened him.

He would always say to himself as he rode through more civilized regions: "Now there, you know, a man can neither live nor die."

The fields of wheat or oats, even in the summer season when they have such a lovely reddish tinge, so like the overheated earth, so like the turbid, gleaming waters of the Rhône, had no attraction for him. They gave him the impression of an obstacle that he must ride his horse around, and Renaud did not recognize the respectability of any obstacle—except the sea!

He was more inclined to look favorably upon the vine, because it seemed to him that it was a glorious thing for his country to produce wine, just at the time when other districts in France had exhausted their producing power. And then, the Rhône, the *mistral*, horses, bulls, and wine, all seemed to him to go together, as things that told of holiday-making, of manly strength and courage and joy. They knew how to drink, never fear, did the men of Saint-Gilles and Arles and Avignon. Renaud had attended wedding-parties more than once on the island of Barthelasse in the middle of the Rhône, opposite Avignon, and there he had tasted a red wine whose color he could still see. It was an old Rhône wine, so they had told him, and he remembered that, being desirous to do honor to the wine as well as to the bride, and being a little exhilarated, he had solemnly thrown his cup into the Rhône after the last bumper. There are, at the bottom of the Rhône, many such cups, dead but not broken, from which joy was quaffed but yesterday. They go gently down, turning over and over, through the water to its sandy bed. There they sleep, covered with sand, and two or three thousand years hence—who knows?—the venerable scholars of that day will discover them, as they are discovering amphoræ of baked earth at Trinquetaille to-day, and now and then beside them a glass urn, wherein all the colors of the rainbow chase one another about as soon as its robe of dust is removed.

Who can say that Renaud's brittle glass, from which he drank the best wine of his youth, will not remain for ages full of the sand and water of the Rhône, and that—in days to come—other youths will not find therein the same delight? For everything begins anew.

Thus did the wanderer's thoughts wander from point to point, from vine to glass. Ah! that glass of his, thrown into the Rhône! His mind recurred once more to that memory of a debauch. It seemed to him now, that, by throwing it into the river on the wedding-day, he had foretold his own destiny, and that he, Livette's fiancé, would never be married! He would drink no more from the discarded glass.

The first impulse of delight that came to him with the newness of the morning had already passed; his sadness had returned as the day lost the charm that attaches to a thing just beginning.

Dreaming thus, Renaud rode across the marshes, Prince splashing through the water up to his thighs.

Yes, my friends, he forgave the vine, did Renaud, for invading Camargue.

Moreover, after the harvest was gathered, did not the red and white vineyards afford excellent pasturage for the bulls? There are some that are all red in the autumn, and others all white, or of a light golden yellow—as if the vines had amused themselves by reproducing the two colors of the wine under the gorgeous sunsets. He has seen nothing who has not seen the beams of the setting sun, in November, now yellow as gold, now red as blood, spreading over a field of red vines, over a field of yellow vines, which themselves spread out as far as the eye can reach. Indeed, is not Camargue the home of the *lambrusque*? The *lambrusque* is the wild, Camarguese vine, different from our cultivated vines in that the male and female are on separate plants. The grapes that grow on the female *lambrusque* make a somewhat tart but pleasant wine, and the shoots of the vine make light, stout staves for the hand.

Arrived at Grand Pâtis, Renaud swam the Rhône three times, from Camargue to Ile Mouton, from Ile Mouton to Ile Saint-Pierre, and from Ile Saint-Pierre to the mainland.

He was now in the swamps of Crau, a stony desert adjoining Camargue, which is a desert of mud.

To the eye these two deserts seem to join hands across the Rhône. From Aigues-Mortes to the pond of Berre is a pretty stretch of flat country, my friends, and the sea-eagle, try as he may, cannot make it less than twenty good leagues in a straight line! And that is the kingdom of King Renaud.

Camargue has its saltwort, its grain and plantains and burdocks, growing in small clumps, with sandy intervals between; it has its *gapillons*, which are green rushes split into bouquets, with thousands of sharp points finer than needles; and here and there tamarisk-trees; and, on the banks of the two Rhônes, great elms, so often cut and hacked to procure wood to burn, that they resemble huge caterpillars sitting erect upon their tails, their short hair bristling as if in anger.

Crau is a land of naked plains and heather. It is, to tell the truth, a veritable field of stones. They have come, people say, from Mont Blanc, all the stones that now lie sleeping there. The Rhône and the Durance have borne them down, then changed their beds, after having jousted together on the vast space at the foot of the little Alps. From beneath the stones of Crau, in May, there springs a rare, delicate plant, the *paturin*, or dog's tooth. The sheep push the stone away with their noses and browse upon the slender stalks while the shepherd stands and dreams in the wind and sun.

But this stony Crau is farther away, beyond the pond of Ligagnou, which skirts the river. Here, in the Crau that lies along the banks of the Rhône, we are in the midst of the marshes, which are dry during the greater part of the year; some of them, however, are very treacherous, and one should know them well.

Renaud rode in a northeasterly direction, and soon reached the neighborhood of the Icard farm.

He drew rein.

"Where is the hiding-place?" he muttered.

And he tried with all his eyes to pierce the thick underbrush of reeds, rushes, cat-tails, sedges, and bull-rushes, springing from the midst of a deep bog. This bog did not seem, to the eye, more formidable than another, but the bulls and mares feared it and carefully avoided it.

On the surface of the water was what looked like a thick crust of mouldy verdure. It was not, however, the leprous formation of duck-weed that lies sleeping on our stagnant ponds. It was a sort of felt-like substance, composed of dead rushes, roots, twined and twisted weeds, which made a solid but movable crust upon the water, swaying beneath the feet that ventured upon it, ready to bear their weight for a moment and ready to give way beneath them.

This crust (the *transtaïère*) was broken with fissures here and there, through which the water could be seen, dark as night, its surface flecked with transient specks of light, gleaming like a mirror of black glass. Around the edges, at the foot of the scattered tamarisks, grew reeds innumerable in thick clusters, always rustling against one another, and incessantly brushed, with a noise like rustling paper, by the slender wings of the dragon-flies with their monster-like heads.

Many of these *canéous* bear white flowers streaked with purple. As they rise above one another on the long stalks, you would take them for the flowers of a tall marsh-mallow. These reeds, with their long leaves, remind one of the *thyrsi* of antiquity, left standing there in the damp earth by bacchantes who have gone to rest somewhere near at hand in the shade of the tamarisks, or to abandon themselves to the centaurs. They make one think, also, of the wand of the fable, which, when planted in the ground, was at once covered with flowers, and thereby had power over marriages.

These *thyrsi* of the bog are reeds besieged by climbing plants. The convolvulus fastens itself to the reed, twines its arms about it, rises in a spiral course, seeks the sunlight at its summit, and robes the long murmuring stalk in brilliant and harmonious colors.

The sharp leaves of the young reeds stand erect like lance-heads. The older ones break off and fell at right angles. The delicate, graceful foliage of the tamarisks is like a transparent cloud, and their little pink flowers, hanging in clusters that are too heavy for the branches, especially before they open, cause the flexible plumes of the gracefully rounded tree-top to bend in every direction.

Through the reeds and tamarisks Renaud sought to discover the hut that he knew, and that Audiffret had spoken of to him the night before. But he could hardly distinguish the little inclined cross placed at the highest point of the roof of all the Camargue cabins, which are built of joists, boards, grayish mud (*tape*), and straw. The cabin was formerly entirely visible from the spot where he stood, but the reeds had grown so thickly on the islet on which it was built, that they completely hid it. The path leading to it was on the opposite side of the bog. He must make a wide détour in order to reach it, the bog *de la Cabane*, so called, being of a very erratic shape.

From the south side of the cabin he went around to the north side. He no longer had the *transtaïère* in front of him; but beneath the surface of the water, where reeds and thorn-broom flourish, was the *gargate*, the slime, wherein he who steps foot is quickly buried.

There are many other dangers in these accursed bogs. There are the *lorons*, a sort of bottomless well found here and there under the water, the location of which must be thoroughly understood. The mares and heifers know them and are clever in avoiding them, but now and then one of them falls in, and now and then a man as well. And he who falls in remains. No time for argument, my man! You are in—adieu!

The drovers will tell you, and it is the truth, that from every *loron* comes a little twisting column of smoke, by which those mouths of hell can be located. A hundred *lorons*, a hundred columns of smoke. There, my friends, is something to dream about, is it not, when the malignant fever, bred in the swamps, smites you on the hip?

Renaud was anxious to know if Rampal was occupying the cabin, but not to attack him there, for it is a treacherous spot. "If he is there, he will come out some time or other. I will wait for him on the solid ground. Ah! I see the path!"

It was a winding path hiding under a sheet of shallow water. The bed of the path was of stones, very narrow but very firm, the right edge being marked, as far as the cabin, by stakes at short intervals, just on a level with the water.

Renaud dismounted, and looked for the first stake, holding his horse by the rein. Although he knew its location, it took him some time to find it. With the end of his spear he put aside the grass, and when he discovered the stake, he felt for the solid road whose width it measured. Bending over, he gazed long and very closely at the grasses and the reeds, which met in places above the concealed pathway, and when he rose he was certain that it had not been used for some time.

He was not mistaken. In truth, Rampal was a little suspicious of that hiding-place, which was too well known, he thought, and to which he could easily be traced. He often slept in the neighborhood, ready to take refuge in the *cul-de-sac*, if it should become necessary, but he preferred, meanwhile, to feel at liberty, with plenty of open space about him.

Renaud remounted Prince, and crossed the Rhône again an hour later.

That night he lay in one of the great cabins which serve as stables—winter *jasses*—for the droves of mares, in those months when the weather is so bad that the bulls can find no pasturage except by breaking the ice with their horns.

The next day, an hour before noon, he saw before him the church of Saintes-Maries standing out like a lofty ship against the blue background of the sea.

Little black curlews were flying hither and thither around it, mingled with a flock of great sea-gulls with gracefully rounded wings.

A cart was moving slowly over the sandy road.

"Good-day, Renaud."

"Good-day, Marius. Where are you going?"

"To carry fish to Arles."

Marius raised the branches which apparently made up his load, but which were simply used to shade a dozen or more baskets and hampers. Well pleased with his freight, he put aside the cloth that was spread over his treasure under the branches. Baskets and hampers were filled to the brim with fish taken in the ponds and the sea. There were mullet and bream, still alive, animated prisms with mouths and gills wide open like bright red marine flowers amid a mass of dark-blue, olive-green, and gleaming gold. There were enormous eels, too, caught for the most part in the canals of Camargue, which are veritable fish-preserves.

The dark-hued, slippery creatures twisted in and out, tying and untying endless slip-knots with their snake-like bodies. By the livid spots upon some of the great eels, Renaud recognized them as *murænæ*, possessors of voracious mouths, well stocked with sharp teeth.

"See how they all keep moving!" said Marius.

At that moment, as if to justify his words, a great flat fish flapped out of one of the baskets and fell to the ground.

With the end of his three-pronged spear the mounted drover nailed him to the earth to prevent his leaping into the ditch, filled with water, that ran along the road.

"Hallo!" said he in surprise, "isn't that a cramp-fish. When I spear one of them with my regular fish-spear, which is longer than this three-pronged one, it gives me a shock I didn't feel at all to-day."

"That's because the fish is in the water then, and your spear is damp," said Marius, laughing. "But let the fellow stay there," he added. "He isn't worth much. The snakes will have a feast on him."

Thereupon, horseman and fisherman went their respective ways.

The drover's thoughts wandered from the cramp-fish and the *murænæ* to the electric fish of America, of which old sailors had spoken to him. They had told him that it was charged with electricity like the cramp-fish, but resembled the conger more in shape, and that it could, with its overpowering current, kill a horse; in order to make it exhaust its stock of electricity, so that it can safely be taken, it is customary to send wild horses into the water against it; they receive the first shock, and sometimes die from the effects.

As he rode on toward Saintes-Maries, Renaud mused in a vague way upon the miracles of life, which there is naught to explain.

XII

A SORCERESS

Livette did not go to sleep. When Renaud had passed out of sight in the darkness, she softly closed her windows, and, throwing herself on the bed with her face buried in the pillow, wept in dismay.

Meanwhile,—while Livette was weeping and Renaud, bewitched, was galloping over the moor, fancying that he was pursued by the gipsy,—the gipsy herself was asleep.

The two beings whose lives she was beginning to destroy were already suffering a thousand deaths, and she, lying, fully dressed, under one of the carts of her tribe, in their regularly pitched camp outside the village, was sleeping tranquilly, her pretty, puzzling face smiling at the stars of that lovely May night.

When Renaud left her, at sunset, all naked on the beach, she had slowly stretched her sun-burned arms, taking pleasure in the sense of being naked in the open air, of feeling the caressing breath of the sea-breeze that dried the great drops of water rolling down her body. Then, still slowly, she had dressed herself,—very slowly, in order to postpone as long as possible the renewed subjection to the annoyance of clothes, in order to enjoy unrestricted freedom of movement, like a wild beast.

She had then walked along the beach, leaving the imprint of her bare, well-shaped foot in the sand, covered at intervals by a shallow wave that gradually washed away the mark.

The last kiss of the sea upon her feet, to which a bit of sparkling sand clung, delighted her. She laughed at the water, played with it, avoiding it sometimes with a sudden leap, and sometimes going forward to meet it, teasing it.

She fancied that she could see, in the undulating folds of the wavelets, the tame snakes which she sometimes charmed with the notes of a flute, and which would thereupon come to her and twine about her arms and neck, and which were at that moment waiting for her, lying on their bed of wool at the bottom of their box in her wagon.

She had already ceased to think of Renaud. She was always swayed by the dominating thought of the moment, never feeling regret or remorse for what was past,—having no power of foresight, except by flashes, at such times as passion and self-interest bade her exert it. Her reflection was but momentary, by fits and starts, so to speak; and her depth, her power, the mystery that surrounded her, were due to her having no heart, and, consequently, no conscience.

The men and women who approached her might hope or fear something at her hands, imagine that she had determined upon this or that course, and try to defeat her plan; but she never had any plan, which fact led them astray beforehand.

She routed her enemies and triumphed over them, first of all, by indifference; and then she would abruptly cast aside her indolence, like an animal, at the bidding of a passion or a whim, and would still render naught every means of defence—her attack, her decisions, her clever wiles, being always spontaneous, born of circumstances as they presented themselves.

No: she made no plans beforehand, in cold blood; she never concocted any complicated scheme; but she could, at need, invent one on the spur of the moment and carry it out instantly, at a breath,—or perhaps she would begin to execute it in frantic haste, and abandon it almost immediately from sheer *ennui*, to think no more of it until the day that some burst of passion should suddenly bring it back to her mind.

She was like a spider spinning its whole web in the twinkling of an eye to catch the fly on the wing; or she would spin the first thread only, and forget it until something happened to remind her to spin a second.

Thus constituted, she was at the same time better and worse than other women, because she was more changeable than the surface of the water,— because she was of the color of the moment.

Being a fatalist, the gipsy said to herself that whatever is to happen, happens, and she had never taken the trouble to devise a scheme of revenge. She would simply utter a threat, knowing well that the terror inspired by a prediction is the first calamity that prepares the way for others, by disturbing the mind and heart and judgment. And then, something always goes wrong in the course of a year, collaborating, so to speak, with the sorcerer, and attributed by the victim to the "evil spell" cast upon him. It is upon him, in reality, because he believes that it is. In short, if opportunity offered, she would assist the mischievous propensities of fate, with a word, a gesture, a trifle—and, if opportunity did offer, it was because it was decreed long ages ago, written in the book of destiny that so it should be!

A true creature of instinct, the gipsy had no other secret than that she had none.

She followed her impulses, satisfied her desire for revenge, her love or her hate, without stopping to consider anything or anybody; and, like the wild beast, she, a human being, became an object of dread to civilized people, as nature itself is. Such creatures are implacable. The gipsy loved life, and lived as animals live, without reflection. It was the paltry yet profound mystery of the sphinx repeated. Her actions were those of a brute, not far removed from the lower types of mankind, notwithstanding her lovely human face, in which the eyes, like Pan's, not clear, seemed veiled with falsehood because they were veiled to their own sight with their own lack of knowledge, their uncertainty and suspense. Look at the eyes of a goat or a heifer. They are as deep as Bestiality, cunning and strong, cowering in the shadow of the sacred wood. Life longs to live. It is lying in ambush there. It is sure of her and bides its time. The human beast not only has more craft than the fox or tiger, but has the power of speech as well. Nothing is more horrible than words without a conscience.

After all, Zinzara was always sincere, although she never appeared so, because her versatility placed her from moment to moment in contradiction with herself.

The caress and the wound that one received from her in rapid succession did not prove that she had feigned love or hate. She did, in fact, love and hate by turns, from moment to moment, or rather, without loving or hating, she acted in accordance with her own fancy, sincere in her contradictions—and very artlessly withal.

She bore some resemblance to the ape, as it sits among the branches, softly rocking its little one in its arms with an almost human air, then suddenly relaxes its hold and lets its offspring fall, forgotten, to the ground, in order to pluck a fruit that hangs near by.

She was a personage of importance in her own eyes, and she saw nobody but herself at all times and under all circumstances.

The gipsy was formidable, as a spirit concealed in an element whose slave it should be. She had the force of a thunderbolt, of an earthquake, of any fatal occurrence impossible to foresee or to ward off.

The viper is not evil-minded. He does not prepare his own venom. He finds it all prepared. Disturb him, and he bites before he makes up his mind to do it.

Like the cramp-fish or the electric eel, the gipsy could discharge a fatal current of electricity as soon as you approached her,—by virtue of the very necessity of existence. It might happen to her also to indulge in the sport of exerting her malignant power around her, for no reason, simply to watch its effects, because it was her day and her hour, her whim.

She had the same means of defence and amusement.

It was not in her nature to be malignant. It simply was not necessary for her to think of you, that was all. As a matter of fact, a man was fortunate if she did not look at him.

Although born of a race that holds chastity in high esteem, she was not chaste; not that she loved debauchery above everything else, but she used it as a means of domination,—the more unfailing because she made little account of it. Always superior, in her coldness, to the passion she inspired, it was in that more than all else that she really felt herself a queen, a sorceress—aye, a goddess, by favor of the devil! The caress of the water in which she bathed afforded her more pleasure than it afforded others. She was like the female plant of the *lambrusque*, which is fertilized by the wind.

Like the mares of Camargue, that often assemble on the shore to breathe the fresh sea air,—when she opened her lips to the salty breeze, on those fine May evenings, she was happier than any man's kiss could make her. The wandering spirit of her race breathed upon her lips, in the air, with the freedom of the boundless waste—a vague hope, vain and unending.

Being thus constituted, she knew that she exercised a disturbing influence upon others, and that she was herself protected by something that relieved her of responsibility. That thought filled her with pride. There was a reflection of that pride in her smile. There was also the constant remembrance of the sensations she had experienced, known to her alone, and a certain number of men, who knew nothing of one another.

Their ignorance, which was her work, also made her smile. And that smile was a mixture of irony and contempt. She knew her own strength and their weakness. So she was always smiling.

With no other policy than this, she reigned over her nomadic tribe, changing her favorite, like a genuine queen, as chance or her own impulses willed, but giving each one of them to believe that he was the only man she had ever really loved, even if he were not her first lover.

To deceive the *zingari*—that was a notable triumph for a *zingara*!

Among the fifteen or twenty children in her party, there was a young dauphin, the queen's offspring; but since he had left her breast, she had bestowed no more care upon him than the bitch bestows upon her puppy some day to become her mate.

When she came near her camping-ground, excited by her recent contact with the waves and the salt, which, as it dried upon her, pressed against her soft, velvety flesh, the gipsy, tingling with warmth in every vein, cast a sidelong glance at one of the male members of the tribe, a young man with a bronzed skin and thin, curly beard.

And, in the darkness,—when they had eaten the soup cooked in the kettle that hung from three stakes in the open air,—the *zingaro* glided to the *zingara's* side.

At that very moment, by her fault, two human beings were suffering in the inmost recesses of their consciences, where Livette and Renaud were gazing at each other with eyes in which there was no look of recognition.

The betrothed lovers, her victims, were struggling under the evil spell cast upon them by her glance, at the moment that that glance seemed to grow tender in response to that with which her lover enveloped her, on the edge of the ditch, beneath the feeble light of the stars.

Renaud at that moment was dreaming that he had seen the naked gipsy again and triumphed over her, and was asking himself, at the memory of that robust, youthful form, if she were not a virgin, even though a child of the high-road; recalling confusedly a strange, overpowering, absolute passion, the triumphal possession of a new being, a heifer hitherto wild and vicious, even to the bulls; of a mare that had never known bit or saddle, and had maintained a rebellious attitude in presence of the stallion.

Renaud was dreaming all that, but Renaud no longer existed for Zinzara.

Zinzara, just at that moment, in the dew-drenched grass, was writhing about like the legendary conger-eel, that comes out of the sea to abandon itself to the labyrinthine caresses of the reptiles on the shore.

Two days Livette waited, wondering what was taking place. Weary at last of seeking without finding, she set out for Saintes-Maries on the morning of the third day.

"There," she thought, "I may, perhaps, hear some news."

Her father saddled an honest old horse for her use.

"You must go to Tonin the fisherman's at noon," said he, "and eat your *bouille-abaisse*. Send him word, when you arrive, with a good-day from me."

Livette, as she rode along, looked about her at the peaceful green fields, joyous and bright in the light that fell from the sky and the light that rose on all sides from the water.

The gnats danced merrily in the sunbeams. When the gnats dance, they furnish the music for the ball with their wings, and on calm days there is a sound like the strumming of a guitar on the golden strings of light over all the plain. There were also in the air long, slender threads,—the "threads of the

Virgin," or gossamer,—come from no one knows where, which waved gently to and fro, as if some of the fragile strings of the invisible instrument on which the little musicians of the air perform, being broken, had become visible, and were floating away at the pleasure of a breath.

It may be that those threads came from a long distance. It may be that the toiling spiders who patiently spun them lived in the forests of the Moors, in Estérel. A breath of air had taken them up very gently, and now they were on their travels.

Livette watched them floating quietly by, and thought of a tale her grandmother had told her. According to the grandmother, the threads came from the cloaks spread to the wind as sails by the three holy women. The wind, as it filled them, had unravelled them a little, very carefully; and the slender threads, taken long ago from the woof of the miraculous cloaks, hover forever above the sands of Camargue, where stands the church of the holy women.—Above the strand they hover night and day, as so many tokens of God's blessing; but they are rarely visible, and if, by chance, on a fine day, you do see them, it means that some great good fortune is in store for you.

In the transparent azure of the morning sky Livette's heart clung to each of the passing threads; but the child tried in vain to acquire confidence,—her heart was too heavy to remain long attached to the fleeting things. She was afraid, poor child, and felt influences at work against her that she could not see.

Alas! while the golden threads floated over her head, the black spider was weaving his web somewhere about, to catch her like a fly.

Still musing, Livette rode on, and could distinguish at last, far before her, the swallows and martins soaring above the steeple. They were so far away you would have said they were swarms of gnats. And with the swallows and martins were numberless sea-mews. This host of wings, large and small, now dark as seen from below, now bright and gleaming as seen from above, turned and twirled and gyrated in countless intricate, interlacing circles. Instinct with the spirit of the spring-time and the morning, they were frolicking in the fresh, clear air.

It occurred to Livette to ride by the public spring in quest of news, for it was the hour when the women and maidens of Saintes-Maries-de-la-Mer go thither to procure their daily supply of water.

As she entered the village, she noticed the gipsy camp at her right hand, but turned her head.

At that moment, she met two women on their way to the spring, walking steadily between the two bars, the ends of which they held in their hands, and from which, exactly in the middle, the water-jug was suspended by its two ears.

"It is just the time for the spring," said Livette to herself, and she followed them at a foot-pace.

"Good-day, mademoiselle," the women said as they passed, for the pretty maiden of the Château d'Avignon was known to everybody.

There was as yet no one at the spring. The two women waited, and Livette with them.

"How do you happen to be riding about so early, mademoiselle? Are you looking for some one?"

"I am out for a ride," said Livette, "and as it's the time for drawing water, I thought I would stop here a moment. My friends will surely come sooner or later."

No more was said, and Livette, having nothing else to do, looked closely for the first time at the carved stone escutcheon in the centre of the high arched wall above the spring. It is the town crest, and it is needless to say that it includes a boat, a boat without mast or oars, in which the two Maries—Jacobé and Salomé—are standing.

"I have often wondered," said Livette, "why they put only the figures of two holy women in the boat. For haven't our mothers always told us there were three of them? Were there three or not?"

"Certainly there were three, my pretty innocent," said the older of the two women, "but Sara was the servant, and no honor is due to her."

"If the third was Saint Sara, then there were not three Marys, eh? But I have always heard it said that the Magdalen was there, and that she went away from here and died at Sainte-Baume."

"Yes, so she was, and many others besides! Lazarus was in the boat, too, but when they were once on shore, every one went his own way: Magdalen went to Baume, and the two Maries and Sara remained with us. That was when a spring came out of the sand, by the favor of our Lord. When they built the church, they walled in the spring in the centre of it."

"Faith, they would have done well to leave the spring outside the church!"

"Why so? is the water spoiled by it?"

"It's only good on the fête-day."

"After so many years! And there's so little of it!"

"We ought to have asked the saints to make it pure and abundant. If we had all set about it with our prayers, they would have done it for us."

"One miracle more or less!"

"The miracles, my dear, are only for strangers."

"And that is just what we need, neighbor. If it wasn't so, you see, strangers wouldn't come any more—and without them what would the country live on? poor we! Where are our harvests? Where are our wheat and our grain, good people, tell me that? If it wasn't for the saints, this would be a cursed country! One fête-day a year, and the pilgrims—God bless them!—fill our purses for us."

"Miracle days are only too few and far between. We ought to have two fête-days a year!"

"What are you saying, you foolish woman? Two fête-days a year! Mother of God! That would mean death to pilgrimages. To keep the custom going, everything must be just as it is and nothing change at all. Our men know that well enough. Remember the visit the Archbishop of Aix and those great ladies paid us twenty years ago."

And once more the story was told of the visit of the Archbishop of Aix to Saintes-Maries-de-la-Mer twenty or thirty years before.

On a certain 24th of May the archbishop arrived at Saintes-Maries with several elderly ladies of the nobility of Aix. But it so happened that that 24th of May was the evening of the 25th! Anybody may be mistaken!—So that, instead of being lowered at four o'clock, the reliquaries were raised again on that day, and when monseigneur entered the church with his fair companions, it was good-by, saints! They had already been hoisted up at the end of their ropes to the lofty chapel, amid the singing of canticles.

"Oh! well!" said the archbishop to the curé, "they must come down again for us."

The curé was about to obey, but a rumor of what was going on had already spread through the village!—Ah! bless my soul, what a commotion!

"What!" said the old villagers. "They would lower the reliquaries on some other day than the 24th, would they? Why, if it is such a simple thing and can be done so often, why do you make the poor devils from every corner of Provence and all the rest of the world come hurrying to us on a special day? No, no, it would be the ruin of the country, that is certain!"

To make a long story short, the people of Saintes-Maries took their guns, and under arms, in the church itself, compelled the prince of the Church to respect the sovereign will of the people of the town.

And they did very well, for rarity is the quality by virtue of which miracles retain their value.

One of the women having told this anecdote, which was perfectly well known to them all, they began, as soon as she had finished, to make up for their long silence by loud talk, vying with one another in their approval of the villagers' revolt against the bishops, who would have abused the good-will of the two Maries.

"We are very lucky, all the same," said one of the old women, "to have a good well with good stone walls instead of the brackish spring the saints had to get their drinking-water from. I can remember the time when we got our water from the *pousaraque* (artificial pond), as the people on our farms do to-day. The Rhône water that was brought into them through the canals was always so thick and muddy you could cut it with a knife!"

"Bah! it had time enough to settle in our jars."

"It is funny, though, to be so hard up for water in such a wet country!" said a young woman who had just arrived. "This water is a nuisance! Saint Sara, the servant, ought to have known from experience that a woman has enough work to do at home without wasting her time waiting in front of closed spigots. Saint Sara, protect us, and make them turn on the water!"

The women began to laugh.

Almost all the housekeepers of Saintes-Maries had assembled by this time. A last group arrived upon the scene. Some carried jars, without handles, upon their heads, balancing them by a graceful swaying of the whole body. With their hands upon their hips, they themselves were not unlike living amphoræ. Others, having one jug upon the head, carried another in each hand—the stout *dourgue*, with handle and mouth; others had wooden pails, others, glass jars, each having selected a larger or smaller vessel, according to the necessities of her household.

"What sort of a pot have you there, Félicité?"

Whereat there was a general laugh.

She to whom the question was directed, replied:

"I broke my jug, poor me! And, as I had to have some water, I took an old thing I found that has always been standing behind the door at our house since I can remember. If it will hold water, it will do for me to-day, my dear!"

"Take it to monsieur le curé for his library; it's an antique, and is worth money!"

81

Félicité had, in fact, come to the spring with a genuine Roman amphora, found in the sandy bed of the Rhône—a jar two thousand years old and hardly chipped!

Each family at Saintes-Maries is entitled to one or two jars of water each day, according to the number of its members.—The water had not begun to flow.

Livette, sitting upon her horse, thoughtful and sad amid the chatter, was still awaiting her friends.

"What were you saying just now?" asked some late comers.

And having been informed, each one of them proceeded to expound her ideas upon the subject of the saints and Sara the bondwoman, paying no heed to what the others were saying—so that the jabbering of the women and girls seemed like a *Ramadan* of magpies and jays assembled in one of the isolated clumps of pines so often seen in Camargue.

"I would like to know if it's fair," cried one of the women, "not to put in Saint Sara's portrait, too! A saint's a saint, and where there's a saint there isn't any servant!"

"The saints aren't proud! and Saint Sara cares mighty little whether her picture's there or not!"

"She may not care, but it was an insult to her!"

"Oh!" said another, "good King René and the Pope knew what they were doing when they arranged things so. Sara was Pontius Pilate's wife, and she was the one who advised her husband to wash his hands of the heathens' crime!"

A murmur of reproof ran from mouth to mouth among the gossips.

"Ah! here's old Rosine, she'll set us right."

Motionless upon her horse Livette listened vaguely. She was absent-minded, yet interested.

When old Rosine, who was very deaf, had finally been made to understand what was wanted of her, and that she was expected to give her views concerning Sara the bondwoman, she began:

"Ah! my children, God knows his own, and Sara was a great saint, for sure _____"

Here Rosine crossed herself, and was at once imitated by all the old women.

"But," added Rosine, "Sara was a heathen woman from Egypt, and not a Jewess of Judea; and the heathens, you see, come a long way after the Jews in the world's esteem. Don't you see that the Jews are scattered all over the world, but they stay everywhere, and become masters by force of avarice. That is their way of being blessed by their Lord. But the heathens of Egypt, on the contrary, are wanderers and poor, although they are thieves, and more scattered and more accursed than the Jews. Well, you see, my children, Saint Sara is their saint, the saint of the Egyptian heathens! She wasn't a very good Catholic saint, to pay the boatman for her passage by a sight of her naked body—with the indifference of an old sinner, I fancy! So it is right that she should come after the two Marys, for there are different ranks in heaven. And that is why Saint Sara's bones are not between the boards of the great shrine in the church, but under the glass of the little shrine in the crypt—or the cellar, you might say. The cellar is a good enough place—under the feet of Christians—for miserable gipsies! And it is right that it should be so."

"What Rosine says is true!" cried one of the women. "These frequent visits of the gipsies are the ruin of the country. When our pilgrims come, rich and poor, do you suppose they like to find all these scamps, who are so clever at stealing folks' handkerchiefs and purses, settled here before them? Don't you suppose that drives people away from us? How many there are who would like to come, but don't care to compromise themselves by being found in such company!"

"Bah! such nonsense!" said a humpbacked woman; "those who have faith don't stop half-way for such a small matter! And those who have some troublesome disease and hope to cure it here aren't afraid of the thieves nor their vermin. Take away my hump, mighty saints, and I will undertake to get rid of my lice and my fleas one by one, without any assistance!"

This speech was greeted by a roar of laughter, which stopped abruptly, as if by enchantment. The little gate to the spring was opened at last, and, at the sound of the water rushing from the pipe, all the women ran to take their places in the line—not without some trifling disputes for precedence.

At last, some of Livette's girl friends arrived. Spying them at some little distance, she went to meet them.

"What brings Livette here so early, on horseback?" said the women, when she had moved away.

"Why, she's looking for her rascal of a Renaud, of course!" said the hunchback. "That fellow isn't used to being tied like a goat to a stake, and the little one will have a hard time to keep him true to her, for all her fine *dot!*— The other day, Rampal—you know, the drover, a good fellow—saw him at a distance on the beach talking with a gipsy who wasn't dressed for winter!"

"Not dressed for winter? what do you mean?"

"She wore no furs, nor cloak, nor anything else, poor me! She was taking a bath as God made her. The plain isn't a safe place for that sort of thing. You think you can't be seen because you think you can see a long distance yourself, but a tuft of heather is enough for the lizard to hide his two eyes behind while he looks."

Again the women began to chuckle and laugh, but for a moment only.

Meanwhile, Livette's friends were saying to her:

"No, we haven't seen your sweetheart, my dear; but they are already putting the benches in place against the church for the branding, and he can't fail to be here soon."

At that moment, a strain of weird music arose not far away. It was produced by a flute, and the notes, softly modulated at first, were abruptly changed to heart-rending shrieks. A strange, dull, monotonous accompaniment seemed to encourage the sick heart, that called for help with piercing cries.

"Hark! there are the gipsies and their devil's music, Livette. Just go and look —it is such an amusing sight. We will join you in a little while."

"What about my horse?" said Livette.

"If you haven't come to stay, there's a heavy iron bracelet just set into the wall of the church to hold the bars of the enclosure for the branding. Tie your horse to that, and don't be afraid that he will disappear. Every one will know he's yours by those pretty letters in copper nails you have had put on your saddle-bow."

Livette fastened her horse to the ring in the church-wall, and walked in the direction of the gipsy music. It seemed to her that she might probably learn something there.

Now, Zinzara the Egyptian had seen Livette ride into the village, and her music had no other purpose than to attract her, and Renaud, her fiancé, with her, if he were there. Why? to see;—to bring together for an instant, with no fixed purpose, upon the same point of the vast world through which she wandered, two of the personages with whom she "beguiled her time;" to look on at the comedy of life, and to watch the sequel, with the inclination to give an evil turn to it, chance aiding. She loved the anomalies that result from the chaotic jumbling together of circumstances.

Zinzara was turning a kaleidoscope whose field was vast like the horizon of her never-ending travels, and whose bits of glass, multicolored, were living souls.—She turned the wheel to see what calamity destiny, with her assistance, would bring to pass. The amusement of a woman, of a sorceress.

XIII

THE SNAKE-CHARMER

Life is an enigma. The everlasting silence of space is but the endless murmuring of invisible circles which, twining in and out, part and meet again, lose and never find one another, or are inextricably interwoven forever. Life is an enigma. We can see something of its beginning, nothing of its close; its meaning escapes us, but all the links make the chain, and some one knows the rest.

That there are two ends to the ladder is certain. Day is not night, and one does not exist without the other. There are joy and sorrow, health and sickness, happiness and unhappiness, life and death—in a word, good and evil, for the beast of flesh and bone. This is a good man, that a bad. Religion and morals have nothing to do with it, and afford no explanation; but little children know that it is so, and fools know it likewise. They who undertake to reason the thing out learnedly, befog it. They who pull the thread break it. There is some one and there is something. Nothing is null, I tell you, my good friends, and yonder drivelling old idiot, sitting on the stone at the foot of the Calvary before the church, and holding out his hand to Livette, knows two things better than we—good and evil. The idiot, when he passed the gipsies' wagons in the morning, talked amicably, yes, he talked for some minutes with two or three gaunt dogs chained up under the wagons; but when he saw Zinzara, the queen, fix her eyes upon him, the idiot was afraid and limped away as fast as he could. He was afraid because *there was*, in Zinzara's look, *something not good*.

And now Livette, as she passes by, glances at him, and the idiot—poor human worm—smiles and holds out to her a glass pearl,—a treasure in his eyes,— which he found that morning in the filth of the gutter near by. The pearl glistens. It is bright blue. The idiot sees beauty in it, and offers it to the pretty girl passing by. Livette smiles at him, and he, the drivelling idiot, the cripple who drags himself along the ground, laughs back at Livette. He laughs and feels his man's heart vaguely opening within him—why?—because of *something good* in Livette's eyes.

God is above us, and the devil beneath us. God? what do you mean by God? Kindly humanity, which is above us and toward which we are ascending; the ideal, evolved from ourselves which, by dint of declaring itself and compelling love, will be realized in our children. The devil? what is that? the obscure beast, the ravenous, blind worm, which we were, and from which we are moving farther and farther away.

There is something nearer the mystery than the mind, and that something is the instinct. Certainly we are nearer to our origin than to our end, and instinct almost explains the origin because it is still near at hand, but the mind cannot explain the end because it is still so far away! Whence come we? The crawling beast may suspect.—Whither go we? How can the beast tell, when he cannot fly?

The bond that binds us fast to earth is not cut. Man bears forever the scar of his birth. He has, therefore, always before him evidence of how he is connected with infinity *behind* him; but how he is connected, by death, with the life everlasting, *before* him, he does not see.

Instinct, like a glow-worm, lights up the depths from which man comes forth, but intelligence casts no light into the boundless expanse on high, wherein it loses itself, just at the point where God begins.—Ah! how mysterious is God!

Yes, between the intelligence and man's origin, instinct stretches like a bridge. Between the intelligence and man's end, there is a yawning chasm. The reason cannot cross it. There is no way but to leap. Man finds it easy to imagine what lies below; his own weight draws him down to a point where he can understand it.

To understand what is above, it is essential to have a power of lightening one's self, a wing which man has not. Here instinct acts upon the mind in a direction opposed to mental effort.

To some minds this faculty of rising sometimes comes, but man's conceptions depend upon his experiences, and the time has passed when reliance was placed upon the "wise men," upon those whose conceptions far outran their experiences. Perhaps it is better so. Perhaps every man ought to form his ideas for himself and no one will know anything *for good and all* until he has earned the right.

Sometimes, for a moment, especially in dreams, but occasionally in his waking hours, man *knows*. He has profound intuition; but nothing is more fleeting than this sudden glimpse of eternity.

The best of us are blind men haunted by the memory of a flash of light.

Which of us has not known, by personal experience, how a man can fly away from himself? The sense of mystery, scarcely detected, has escaped us, but who has not been conscious of it for a second?

Truth, like love, reveals itself for a second only, but we must believe in it—

forever.

These thoughts are properly presented here, for everything is in everything. One man studies the hyssop, another the oak; Cuvier the mastodon, and Lubbock the ant, but they all arrive at the same point, a point which includes everything.

Do you know why the gipsies, Bohemians, gitanos, zincali, zingari, zigeuners, zinganes, tziganes, romani, romichâl,—all different appellations of the same wandering race,—arouse such intense interest on the part of civilized peoples?

There are two reasons.

The first is, that the gipsy, being very primitive and wild, appears among civilized beings as the image of themselves in the past. It is as if they were our own ghosts.

When we see them among us, we amuse ourselves, in the shelter of our established homes, by thinking regretfully that we no longer have before us the broad plains so dear to the beasts we are; that we are no longer in constant contact with the earth, the plants, the animals, which are the *mothers* that bore us, and whom we love for that reason. They have remained what we were when we left them, and that touches us.

The second reason is that they really discovered long ago something of the meaning of life.

It is certain that they are magicians. They have seen the hidden spring and have a vague remembrance of it; they have retained its dark reflection in their glance.

The glance! they know its dormant and insinuating power. They know how to subdue weak minds by a glance.

The least skilled in magic among them still believe that the "secret" of things is hidden away somewhere under a stone, and in their travels through every country on earth they often raise heavy boulders, whose peculiar shapes seem to indicate that they may conceal the mystery. They never find under the boulders anything but toads and snakes and scorpions, but they are skilled at making powerful potions from the blood and venom of the reptiles.

They know, also, the secret properties of plants, and that the hemlock and belladonna vary in their effects when cut at certain times of the year and at certain hours, according to the influence of the seasons and the moon's rays.

The gipsies are skilled in the science of poisons. Men and women—*roms* and *juwas*—excel in the art of giving diseases to cattle.

Their trades are only pretexts for calling at the houses they pass. They are coppersmiths simply because the art of subjecting metals to the action of fire was invented by the son of Cain, the progenitor of all accursed mortals. And they are saddlers because they like to be about horses, dear to all vagabonds.

The gipsies, who were originally worshippers of fire, and now have no religion of their own, but always adopt that of the country they are passing through, are to mankind what Lucifer is to the angels.

"We come from Egypt, if you please," Zinzara would sometimes say to the people of her tribe. "Indeed, that is where we had our homes and were a powerful race in the days of Moses. Then our ancestors were magicians to the kings of Egypt, who overcame death; but our origin is higher and farther away.

"We come from a country where the *Secret Power of the World* was discovered: a dragon guards the mystery on the summit of a lofty mountain, in a cavern, out of reach of whatever floods may come.

"Our ancestor Çoudra learned from the high-priests the method of compelling the dragon to obey him. He entered the cavern and conceived the idea of universal knowledge, and resolved to avail himself of it in the outside world, in order that he might become a king and mighty among men—for why was he poor? Why does poverty exist, why death?

"He had no sooner conceived his project of justifiable rebellion than the dragon sought to devour him. Our ancestor eluded him, and believed that, by virtue of the secrets he had discovered, he would be omnipotent on earth, but suddenly he found that he had almost forgotten them all, as if by magic. He no longer remembered any of them except those that do harm, those that produce disease, sorrow, misery, and death—all the evils from which he would have liked to free himself.

"And the high-priests cursed him and his sons. Manou spoke against them thus: *They shall dwell outside of cities; they shall possess none but broken vessels; they shall have nothing of their own, except it be an ass or a dog. They shall wear the clothes they steal from the dead; their plates shall be broken; their jewels shall be of iron. They shall journey, without rest, from place to place. Every man who is faithful to his duty shall hold himself aloof from them. They shall have no dealings except with one another. And they shall marry only in their own race.*

"And the *Tchandalas* were able to flee the country, but not the sentence.

"And that is our present case.

"The crown of Çoudra is a broken ring—with sharp points, like a dog's collar, and his sceptre is an iron staff, broken but formidable. For why does want exist, and pain and death? God is wicked!"

With this tale, set to music, the gipsy queen sometimes lulled her son to sleep.

And when, at the entrance to some château, she cast a long, malevolent glance upon a young mother, who, upon catching sight of her, quickly carried her little child within, such thoughts as these would run through Zinzara's head: "The secrets that are known to our prophets, our dukes and princes and kings, will cause all your cities, your churches, and your thrones to tremble on their foundations, for why does want exist, and pain and death? The hour will come —we await it—when your nations will be scattered to the winds of wrath, unless the wise men who invoked a curse on us become their masters—but you are too far from their wisdom for that! You will be ours.

"Meanwhile, woe to those of you whom we find alone! We look fixedly at them, and the spirit of evil does the rest."

And this is what little Livette saw when she approached the gipsy camp.

The whole tribe was there. Their numerous wagons were of different sizes, most of them being made in the shape of small oblong houses, with little windows, very like the Noah's arks made for children in Germany. The gipsies had arranged their wagons side by side, in a line, each one opposite a house in the village. Thus the line of wheeled houses formed with the houses of the village a winding street, which, if prolonged, would have surrounded Saintes-Maries like a girdle. Thus, while their sojourn lasted, the gipsies could cherish the illusion that they were settled there, that they were inhabitants of the village, one dwelling opposite the baker, another opposite the wine-shop; but no one forgot that the gipsy houses were built upon wheels that turn and can make the tour of the world.

"I pity the tree," says the gipsy, "it looks enviously at me as I pass. It is jealous of my ass's feet."

Most of the wagons were patched with boards of many colors, picked up or stolen here and there.

As a matter of fact, the wagons of the tribe were placed in the rear of the village houses, so that the occupants of those houses, the innkeeper or the baker, being busy in the front part of their establishments, could naturally dispense with a too frequent appearance in the gipsy street.

The nomads alone swarmed there undisturbed. They passed but little time in the wagons, except when they were on the road or tired or sick; their days were passed in the open air, squatting in the dust, or on the steps of the little ladders which they lowered from the doors of their wagons to the ground; or else they passed long hours lying in the shade under the wagon—smoking their pipes and dreaming.

For the moment, some of the women here and there through the camp were intent upon the same occupation: searching, in the bright morning light, for vermin among the matted hair of their children, whom they held tightly between their knees as in a vise.

From time to time, one of the little fellows would howl with pain, when his mother inadvertently pulled or tore out one of his wiry, coal-black hairs. Then he would wriggle and squirm to get away, but the vise formed by the knees would nip him again and hold him tight, and there would be a squealing as of sucking pigs loth to be bled. Then blows would rain down and the shrieks redouble. Suddenly the urchin that was howling most lustily would cease, and follow, with a lively interest, the movements of a chicken from some neighboring coop, or the antics of a hunting-dog that had wandered that way and was well worth stealing.

The mothers went through with their matutinal task in an automatic way that said as clearly as possible: "It is of no use to try to do this, for the vermin breed and always will breed; but we must do something. It is always a good thing to be busy; and then it makes an excellent impression, here under the eye of civilized people. They see that we are clean and neat."

"Buy my dog," said one of them with a leer to an open-mouthed villager. "You will be well satisfied with his fidelity. He is faithful, I tell you! so faithful that I have been able to sell him four times.—He always comes back!"

All these women had a coppery, sun-burned, almost black skin, and hair of a peculiar, dull charcoal-like black.—Some wore it twisted in a heavy coil on top of the head. Several of the younger women let it hang in long, snake-like locks over their breasts and backs. Their eyes also were a curious shade of black, very bright, like black velvet seen through glass. Life shone but dully in them, without definite expression. Some mothers were attending to their duties with a child on their back, wrapped in a sheet which they wore bandoleer-fashion, with the ends knotted at the shoulder. The little one slept with his head hanging, tossed and shaken by every movement.

Red, orange, and blue were the prevailing colors of their tattered garments, but they were tarnished and faded and almost blotted out by layers of dust and filth;—a smoke-begrimed Orient.

Many of the women had short pipes between their teeth. The men who lay about here and there, with their elbows on the ground, were almost all smoking placidly, their Sylvanus-like eyes fixed on vacancy. They made a great show of pride under their rags. Some were asleep under the rolling cabins.

The line of wagons along the outskirts of the village was still in shadow, but at the head of the line, the first of the wagons, standing a little apart, beyond the line of the houses, was in the sunlight. This wagon, which was painted and kept up better than the others, was Zinzara's, and a few of the villagers had collected in the sunshine in front of it, attracted by the notes of the flute and tambourine.

Livette, as she approached the group, had no suspicion that, in the wine-shop facing the wagon, behind the curtains of a window on the first floor, Renaud had stationed himself, there, at his ease, to watch the gipsy, who was playing the flute and dancing at the same time, her feet and arms bare.

Zinzara held the flute—a double flute with two reeds diverging slightly—with much grace, and blew upon it with full cheeks, raising and lowering her fingers to suit the requirements of a weird air, sometimes slow, sometimes furiously fast and jerky. Her head was thrown back, so that she appeared more haughty and aggressive than ever.

As she played upon her flute, Zinzara danced—a dance as mysterious as herself. With her bare feet she simply beat time on the ground. Her dance was naught but a play of attitudes, so to speak. She constantly varied the rhythmical undulations of her flexible, vigorous body, whose outline could be traced at every movement beneath the clinging material of her dress. When the movement quickened, she stamped her feet faster, still without moving from where she stood, as if in haste to reach a lover's rendezvous, where languor would replace activity.

Seated a few steps from the dancer, a young gipsy, with a vague, dreamy expression, was pounding with his fist, thinking of other things the while, upon a large tambourine, to which amulets of divers kinds were attached,— Egyptian beetles, mother-of-pearl shells, finger-rings, and great ear-rings,— which danced up and down as he played.

And the tambourine seemed to say to the double flute:

"Never fear: your mate is watching over you. I am here, father or betrothed, I, your strong-voiced mate, and you can sing freely of your joy and sorrow; no one shall disturb you; I am on the watch, and for you my heart beats in my great, sonorous breast."

But to the gipsy's ear the music of the tambourine said something very different; and with a smile upon her lips, blowing into her flute with its diverging reeds, raising and lowering her slender fingers over the holes,

Zinzara, exerting a subtle influence over all about her, dressed in soft rags that clung tightly to her form and marked the outlines of her hips and of her breast in turn; displaying her tawny calves beneath her skirts, which were lifted up and tucked into her belt,—Zinzara seemed not to see the spectators.

Twenty or thirty people were looking at her, and still she seemed to be dancing for her own amusement; but her witch's eye followed, without seeming to do so, the slightest movement of Renaud's head, the whole of which could be seen at times between the serge curtains with red borders, behind the windows of the wine-shop, under the eaves of the house across the way.

When she saw Livette approach, the dancer beat her feet upon the ground more rapidly, as if annoyed, and the flute emitted a cry, a shrill war-cry, like the sound made by tearing silk quickly.

Livette involuntarily shuddered, but she mingled with the group, momentarily increasing in size, and looked on.

Zinzara made a sign, and uttered some strange, guttural words between two loud notes—words that were, evidently, a precise command, for a gipsy child, who had come to her side a moment before, glided under the wagon, whence he emerged armed with a long white stick, with which he motioned to the spectators to fall back a little. Then he stationed himself in front of Zinzara, in the centre of the first row of spectators, and, turning toward them, enjoined silence upon them by placing his finger on his lips. The word was passed along, and the bystanders ceased their conversation, realizing that *something* was about to happen.

The dance was at an end.—The tambourine ceased to beat time. The flute alone sang on in Zinzara's hands, as her fingers moved slowly up and down.
—Now it gave forth a thin, clear note, like the prolongation of the sound made by a drop of water falling in a fountain; it was a sweet, insinuating appeal, as melancholy as the croaking of a frog at night, on the shores of a pond, at the bottom of an echoing, rocky valley.

And, with the end of his wand, the child pointed out to one of the spectators something that came crawling out from under the wagon. It was a tiny snake, with red and yellow spots, and it drew near, evidently attracted by the notes of the flute. Another followed, and soon there were several of them—five in all.

When they were in front of the flute-player, between her and the boy with the wand, they raised their heads and waved them back and forth, slowly at first, then more quickly, keeping time with the flute. The serpents danced, and the mind of every spectator involuntarily compared their dance with the woman's that he had seen a moment before. There was the same undulating movement, the same evil charm, and every one was conscious of an uncomfortable feeling at the sight.

Livette, surprised and strangely moved, thought that she was dreaming. The spectacle before her was curiously, deplorably in accord with the state of her heart. She did not understand its hidden, intimate connection with her own destiny, but she felt its baleful effects. Zinzara's glance, from time to time, swept over the girl's face, but did not rest upon it. On the subject of her own influence, Zinzara knew what she knew.

Soft, soft as spun silk, the notes of the flute arose, very soft and prolonged, like threads extending from the instrument and winding about the necks of the little snakes; and the little snakes followed the notes of the flute, which drew them on and on. Zinzara walked backward. The little snakes followed her as if they were held fast by the notes of the flute as by silken threads. The gipsy stopped, and the notes *grew shorter*, so to speak, like the threads one winds about a bobbin. Then the snakes approached the sorceress, and as Zinzara stooped slowly over them, and put down her hands, still holding the flute, upon which she did not cease to play, the snakes twined themselves about her bare arms. Thence one of them climbed up and wound about her neck, letting his little head, with its wide open mouth and quivering tongue, hang down upon her swelling breast. And when she stood erect again, two others were seen at her ankles, above the rings she wore on her legs. Then she laid aside her flute and began to laugh. Her laugh disclosed her regular, white teeth.

"Now," said she, "if any one will give me his hand, I will tell his fortune!"

But no hand was put forward to meet hers because of the little snakes.

Zinzara laughed aloud, and her laugh, in very truth, recalled certain notes of her double flute.

At that moment, Livette started to walk away.

"Come, you!" said the gipsy quickly,—"you refused to listen to me once, but to-day you must be very anxious to find out where your lover is, my beauty! Give me your hand without fear, if you are worthy to become the wife of a brave horseman."

Livette blushed vividly. Her two young friends arrived just then and heard what was said. "Don't you do it!" said one of them in an undertone, pulling Livette's skirt from behind; but, Livette, annoyed by the gipsy's expression, in which she fancied that she could detect a touch of mockery, put out her hand, not without a mental prayer for protection to the sainted Marys. The gipsy took the proffered hand in her own. The snakes put out their forked tongues. Livette was somewhat pale.

They were both very small, the fortune-teller's hand and the maiden's.

Renaud looked on from above with all his eyes, greatly surprised and a little disturbed in mind.

The gipsy held Livette's hand in her own a moment, exulting to feel the palpitations of the bird she was fascinating. She had hoped to intimidate Livette, and the courage the girl displayed annoyed her.

"Your future husband isn't far away, my beauty," said she, "but he is not here on your account, never fear! On whose, then? That is for you to guess!"

Livette, already somewhat pale, became as white as a ghost.

"That alone, I fancy, is of interest to you, my pretty sweetheart! Then I'll say no more to you except this: Beware; the serpent on my left wrist just whispered something to me. Look well to your love!"

A shudder ran through the spectators like a ripple over the surface of a swamp. One of the snakes was, in fact, hissing gently.

The gipsy released Livette's hand; as the girl turned to go away, she came face to face with Rampal. He had been wandering about the village since early morning, and had just joined the group, unseen by any one, even by Renaud.

Livette recoiled instinctively and in such a marked way that Rampal might well have taken it for an affront. Unfortunately, having left the front row, she was hemmed in by the crowd on all sides of her.

"Oho! young lady," said Rampal, "so we don't recognize our friends!"

"Good-day, good-day, Rampal," replied Livette, repeating the salutation as the custom is in the province; "but let me pass! Make room for me, I say!"

"*Sur le pont d'Avignon*," sang the gipsy, with a laugh, "*tout le monde paye passage!*"[2]

Renaud, still behind his window, had at last recognized Rampal. Fuming with rage, but naturally wary, he considered whether he should rush down at once and attack him or wait until Livette had gone.

Rampal did not always need a pretext to kiss a pretty girl,—but here was one ready-made for him!

"Do you hear, demoiselle?" said he. "You must pay the tollman of your own accord, or else he will pay himself!"

He threw both arms about the poor child's waist. She bent back, holding her body and her head as far away from him as possible, but the rascal, hot of breath, holding her firmly and forcing her a little closer, kissed her twice full upon the lips.

A fierce oath was uttered behind them in the air. Everybody turned, and, looking up, discovered Renaud shaking the old-fashioned window, which was reluctant to be opened. Two more wrenches and the window yielded, flew suddenly open with a great noise of breaking glass, and Renaud, standing on the sill, leaped to the ground.

"Ah! the beggar! the beggar! where is the vile cur?"

But Rampal had already leaped upon his horse that was hitched near by to the bars of a low window, and was off at a gallop.

He rode as if he were riding a race, half-standing in his stirrups, his body bent forward, and plying incessantly and very rapidly a thong that was made fast to his wrist, and that drove his horse wild by the way it whistled about his ears.

"Coward! coward!" one of the young men present could not refrain from shouting after him.

"Coward? oh! no!" said Renaud—"simply a thief! for if he weren't riding a horse he never intends to return, the fellow wouldn't run away—I know him!"

He turned to poor, frightened Livette.

"Never fear, demoiselle," said he, "he shall not carry our horse to paradise with him."

Was it Renaud's purpose, in saying this, to make the gipsy think that he was bent upon taking vengeance for the theft of his horse rather than for the insult put upon his fiancée? Perhaps so; but the devil is so cunning that Renaud himself had no idea that he was capable of such craft.

As to the gipsy, she said to herself that Renaud, by jumping out of the window, instead of coming quietly down the stairs, had compromised his prospects of revenge for the satisfaction of exhibiting his gipsy-like agility to her. He did, in truth, jump like a wild cat, and rebound as if he were equipped with elastic paws! He was as agile as a true *zingaro*! He was as handsome and bold as a highwayman! They are gipsies, to all intents, these wandering guardians of mares and heifers!

Renaud, who had disappeared long enough to buckle his horse's girth, rode by in a few moments upon Prince; the witnesses of the scene just enacted were still discussing it.

"Catch him! catch him! eat him, King!" cried twenty young men's voices in chorus.

"With the King and the Prince arrayed against him, Rampal is a dead man," some one remarked, with a laugh.

Renaud was already at a distance. He had not looked at the gipsy, but he felt that her eyes were upon him, and he felt now that they were following him from afar; and the feeling caused a pleasurable thrill, of which he was conscious, and for which he reproved himself vaguely on Livette's account, but without seeking to repress it. Yes, as he galloped along in his wrath, he galloped in a particular way in order that his wrath might show to good advantage, so that he might appear a handsome and graceful horseman, as he was in fact. He was conscious of every movement that he made—he fancied that he could see himself, and was desirous to make a good appearance, he, the King!

The peacock, in the mating season, has more gorgeous plumage, and makes the greatest possible display of it. The nightingale and the redbreast have sweeter voices. All alike take pleasure in so arraying themselves as to give pleasure.

"Where are you going, Livette?" her two friends asked her.

"I am going to see monsieur le curé. I must have a talk with him, poor me! for it was a great sin to listen to that sorceress, you know!"

XIV

JOUSTING

Both Renaud and Rampal had spears.

As he rode by the Neuf farm, half a league from Saintes-Maries, Rampal, who owned nothing in the world but his saddle, and had no spear, being at that time simply a drover out of a job, had spied one leaning against a fig-tree, and had appropriated it without dismounting, had "borrowed it without a word," thinking that he should probably need it to defend himself.

Now he was galloping across the fields, leaning forward on his horse's neck, with his thong in his boot and the spear resting in the stirrup.

Renaud had mistaken the road in his hot pursuit. Perhaps the gipsy was the cause of it, for, in spite of himself, in order to remain within her range of vision, Renaud had ridden straight toward the Vaccarès, while Rampal had just taken the road to Arles, avoiding stratagem in order to mislead his pursuer more effectually, for he said to himself that Renaud would surely argue that he had made for the middle of the island to take refuge in some deserted *jass*.

Renaud divined Rampal's plan.

"He will keep to the road," he suddenly thought, and feeling certain that he was right, he turned to the left and rode due west. Rampal, having the start of him by a full league, drew rein in the vicinity of Grandes-Cabanes, and having planted his spear-head in the ground, rested both hands upon it, then placed his feet, one after the other, on the hind-quarters of his horse, and stood there for some moments, scanning the plain behind him. Between two clumps of tamarisks he caught a glimpse of a horseman, like a flash of light, or like a rabbit scuttling between two wild thyme bushes—Renaud, beyond question! Rampal saw that Renaud, if it were he, was about to take to the road, and he himself thereupon left it and rode in the opposite direction on a line parallel to that his enemy was following in the distance. When Renaud reached the road and turned into it, Rampal had the Vaccarès in front of him, and there he turned to the left and followed the shore. His plan was to cross the main stream of the Rhône, and reach the Conscript's Hut, in the middle of the *gargate*, the spot where he was confident of finding safe shelter in times of serious danger. Unluckily for him, he had been seen—when he was standing on his horse watching his man—by a fisherman who was crouching

98

on the edge of the canal, fishing for eels with a reed and a short line, at the end of which was a bunch of worms, strung and twisted together.

"Have you seen Rampal, friend?" said Renaud, stopping his horse short as soon as he saw the fisherman, who was just about changing his place.

"Ah! King, are you the man who is looking for him?" said the fisherman, an old man. "If he has kept to the road he took to get away from you,—for I saw he was watching some one behind him,—he ought to be on the shore of the Vaccarès by this time, and from there, if he doesn't go back to Saintes-Maries, he will surely go up toward Notre-Dame-d'Amour. You have a good horse, and you can catch him between the Vaccarès and the Grand' Mar."

Renaud darted away as if he had wings.

After an hour and a half of furious riding,—he was wise enough, however, to change his gait several times,-he drew rein, a little discouraged; then, after a brief halt and a draught of brandy from the flask that never left his holsters, he resumed his headlong race—but not until he had thoughtfully allowed his horse to drink a swallow of water from the canal.

When he was between the Grand' Mar swamp and the Vaccarès, he found his own drove taking their midday rest there, under the guidance of Bernard, his young assistant.

Horses and bulls were lying motionless on the shore of the Vaccarès, in the twofold glare from sky and water, for it was well-nigh noon, and the light was dazzling.

Bernard was resting likewise, lying on his back with his head on the saddle, not far from his horse, which was fettered near by, learning to amble.

In front of Renaud lay the pearl-gray Vaccarès, gleaming like a huge table of polished steel, in the centre of which a veritable white islet of sea-mews were sleeping, motionless as statues.

Behind him stretched an ashen-gray plain, which could be seen only in spots —where the salt emerged in efflorescent crystals—glistening through a vast violet net-work of flowering *saladelles*; for the *saladelles* spread out in broad, graceful tufts, with many ramifications, but without foliage, dotted with a multitude of lilac blossoms, between which the ground can be seen. And farther away the fields of glasswort began, with their plump, juicy leaves; they are a beautiful rich green when they are young, but the salt air soon turns them blood-red, so that the oldest and those nearest the sea are the darkest.

Here and there the stunted tamarisk, with its gnarled trunk, dotted the plain, its sparse foliage tinged with pink by the blossoms hanging in tiny clusters, which, tiny though they be, are a heavy burden for its flexible branches.

And in the dry, seamy bottoms were great patches of *siagnes*, *triangles*, *apaïuns* of every kind, *canéous* or dwarf reeds used in making roofs and matting, thorn-broom and all sorts of aquatic plants, bright green, and straight as fields of grain; their angular battalions, harvested in summer, go down before the scythe in broad half-circles. Above these patches of verdure, which bend and rustle with the faintest breath of air, hovered dragon-flies with enormous heads,—swallow-like insects, voracious devourers of gnats. They flew about with the swallows over the waters where the mosquito is born, making a metallic sound among the reeds when their wings of transparent, black-veined mica came in contact with them.

Renaud gazed at these familiar things and forgot himself in them. For a second he fancied that he was watching his drove there, and that he had nothing else to do but remain with his beasts, absorbed, as they were, in calm, unreasoning contemplation of the desert that surrounded him. He ceased to love, to hate, to desire, and to pursue.

The shadow of wings passed him by. He raised his eyes and saw, above his head, two red flamingoes.

"They built their nest here this year," he thought.

But Prince, the good horse, had recognized his favorite mares, and, stretching out his neck, opening his nostrils wide to inhale the fresh breeze of the swamp and the plain, raising his lips and displaying his teeth, he gave a neigh that made all the mares spring to their feet at a single bound, the bulls raise their heads, and Bernard himself jump up from the ground, spear in hand.

Renaud, pressing his knees together and pulling his horse back, held him in hand, although he trembled under him and pranced up and down in the soft sand.

At the same time, a sudden gust of the *mistral* swept across the plain and broke the mirror-like surface of the Vaccarès into little waves.

"If it is Rampal you are looking for," said Bernard, "he isn't far away, you may be sure. When he saw me here, all of a sudden—just a moment ago—he rode off that way. And as he went out of my sight very soon, I believe he has gone into some cabin. You had better look around the Méjeane tower."

Renaud was off again.

Suddenly his eyes fell upon a low cabin with its rush-covered roof, shaped like a pyramid, or like a stack of straw, and surmounted, as they all are, by its wooden cross, bending back as if the *mistral* were gradually blowing it over.

The thought came to him: "Rampal is there! His horse must be tired. He retraced his steps a short distance without Bernard's seeing him, and went into hiding there—hoping that I should be thrown off the scent and would ride by. Yes, he is surely there!"

Renaud turned about, and rode straight toward the cabin, keeping a sharp lookout; whereupon Rampal, who was really hidden there, watching his pursuer through the holes in the wall, rushed out, frightening an owl that flew away in dismay, and leaped upon his horse which was browsing in hobbles near by, but out of sight, at the bottom of a ditch.

The *mistral*, which comes like a cannon-ball when it makes up its mind to blow at that time of day, suddenly began to roar. Renaud had put his head down to meet the squall, so that he did not perceive this manœuvre of the enemy.

So it was that Rampal seemed suddenly to come up out of the ground, not twenty feet from Renaud, who was not taken by surprise, however, but rushed at him, brandishing his spear, for all the world like one of the knights of the time of Saint Louis, of whom our legends tell. (Aigues-Mortes was then in its prime.)

But Camargue is, as every one knows, the mother of the *mistral*—the vast sunny plain, with Crau, which, after sending the air up by dint of overheating it, is compelled to summon other air in order to breathe at all. And thereupon, down the Rhône valley, at the summons of the desert, comes a torrent of fresh air, which is the companion of the river, and is called the *mistral*. It roared through Renaud's open vest as in the belly of a sail, and, taking Prince sidewise, kept him back a little. It was no easy matter to leap the ditch. That gave the advantage to Rampal, who was now trotting freely along, face to the wind.

The ditch was now between the two men, and Rampal's only purpose in trotting along the edge of it was to limber up his horse's legs. Renaud, abandoning the idea of crossing the ditch for the moment, decided to follow along on his side. The two horsemen rode thus for a few moments. Rampal had prudently protected his face from the *mistral* with a red silk handkerchief, the ends of which flapped about his neck.

Suddenly, taking advantage of a spot where the banks came somewhat nearer together, Renaud lifted his horse and landed on the other side of the ditch at the very instant that Rampal, having executed the same manœuvre in the opposite direction, landed on the side Renaud had left.

Renaud did not find a favorable spot for crossing at once, and Rampal gained upon him.

Having at last crossed the obstacle once more, Renaud pursued Rampal at full speed, and so rapidly that, when Rampal turned to judge the distance between them, he saw Renaud hardly fifty paces behind him.

He had just time to turn about, and waited for his foe, with lance in rest, leaning forward in his saddle, his feet planted firmly in the broad stirrups.

Renaud, unluckily, was charging against the *mistral*. A sort of hail, consisting of sand and of the little snails that cling in myriads to the leaves of the *enganes*, beat into his face and angered him.

Five hundred feet away, Bernard was looking on—not saying a word, for fear of Rampal, but praying fervently for Renaud, and he fancied that he was watching two champions standing on the long ladders in the prows of the jousting boats, with their lances held firmly under their right arms. Rampal's spear, being suddenly lowered too far by a false step of his horse, pricked the heel of Renaud's boot and grazed Prince's flank, whereupon he jumped violently aside, as if he were avoiding the horns of a heifer.

Renaud's spear tore the sleeve of his enemy's blue shirt and carried away the piece.

The horsemen met and passed each other.

Rampal was the first to turn, and rode after Renaud, ready to strike him from behind, while he was struggling to stop Prince, who had acquired too much momentum; and Prince, hearing the other horse's hurried step, and feeling his hot breath behind him, furious at being held back, fearing that he would be overtaken, turned about so quickly and unexpectedly in his wrath, that Rampal took fright and turned again, but involuntarily.

Renaud, finding that his pursuer had once more become a fugitive, gave Prince a free rein.

The stallion was off like the wind.

The horsemen sped along, pushed on by the gusts, the wind being now behind them.

The mares and heifers, the whole drove, in fact, stood with their heads in the air, staring eyes, and nostrils distended, watching the two men come down toward them, bending over their horses' necks, reins flying, as if pursued by the tempest along the shores of the pond, whose waters were dancing and rippling in the wind.

Here and there the little tamarisks, bent almost double, seemed likewise to be fleeing from the storm. There were no more gnats or dragon-flies in the air. Above the Vaccarès the spray was flying. The *mistral* swept everything clean.

Two minutes later, powerless to control their enervated beasts, excited as they were by the struggle and the wind, the two adversaries rode at full speed through the drove.

Thereupon, inflamed by the sight of their two stallions racing madly by, alarmed at the sight of the waving spears, intoxicated by the wild wind that found a way into their bodies through their fiery nostrils, the mares neighed and reared and started off together on the gallop. The heifers followed. Hundreds of hoofs and cloven feet beat the ground with a noise like the roaring of a tempest, and the whole drove, lashed by the *mistral*, which howled behind them, biting them and urging them forward, rolled across the plain like a second Rhône. And while Bernard was saddling his horse in hot haste to overtake them, the two enemies galloped in the midst of the hurricane as if borne on by the stamping of eighty beasts, whose hoofs raised clouds of sand and showers of spray and mud in the wind that travelled faster than they!

At the head of this whirlwind, and still in the midst of it, Renaud succeeded in overtaking Rampal. When he was near enough to touch him, he selected the precise moment when his horse was raising his left hind foot, to strike him on the right hind-quarter. The right leg, just as it was about to strike the ground, bent double under the blow of a spear directed by a man riding at a gallop, and Rampal and his horse rolled over among the countless galloping hoofs that shook the earth.

Bulls and horses leaped over the two bodies lying there, man and beast, and when the drove, tired and subdued, came to a stop half a league farther on, Renaud, still riding Prince, was holding by the bridle his recaptured horse, bleeding only in the flank and at the nose.

Standing beside him, with rage in his heart, stained with mud and dust, his face bleeding and the skin torn from the palms of the hands, Rampal, red as fire, was occupied in rearranging his breeches and fastening his belt.

"Wait till next time, Renaud! After this you would expect a man to seek revenge, eh?"

But his shrill voice was drowned in the howling of the *mistral*.

"Give me back my saddle!" he shouted in a louder tone.

The drover's saddle is his whole fortune. He cherishes it, loves it, takes pride in it.

"Your saddle?" rejoined Renaud suspiciously. "Come with me and get it! Bernard will give it to you."

He shrugged his shoulders, and without another word rode after the drove, leading back to it the emaciated horse which Rampal had sadly misused.

He was extremely glad that Blanchet had had no part in this duel. He recognized Blanchet from afar in among the mares, but sleeker and better cared for than the others. A true lady's horse, staunch as he was!—And now he would be able to return him to his mistress, as he had his former horse, in addition to Prince. And his nostrils dilated with the pride of victory. He inhaled long draughts of the bracing salt air.

He was thinking of two women—yes, of two, not one only!—who would say of him when they heard what had taken place: "That is a man!" And Renaud's noble horse shared his master's pride, as he capered about, in the liberty accorded him to choose his own pace, with the proud bearing of a stallion that had won the race in the sight of his whole drove.

XV

MONSIEUR LE CURÉ'S ARCHÆOLOGY

The curé of Saintes-Maries was a man of about sixty, well preserved, very tall and stout, with bright eyes whose light he quenched with spectacles, and energetic gestures which he purposely restrained.

The parsonage was near the church, the doorway shaded by a number of elms. The house, in accordance with the prevailing custom of the province, was whitewashed once a year, outside and in, like the houses of the Arabs.

The houses in Saintes-Maries are low. The streets are narrow, and wind about to escape the sun. The shadows under the awnings of the little shops have a bluish cast. In front of the doors, which open on the street, hang transparent curtains of common linen, in some cases of very fine net-work, to stop the flies and admit the light after it has passed through the sieve, so to speak. And, behind them, the maidens of Saintes-Maries are confined like birdlings in a cage, or like very dangerous little wild beasts. Are not all maidens to be looked upon with more or less suspicion?

The maidens of Saintes-Maries wear the Arles head-dress and the neckerchief, with fold upon fold held in place by hundreds of pins, by as many pins as a rose-bush has thorns; and where the thick folds of the handkerchief open, in the depths of the *chapelle*, you can see the little golden cross gleaming upon the firm young flesh rising and falling with the maidenly sigh. The apron worn over the ample skirt seems like a skirt itself, it is so broad and full, and slender feet peep out from beneath it, as agile as the Camargue partridge's red claws, that love to scamper swiftly over the fields to escape the hunter, knowing that Camargue is broad and space is plentiful.

Many are the pale faces at Saintes, for, whatever they may say, the marshes still breed fever, and this country, to which people come to be miraculously cured, is, generally speaking, a country of disease; but pallor goes well with the wavy black hair, worn in broad puffs on the temples and falling upon the neck in two heavy masses which are turned up to meet the *chignon*. To help them to forget what is depressing in their lives, they resort, here as elsewhere, to coquetry—and the rest!—And then they are accustomed to the fever, which gives birth to dreams and visions; they tame it, as it were; it is not cruel to the people it knows, and does not lead them to the cemetery until they are old and gray.

The cemetery is a few steps from the village, a few steps from the sea. It lies at the foot of the sand-dunes, surrounded by a low wall. The dead and gone villagers of Saintes-Maries lie sleeping there between the sea and the desert of Camargue: many fishermen who lived in their flat-bottomed boats; many herdsmen who lived on horseback in the plain.

All of them alike find there, in death, the things amid which their lives have been passed: the salt sand, filled with tiny shells, the *enganes* that grow in spite of everything, reddened by the salt-laden winds, and heavy with soda,— and the thin shadow of the pink-plumed tamarisk. There they hear the neighing of the wild mares, the shouts of the herdsmen contending on the race-course on fête-days, or stirring up the black bulls in the arena under the walls of the church. They hear the sails flapping, and the *han* of the bare-legged fishermen pushing their flat-bottomed boats or barges into the water; and night and day, the pounding of the sea in its efforts to push back the island of Camargue, while the Rhône, on the other hand, is constantly pushing it into the sea, and adding to its bulk with mud and stones brought down from its head-waters. The sea smites the island as if it would have none of it, but all in vain,—it, too, can but augment its size with the sand it casts up.

And the sand from the sea makes a broad hem of dunes along the shores of Camargue.

No one can fail to see that the dunes, those shifting, tomb-like hills of sand, must have served as models for the massive pyramids, the tombs of kings, in the Egyptian desert.

At the feet of the little pyramids of sand sleep the dead of Camargue.

But whither has the thought of death led us? Why do we tarry here, while Livette is timidly lifting the knocker at monsieur le curé's door?

The blow echoed within the house, in the empty hall. Livette was much perturbed. What was she to say? Where should she begin? The beginning is always the most difficult part. She would like to run away now, but it is too late. She hears steps inside. Marion, the old servant, opens the door.

Marion has a practised eye. When any one knocks at Monsieur le curé's door, she knows, simply by examining his face, what he wants, and frames her answers accordingly, on her own responsibility; for Monsieur le curé is subject to rheumatism: he suffers from fever, too, and Marion nurses Monsieur le curé! If he listened to Marion, he would nurse himself so carefully that all the sick people would have to die unshriven, without extreme unction, for Marion would always have a good reason to give to prevent him from going out by day or night, when the *mistral* was blowing or the wind was from the east, summer or winter, rain or shine.

But Monsieur le curé would smile and do just what he chose. He was a good priest. He never failed in his duty. He loved his parishioners. He assisted them on all occasions with his purse and his advice. He was beloved by them all.

He loved his parishioners, his commune, and his curious church, which was once a fortress; he was familiar with the shape of its every stone. He loved it both as priest and as archaeologist, for Monsieur le curé is a scholar, and his church is, in very truth, one of the most interesting monuments in France, with its abnormally thick, high, and threatening walls, crowned with jutting galleries and surmounted by crenelated battlements, with an unobstructed view of sea and land in all directions, and overlooked by four turrets, and a tower in the centre,—the highest of all,—from whose belfry the alarum bell, in the old days, often aroused the country-side, repeating in its shrillest tones: "Here come the heathens, good people of Saintes-Maries! Attention! Come and shut yourselves up here! Make ready your arrows and the boiling oil and pitch!"—Or else: "Hasten to the shore, good people of Saintes-Maries! A French vessel is sinking!"

And to this day it seems still to say, to all, far and near: "I see you! I see you!"

One could go on forever describing the church of Saintes-Maries, and relating anecdotes concerning it.

Behind the battlements at the top, and enclosing the roof of flat stones, runs a narrow pathway, where the archers and patrols in the old days used to make their rounds, surrounded by countless sea-swallows. Along the ridge-pole of the roof, of overlapping broad flat stones, between which thick tufts of *nasques* are growing, rises a high carved comb, in ogive-like curves, surmounted by fleurs-de-lis.

All this is beautiful and grand, but there is a little thing of which the villagers are as proud as of the bell-tower and the turrets, and that is a marble tablet, about five courses in length by three in height, on which two lions are represented. One is protecting its whelp; the other seems to be protecting a little child, as if it were its own offspring. It seems that this tablet was carved by a Greek workman long, long ago.

The marble is set into the southern wall of the church, beside the small door.

You enter. The ogive arch of the nave compels you to raise your eyes to a great height. And as you enter by the main door, your attention is attracted by a romanesque arch, directly in front of you, at the far end of the church, at least five metres below the ogive arch of the nave; in the centre of this arch are the blessed reliquaries, resting upon the sill of an opening like a window, flanked by two columns. From that position they are lowered once in every year at the ends of two ropes.

The choir is some few feet higher than the flagging of the church. It is reached by two symmetrical staircases, between which is the grated door leading down into Sara's crypt. That door you can see, directly in front of you, at the end of the passage through the centre of the church, between the rows of chairs. One would say that it was the air-hole of a dungeon.

Down below, in the damp crypt, with its low arched roof and naked walls,—a veritable dungeon,—upon a mutilated marble altar, is the little glass shrine containing the relics of Saint Sara, the patron saint of the gipsies. There, amid the smoke of their candles, in an atmosphere made foul by human exhalations, you can see them once a year, huddled together in a dense crowd, mumbling their questionable prayers.

In the days of the Saracen invasions this crypt served as a storehouse for supplies, when all the inhabitants of the little village were forced to take refuge in the fortress-church.

Aigues-Mortes has her walls and her Constance Tower, massive as Babel; Nîmes has her Arena and her Fountain—and the Pont du Gard, superb in its beauty, is also hers; Avignon her bridges, her ramparts, and her clocks with figures of armed men to strike the hours; Tarascon her Château, mirrored in the Rhône; Baux the fantastic ruins of her houses, hollowed, like the cells of a bee-hive, out of the solid rock of the hill-side; Montmajour has her tombs of little children, also dug, side by side, in the solid rock, and to-day filled with earth and flowers, like the troughs at which doves drink; Orange has her theatre and her triumphal arch; Arles has her theatre with the two pillars still upright in the centre; she has Saint-Trophime, too, with its sculptured façade and its *Allée des Alyscamps*, bordered with Christian sarcophagi and lofty poplars. But Saintes-Maries-de-la-Mer has her church, which Monsieur le curé would not give for all the treasures of the other towns!

Marion saw plainly that Livette was depressed; Marion was touched when Livette said: "I must see Monsieur le curé," and as her master would not be seriously discommoded, there being no occasion for him to leave the house, Marion ushered Livette into the parlor.

It was a whitewashed room, but the curé had transformed it into a veritable museum, and the walls were completely hidden behind wooden cabinets, made by himself, and all filled with his collections.

There were pieces of antique pottery and of rainbow-hued antique glass. There were old medals.

One of the latter attracted Livette's attention. It represented a bull in the act of falling; one of his fore-legs had given way. A man, his conqueror, had seized him by the horns. That Grecian medal was struck centuries upon centuries ago. A label explained it to Livette, who thought at first that it was Renaud. Life is all repetition.

There were collections of plants and boxes filled with shells, and also many stuffed birds, all the varieties found in Camargue. For more than thirty years, fishermen and hunters had presented Monsieur le curé with curious objects and animals. Here was an otter from the Rhône, there a beaver, with his trowel-shaped tail and hooked teeth. It is a question of serious importance whether the beavers do not injure the dikes of the Rhône. The important point, you see, is that the water from the swamps should empty into the river or the sea through the canals, which run in all directions. Therefore, the dikes must hold firm and not let the Rhône overflow the swamps. And the beavers, they say, destroy the dikes. They gnaw into them when the great freshets come, to avoid the drift, and take refuge inside; and when the water comes in after them, they make a vertical hole through which to escape, and there is your dike, undermined, eaten into by the water! That is a bad state of affairs.

Livette raised her eyes. A reptile, with his mouth open, was hanging from the ceiling; he was very fat, and well he might be! he was a little crocodile, the last one killed in Camargue, a very long while ago!

In every nook left free by the natural curiosities some pious image was to be seen. Here the two Maries in their boat. There the Holy Women wrapping the Christ in his shroud. In another place, Magdalen at La Baume, kneeling in front of the death's-head. But Livette saw no image of Saint Sara.

Livette sat down and waited. Monsieur le curé did not come. The fact was, that Monsieur le curé, who had already written two monographs, one entitled *La Cure de Boismaux*, and the other *La Villa de la Mar*, was at that moment at work upon a third: *Concordance of the Legends of the Blessed Maries*, with this sub-title: *Concerning the strange and regrettable confusion that seems to exist between Saint Sara and Marie the Egyptian.*

La Cure de Boismaux also had a sub-title: *Monograph concerning the domains of the Château d'Avignon in Camargue.* Monsieur le curé recalled the fact that the domains of the Château d'Avignon formerly constituted a separate commune. That commune naturally had a curé, and in those days the proprietor of the Château d'Avignon was General Miollis, brother of the Bishop of Digne mentioned by Monsieur Victor Hugo in *Les Misérables* under the name of Myriel.

In a special chapter, Monsieur le curé sought, to no purpose, to find a reason, telluric or otherwise, for the fact that the estates of the Château d'Avignon are particularly subject to invasion by locusts, which sometimes have to be fought in Camargue, as in Africa, by regiments.

As to the *Concordance*, that was a very important and very necessary work. It was based, in great measure, upon the authority of the *Black Book*. That Latin work, preserved in the archives of Saintes-Maries, was written, in 1521, by Vincent Philippon, who signed himself: 2000 Philippon![3] (Jesus himself did not disdain the pun.) There is a French translation of the *Black Book*. It was published in 1682, and begins thus:

"Au nom de Dieu mon œuvre comancée
Par Jésus-Christ soit toujours advancée.
Le Saint-Esprit conduise sagement
Ma main, ma plume, et mon entendement."[4]

Here follows the true version of the story of the patron saints of Notre-Dame-de-la-Mer.

Marie Jacobé, mother of Saint James the Less, Marie Salomé, mother of Saint James the Greater and of Saint John the Evangelist, came not alone to the shores of Camargue. The boat without sail or oars contained also their servants Marcella and Sara, Lazarus and all his family, and several of the Christ's disciples.

Monsieur le curé would prove, with documents to sustain him, that Mary Magdalen was not in the boat. She came to Provence by some other means, no one can say by what miracle.

With the exception of the two Maries and Sara, all the passengers upon the miraculous craft dispersed in different directions, preaching and making converts.

The holy women did not leave Camargue, the island in the Rhône, divided at that time into a great number of small islands by the ponds—a veritable archipelago, called *Sticados* and inhabited by heathens. In those days, all these small islands, formed by the swamps, were covered with forests and filled with wild beasts. And this delta of the Rhône was infested with crocodiles.

Now, a long, long time after the death of the holy women, a hunter, followed by his dogs, was passing over the spot where they lay buried in unknown graves; he fell in with a hermit there, beside a spring.

"My lord," said the hermit, "I had a revelation in a dream last night. In the sand beside this spring repose the bodies of three sainted women!"

The hunter was a Comte de Provence. His palace was at Arles, and the curé had every reason to believe that he was Guillaume I., son of Boson I., famous for his liberality to the church.

It was in 981. This Guillaume had overcome the Saracens, and Conrad I., King of Bourgogne, his suzerain, loved and respected him.

The prince, having listened to the hermit's tale, rode away musing deeply; not long after, he returned and caused a church in the form of a citadel to be built at that point of the coast, in the very centre of a spacious enclosure surrounded by moats.

Then he made known throughout Provence that special privileges would be accorded to all those who should build houses between the church and the moat.

Thus was founded the Villa-de-la-Mar—which is in fact a town (*ville*), although it is too often spoken of as a village, under its other name of Saintes-Maries.

The Comtes de Provence have always granted special privileges to the town.

Under Queen Jeanne, a guard was stationed all the time at the top of the church-tower to watch the ships and make signals. Sentinels were obliged to call to one another and answer every hour during the night. The people of Saintes-Maries were also exempted by the queen from payment of tolls and the tax upon salt.

Monsieur le curé explains all these things in his book, which is very interesting. He also describes therein, "as in duty bound," the discovery of the sacred bones. In 1448, King René, being then at Aix, his capital, heard a preacher declare that Saintes Marie-Jacobé and Salomé were certainly buried beneath the church of Villa-de-la-Mar.

René at once consulted his confessor, Père Adhémar, and sent a messenger to the Pope, asking that he be authorized to make search underground in the church. The authorization was given in the month of June in the same year. The Archbishop of Aix, Robert Damiani, presided at the search.

They found the spring; near the spring was an earthen altar; at the foot of the altar a marble tablet with this inscription, upon which the good curé descants at great length:

D.   M.

IOV. M. L. CORN. BALBUS

P. ANATILIORUM

AD RHODANI

OSTIA SACR. ARAM

V. S. L. M.

Lastly, they found the bones of the saints, perfectly recognizable, and, in addition, a head sealed up in a leaden box, which, according to the curé, was the head of Saint James the Less, brought from Jerusalem by Marie-Jacobé, his mother.

The bones, having been devoutly taken from their resting-place, were with great ceremony bestowed in shrines of cypress wood. The king was present with his court. The papal legate was also there, and an archbishop, ten or twelve bishops, a great number of ecclesiastical dignitaries, professors, and learned doctors. The chancellor of the University of Avignon, too, and—so the reports of the proceedings set forth—three prothonotaries of the Holy See and three notaries public.

And so nothing is more firmly established than the authenticity of the relics of the saints.

But various apocryphal legends had appeared to throw doubt upon the truth, and Monsieur le curé was at work upon the following passage while Livette, with increasing uneasiness, was awaiting him in the parlor.

"Among the popular fallacies," wrote the curé, "which destroy pure tradition, we must stigmatize as one of the most deplorable, I may say one of the most pernicious, that one which insists that among the passengers of the miraculous craft was a third Saint Marie, surnamed the Egyptian. It is downright heresy! How could it have taken root, and how far does it extend?"

Monsieur le curé proposed to retouch that last phrase forthwith, and for a very good reason.

"Without doubt," he continued, "the Egyptians, or Bohemians, or gipsies, by manifesting, from remote times, particular veneration for Saint Sara, who was, according to their ideas, an Egyptian and the wife of Pontius Pilate, have contributed to the formation of an absurd legend, but this one has its source, or its root, in something different; there is an episode of a boat in the life of the Egyptian, which assists the error by causing confusion."

Monsieur le curé proposed to return to that paragraph also.

"Born in the outskirts of Alexandria, Marie the Egyptian left her family to lead the life of shame she had chosen, in the great city. Coming to a river, she desired to cross it in a boat, and having not the wherewithal for her passage, she paid the boatman in an impure manner.

"Later, she undertook a journey to Jerusalem with a great number of pilgrims, and on that occasion again she paid the expenses of her journey in diabolical fashion, especially if we remember that those whom she enticed into evil ways were devout pilgrims! And so, when she presented herself at the door of the temple, an invisible and invincible force held her back. She could not gain admission there."

Monsieur le curé was better satisfied with that, and took a pinch of snuff.

"She thereupon withdrew to the desert, where she lived forty-seven years. Her image appeared one day to the monk Sosimus at Jerusalem. She appeared before him naked and begged him to come and confess her. He obeyed, and went into the desert. He found her, naked, indeed, but very old. And Sosimus was convinced of her saintliness because she had the power of walking on the water. He listened to her confession. She died in the odor of sanctity, as decrepit and horrible to look upon as she had been fair and pleasant to the sight. A lion dug a grave for her with his claws in the sand of the desert.

"The Egyptian's long penance had redeemed her life, therefore, and under Louis IX. the Parisians dedicated a church to her, which bore the name of Sainte-Marie-l'Égyptienne,—corrupted at a later period to *La Gypecienne* and then to *La Jussienne*. This church was on Rue Montmartre, at the corner of Rue de la Jussienne.

"The church contained a stained window representing the saint and the boatman, with this inscription: *How the saint offered her body to the boatman to pay her passage.*[5]

"We must not, then, in any case, confound Saint Sara, a contemporary of the Christ, with Marie the Egyptian, who lived in the fifth century,—a fact that cuts short all controversy.

"It is very fortunate," continued Monsieur le curé, well pleased with his somewhat tardy conclusion, "that such a sinner was not among those on board the boat of our Maries-de-la-Mer, for in that boat, as we have said above, there were several of the Christ's disciples. *Spiritus quidem promptus est; caro autem infirma.*"[6]

Monsieur le curé took snuff, he removed and replaced his spectacles. Monsieur le curé forgot himself. He went over all the early pages of his treatise, he struck out and interlined; he struggled with rebellious words. From time to time, he adjusted his spectacles more firmly, and opened and consulted an ancient book of great size. He was very busy, very deeply absorbed in his favorite employment. He forgot that somebody was waiting for him, and poor Livette, all alone in the parlor, with the dead birds and the shells, was sadly disturbed in mind. The melancholy that possessed her was not dissipated—far from it!—by the place in which she found herself.

All the dead birds, most of which she recognized as birds of passage, reminded her of the weariness of winter, the season when the wave-washed island is immersed in fog.

There were screech-owls, the pale-yellow owls that live in church-steeples and at night drink the oil in the church-lamps; vultures that come down from the Alps and Pyrenees in times of excessive cold; the ash-colored vulture that lives at Sainte-Baume. There are little tomtits, called *serruriers* (locksmiths), which are found only on the banks of the Rhône, and *pendulines*, so called because they hang their nests like little pendulums from the flexible branches swaying to and fro above the water; and *stocking-makers*, whose nests resemble the tissue of a knitted stocking; and the *alcyon*, that is to say, the *bleuret* or kingfisher; and the *siren*, of the brilliant diversified plumage, called also *honey-eater*, which flies north in the month of May, and spends its winters by preference in Camargue. There was a stork, that probably considered Camargue, between the dikes of the Rhône, a little like Holland. There, too, was the heron with its frill of delicate feathers, falling like a long fringe over its throat. Livette knew it only by the name of *galejon*, bestowed upon it in that neighborhood because the herons' favorite place of assemblage was the pond of Galejon. There was one that bore on its pedestal the date: 1807, and the words: *Purchased at Arles market*; it was of a bluish slate color, and had on its head three slender black feathers, a foot in length. Then there were flamingoes galore, for they sometimes build their nests by myriads in the marshes of Crau, sitting astride their nests which are as tall as their legs. And the divers! and grebes! and penguins, which are seldom seen! And the rascally pelican, called by the people thereabouts *grand gousier*!

Livette fancied that she could hear in the distance the mournful, heart-rending cry of the birds of passage, rising above the roar of the wind and the sound of the river shedding its tears into the ocean; dominating the mysterious sounds that fill the darkness. How many times had she heard the cries of cranes and petrels and Egyptian curlews over the Château d'Avignon in the season when the nights are long, when the sight of the fire rejoices the heart like a living thing full of promise, when the blackness of death envelops the world. The birds remind her also of the Christmas evenings, the evenings when the logs blazing in the huge fire-place and the many lamps seem to say: "Courage! the night will pass." And it is then that the wheat shows its green stalk, saying likewise: "Yes, courage! bad weather, like all other, comes to an end at last."

Livette mused thus, and mechanically raised her eyes to the ceiling, from which the crocodile was hanging.[7]

Livette did not say to herself that there was, somewhere on the other side of the great sea, in the same Egypt to which Saint Joseph and the Virgin Mary fled to protect the Child Jesus from the persecution of King Herod, a great river, the mighty brother of the Rhône, and that in the hottest hours of the day, on the islands in the Nile, the crocodiles crawl in great numbers out upon the overheated sands to expose their backs to the rays of a sun as hot as any oven.

She did not say to herself that Saint Sara, the swarthy patron saint of the gipsies, is called by them the Egyptian, and that they water their gaunt horses in the Nile as well as in the Rhône. She could not say to herself—because she knew it not—that the Egyptians inherit from the Hindoos a debased sort of magic, and that it was the same sort, even more debased without doubt, that gave Zinzara her power.

Nor did Livette know that Zinzara carried in one of the boxes in her ambulatory house—between a crocodile from the Nile and a sacred ibis, both found in an Egyptian crypt—the mummy of a young girl, six thousand years old, whose face, from which the bandages had been taken, wore a mask of gold. She could conceive no connection between the ibis of the Nile and yonder creature of the same name killed within the year on the shore of the Vaccarès, but she underwent the influence of all these mysterious connecting currents to which space and time are naught.

The lifeless creatures, scattered all about her, lived again by virtue of the power of retaining their form forever. And fear seized upon her, for suddenly the mad idea, at once vague and precise, entered her mind of a resemblance between the profile of the great reptile hanging from the ceiling and the lower part of the gipsy queen's face.

Livette thought that she must be ill, and rose to go, determined to wait no longer, but as she put out her hand to the door she uttered a cry. A centipede was crawling along the key, as lively as you please. She recoiled, and saw upon the white wall, at about the level of her head, a *tarente*, that seemed to be watching her with its pale-gray eyes. The *tarente* is inoffensive, but Livette knew nothing of that. It is the Mauritanian *gecko*, which abounds in Provence, a reptile repugnant to the sight, with gray protuberances on the head and back like those upon cantaloupe melons. And then the little fellow, the tiny creature, resembles the crocodile!—Surely, Livette has the fever.

"What's the matter, my child?"

Monsieur le curé has entered the room. He has a kindly air that comforts the poor child at once.

He points to a chair. She sits down and dares not say a word. Where shall she begin?

He urges her.

"Well, my child?"

He closes his eyes, that he may not embarrass her by his glance, which he knows to be searching. He has left his spectacles up-stairs on his great book. He closes his eyes; and with compressed lips, presses his jaws against each other to a sort of rhythm, so that you can see his temples bulge out and subside like a fish's gills. It is a nervous affection. His hands are folded on his waist; he clasps his fingers and plays at making them revolve about one another, mechanically; but he is keenly attentive. Monsieur le curé loves the souls of his fellow-men. He knows that they suffer, that life is infinite, and that they veer about and call to one another in the boundless expanse of space and time, like birds in a storm. He is reflecting. He is a kind-hearted priest. He is imbued with the spirit of the Gospel. He is indulgent. Does he not know that some great saints have been great sinners? He desires to be kind. He knows how to be.

What can be the matter?

At last, Livette speaks. She tells him everything; the gipsy's first appearance, her refusal to give her the oil she asked for insolently, with jeering remarks about extreme unction; then of the ominous spell she cast upon her, realized even now perhaps; the change in her Renaud's character, his coldness, his flight; and then, that very morning, the scene of the snakes; how she had been attracted—partly by curiosity, no doubt, but also by her conviction that she should hear something of Renaud. And how she gave her hand to the gipsy to have her fortune told! That, she had done against her inclination! She knew that it was wrong. Who would have dared say a moment before that she would commit such a sin? But she was afraid of seeming cowardly, not because of what the world would say, but because of *her*, the gitana, in whose presence she deemed it her duty to display pride and courage. She felt that she was very hostile to her. She was afraid of her, and yet, in her despite, she would defy her. She was the stronger of the two.—At last, she arrives at her most shocking avowal—she is jealous. A terrible thought has come into her mind; is it possible that Renaud could——? But no. Did he not, to save her from Rampal, risk his life by leaping down from a first-floor window the whole height of the house? To be sure, Rampal had stolen a horse from Renaud, and Renaud had been looking for him for a long time——

Livette is undone. She has glanced at Monsieur le curé, who, before replying, is listening to his own thoughts, in order not to be diverted from the matter in hand. He is still playing with his clasped fingers, making them revolve about one another.

Around them the swans, the pelican, the red flamingo, the petrel, the ibis, look on with their eyes of glass imbedded in those heads that have lived! There they stand, those phantom birds, with wings outspread and one claw put forward, exactly similar in shape, color, and plumage to the birds that are soaring above the Nile and the Ganges, beyond seas, at this moment, and no less like other birds that lived six thousand years ago.

The reptile on the ceiling, laughing down at them with his numerous long, sharp teeth, does, in very truth, resemble some one a little—butwhom?

Livette, as she puts the question to herself, suddenly comes to the conclusion that she is insane, utterly insane, to have had such an idea! She smiles at it herself. And she seems to *feel* her smile. She does feel it. She fancies she can see it!

And at the moment she is conscious of a sensation—and a painful sensation it is—of being there, in that same room, surrounded by those creatures and in the presence of a priest—*for the second time in her life*!

Yes, all her present surroundings *she has seen before*—this that is happening to her *has happened before*. But the first time was a long while ago, oh! such a long while! The great reptile on the ceiling remembers, perhaps. That is why it laughs.—But she has forgotten *all about it*. Why is she here? She no longer knows even that. She was a fool to come here!

This Camargue country, you see, is the home of malignant fever. It rises from the swamps in the sunshine, with fetid odors, exhalations that disturb the brain and the action of the blood. From the dead vegetation, from the dead water, bad dreams and fever rise like vapor. There is an *evil atmosphere* there; and the *evil eye* too, thinks Livette.

But who can say of what the mummy lying in Zinzara's wagon is thinking all this time—the mummy of which Livette knows nothing, and which is of the same age as Livette, plus six thousand years? Like Livette, it has wavy hair, very long, but somewhat faded by time. It was once as black as jet like that of the women of Arles. The mummy is of the same age as Livette, plus six thousand years! The gipsies believe that so long as the dead body retains its shape, something of its spirit continues to dwell within it. Zinzara affirmsthat this mummy, which she procured in Egypt, speaks to her sometimes and tells her things.

Ah! if we should undertake to go to the bottom of the simplest facts, how they would puzzle us! Our Saracen mares of Camargue, sisters of Al-Borak, Mahomet's white mare, and the bulls of the Vaccarès, brothers of Apis, sometimes absent-mindedly take into their mouths, in the heart of the swamps, the long, gently-waving stalk of the mysterious lotus that lives three lives at once, in the mud with its root, in the water with its stalk, in the blue air with its flower.

Not without reason do the zingari, descendants of Çoudra, flock to the crypt of the three-storied church, there to adore the shrine of Sara, Pilate's wife—the Egyptian woman.

Monsieur le curé, who is a profound student, is revolving all these things confusedly in his mind—with no very clear understanding of them himself—and pondering them.

Ah! if he could, how quickly he would sweep the island clear of the gipsy vermin! But he cannot. Tradition forbids. Sara in the crypt is their saint. There is a mixture of pagan and Christian in the affair, painful to contemplate certainly, but with which he has no right to interfere. The essential thing is that the Christian shall triumph over the pagan, that God shall prevail against Satan—for certain it is, whatever the gipsies may say, that they are not descended from the wise king who was a negro and who brought the myrrh to Jesus.

How to protect Livette?

"Do not remain alone with your thoughts, my child. Carry your rosary always with you, and tell your beads often, not mechanically but with your whole heart. Confide your sorrows to your good grandmother, whose Christian sentiments I well know. That simple-minded old woman has a great heart.

"Avoid the town. Tell your father—who has always done as you wished, nor has he had reason to repent of so doing—to have an eye to his house, and never to leave you alone. Avoid Renaud for some little time; at all events, do not seek him. He must have an opportunity to read his own heart clearly; we must not—by trying to bring him back to you—help him to mistake his affection for you, which is not, perhaps, so deep as it should be. I will speak to him myself when I have an opportunity. The day after to-morrow is the day of the fête at Saintes-Maries. Do not fail to be present; bring us that day a heart filled with faith and with the desire to do what is right. You will meet many unfortunates there. Turn your eyes toward those who are more wretched than yourself, and by comparing their lot with yours, you will see how fortunate you are, who have youth and good health.

"The health of the soul depends upon ourselves. You will save yours.

"You will be the one, on the day of the fête, to sing the solo of invocation just as the reliquaries descend—I ask you to do it, and, if need be, I will lay the duty upon you as a penance.

"She who thinks on God and the holy women forgets all earthly ills. Knock, and it shall be opened unto you. They who fear shall be reassured. Blessed are they who weep, for they shall be comforted——"

Monsieur le curé broke off abruptly. He realized, the kind-hearted man, that his discourse was, by force of habit, degenerating into a commonplace sermon, and, rising from his chair, he walked quickly toward the door, bestowing an affectionate tap on the trembling maiden's cheek with two fingers of the hand that held his snuff-box, saying to her in a fatherly tone:

"Go, little one; you have a good heart. The wicked can do naught against us. I will pray for you at Mass. Everybody in the country loves you. Have no fear, my daughter."

Livette took her leave. The curé, left to himself, sighed. He saw that Livette was confronted by an ill-defined, strange, diabolical peril, of the kind that cannot be turned aside, that God alone can avert.

"It is fate," he muttered, employing unthinkingly a word of twofold signification.[8] "It is fate," he repeated. "Life is a sea of troubles, and God is mysterious."

XVI

ON THE ROOF OF THE CHURCH

Renaud, after his victory, dismounted for a moment, and, sitting down beside Bernard, on the shore of the Vaccarès, where the cattle and mares of his drove had resumed their attitude of repose, he set about reviewing recent events in his mind.

To overturn his projected marriage, to ruin his future for the sake of the gipsy, for the sake of the unworthy passion that was at work within him—most assuredly Renaud had no such idea.

When the first fury of his desire was worked off by wild leaps and bounds, after the fashion of his horse Prince, he found a way to be reconciled with himself. His rugged honesty was impaired. He would try to satisfy his passion for the accursed gipsy when occasion offered; and that, he felt very sure, would do Livette no wrong!

Like a clever casuist, he combated his own instinctively honest impulses with arguments which he invented with much labor, and then complacently refined and elaborated, playing tricks upon himself.

Now that he could boast of having fought Rampal on Livette's account,—omitting in his thoughts the other two reasons he had had for fighting, namely, his determination to recover the stolen horse and his desire to display his strength and courage to Zinzara,—he could return to the Château d'Avignon with his head in the air, and meet his fiancée again as if nothing had happened.

Why, after all, should he be ashamed? Had he not established a fresh claim to Livette's gratitude and the esteem of her relatives?

He would take poor Blanchet back to her,—Blanchet, of whom she was so fond,—and he could tell old Audiffret that the stolen horse was once more browsing, with the drove, on the reed-grass of the estate.

No: after mature reflection, he was sure that there was nothing that need make him ashamed.

Indeed, when one is not married, is he required to be so absolutely faithful? And what is a man to do, when things fall in his way?

The eyes see before one has had an opportunity to prevent them! Even after marriage, can one refrain from being moved by the sight of youthful loveliness? Can one control the movements of his blood? Desire is not a sin, and so long as Livette knew nothing, so long as she did not suffer through him, what reason had he, in all frankness, for self-reproach?

Nothing had come about by his procurement. He was still determined not to speak to the gipsy woman—but he would be a great fool not to put out his hand if the golden peach should offer itself to him voluntarily.

And the salt breeze that blew across the rushes, arousing the passions of the wild cattle, rushed through his veins, causing the blood to rise in sudden flushes to his cheeks.

Of what avail against that breeze, which the heifers inhale with delight, is the "I will not" of a young man who feels his youth? The good Lord forgives it in others. "I have been worrying a great deal over a very small matter of late," thought Renaud. And he sagely concluded that he would return at once to Saintes-Maries, to set Livette's mind at rest, as it was his duty to do first of all, without avoiding or seeking out the other.

Meanwhile, what had Livette been doing?

When she left the curé, almost at the same moment that Renaud was unhorsing Rampal, Livette had no wish but to take her horse and ride home at once, without even waiting for dinner.

She felt that she was lost in such close proximity to the ill-omened gipsies.

Her first thought was that Renaud, if he had overtaken Rampal, whom he could not fail to master, would go without loss of time to the Château d'Avignon.

But her second thought was that he would return to Saintes-Maries to make the most of his triumph. She knew Renaud well! He was proud of his strength and address. He was spoiled by the public at the races, who applauded with hands and voice, and he loved to hear the "Bravo, Renaud!"—He would return to the town, yes, he surely would!

He might imagine, indeed, that she, Livette, had remained there, and return on her account—and a little on the other's account, at the same time!—Ah! poor child! suspicion was just beginning to creep into her mind. Just God! suppose that that zingara woman should fascinate her Renaud!

Livette, having found her horse still tied to the church-wall, sent him to the stable at the inn and went to the fisherman Tonin's to share his *bouille-abaisse*.

"You did well, Livette," said Tonin, "you have avoided a sharp squall of the *mistral.* But I know what I'm talking about; it's nothing but a squall, and you can go home this afternoon quietly enough. It will be too hot, if anything. But what's the matter, that you're so thoughtful?"

Livette heard but little of all that was said at the fisherman's table, and, after due reflection, returned to Monsieur le curé's after the meal was at an end.

"Are you still at Saintes-Maries, little one?" he said, with a sad smile.

"I had a fright, my father——"

Livette sometimes addressed the curé thus, because of the custom in confession.

"A fright? how was that?"

"Suppose they have fought, who knows what may have happened? *Mon Dieu!* chance is uncertain, and that Rampal is so treacherous that Renaud may be the loser. I would like, with your permission, Monsieur le curé, to go up on the roof of the church at once; from there I could see Renaud much sooner if he comes back here."

The happy thought had come to her of watching her betrothed, as he himself had, that same morning, watched Rampal from the wine-shop window.

The curé smiled again and good-humoredly took down the keys of the little staircase that leads to the upper chapel and thence to the bell-tower.

He left the house, followed by Livette.

At the foot of the great bare wall of the church, so high and cold,—a veritable rampart with its battlements sharply defined against the blue of the sky,—the good curé opened the small door.

They ascended the stairs.

When they reached the upper chapel, which is just above the choir of the church, as we know, the curé said:

"I will remain here, little one, to offer up a prayer to the holy women; you can go on alone."

But Livette, without replying, knelt devoutly beside the curé for an instant, before the relics.

The relics were there, behind the ropes coiled about the capstan, by means of which they were lowered into the church, as the little jug from which the lips of the faithful drank so eagerly was lowered into the miraculous well below; —there they were, on the edge of the opening through which they were launched into space.

Through this window-like opening into the body of the church Livette could see the chairs systematically arranged below, and, higher up, the galleries, the pulpit, and the pictures—all well-nigh hidden in the dark shadow, intersected by two rays of light that darted in, like arrows, through the narrow loopholes.

Away down, below the gallery at the rear, opposite where she stood, the chinks in the great square door were marked like fine lines of fire by the sunshine without.

She gazed for a long moment at the blessed shrines, and conjured them to turn aside the evil spell that she could feel about her.

And, do what she would, as she gazed at the shrines, which had the appearance of two coffins laid side by side and welded together, Livette was conscious that her thoughts became more melancholy than ever. Had she not seen, year after year, some poor, infirm wretch in despair lie at full length on cushions in the acute angle formed by the two lids of the double coffin? And how many of them had been cured? One in fifty thousand, and only at long intervals?

And yet, what scores of votive offerings that lofty chapel held,—pictures, commemorative marble tablets, crutches, guns with shattered barrels, and small boats presented by sailors saved after shipwreck! Aye, but in how many years have the miracles been performed of which these offerings are the tokens?—One shudders to think how many.

And Livette, well content to divert her thoughts from such painful subjects, left Monsieur le curé at his prayers, and went up on the roof of the church.

The bright glare of the sky, bursting suddenly upon her, dazzled her. She had to close her eyes; then she looked down upon the plain. The plain was a flood of light.

The rascally *mistral*, that blows three, six, or nine days at a time when it has fairly buckled down to work, had simply taken a whim, as Tonin had foreseen. Not a leaf was stirring now. The sea had not had time to grow angry below the surface. It was laughing. The ponds were as smooth as mirrors. The sun shone hotter than ever in the clearer air.

The swallows and martins circled about Livette's head, uttering in endless succession shrill, piercing cries that constantly came nearer and again receded. The pointed wings of the martins, also called *arbalétriers* or cross-bowmen, brushed against the turrets and shot into the loopholes like arrows.

Livette looked off into the desert straight before her, and, not seeing what she expected, she let her glance wander here and there over the vast expanse, attractive but monotonous, which one can traverse, from end to end, without ever seeing aught but endless repetition of the same sand, the same tufts of grass, the same gleaming waters.

From the top of the church the horizon seemed almost limitless in every direction, for the golden peaks of the little Alps, vaguely outlined down in the northeast, seem to be no more than jagged bits of cloud.

When you are looking at them from that point, you have at your right, to the eastward, Crau and the *sansouïres*, Martigues, and Marseilles beyond the salt marshes of Giraud, cut into rectangular mounds of glistening salt. In the west is little Camargue, with its temporary ponds, its rare groves of pine, its euphorbium and branching asphodel, and its Étang des Fournaux, the father of mirages, and filled with shells, although it has no connection with the sea.

In this vast, flat region, the mind and the eye fall into the habit of looking always to the horizon, embracing as much space as possible in the hope of finding some inequality.

But they cannot escape the unchanging monotony, even less varied than the monotony of the sea, for the sea changes color, and is by turns black, blue, pale-green, dark-purple, or golden.

In our desert there are everywhere the same tamarisks, the same reeds, and— round about the six thousand hectares covered by the waters of the Vaccarès —always the same horizon lines, nowhere absolutely unbroken, but almost everywhere festooned with clumps of tamarisks; the mirage will always show you a pond gleaming in some spot of the plain where none is to be found; and the fisherman, walking along the shore, increases enormously in size as he recedes, because of the refraction.

Sometimes the month of May is as hot in Camargue as August.

"Au mois de Mai
Va comme il te plaît."

Livette was dazzled by the glare, and lowered her eyes to scan, with her keen glance, the most distant clumps of tamarisks, to follow the almost invisible ribbon of the cart-road that leads from the Vaccarès to Saintes-Maries. Her eyes are tired, and scorching in her head. There is nothing in the landscape to give them rest.

Everywhere the treeless soil exhales a burning breath that rises in visible vibrations. The spirit of the earth breaks its bonds and hovers over her. She can see it ascending in hot waves. Her eyes perceive the transparent undulations, the heat trembling in the cool air, the very soul of the interior fire that trembles so to the sight that one fancies he can hear it rustle. It is the never-ceasing dance of the reflected light.

Weary of the glare of the plain, Livette turned toward the sea, but the sea was simply an immense burnished mirror which flashed back at the eyes, from the countless facets of its swiftly moving fragments, the glow of the blazing sky multiplied beyond expression.

When she looked down once more upon the plain, she saw, about a league away, a horseman trotting briskly toward the Saintes-Maries. By an indefinable something in the bearing of that tiny speck she recognized her Renaud.

So no harm had come to him!

She was on the point of going down again, when suddenly she forced herself to bide a little there, to see what he would do when he arrived.

He was already passing the public spring. He turned to the left, and disappeared for a moment behind the houses. He was coming toward the church.

From embrasure to embrasure she ran, to follow him with her eyes; and in a few seconds he rode out into the square in front of the church, at the foot of the Calvary erected there.

She leaned over and watched him. Where was he going? He had stopped. His tired horse was standing quite still, simply moving his long tail from side to side to drive away the gnats and gadflies that were riddling his bleeding flanks with wounds, for, after the *mistral*, the gadflies dance! And then? Nothing. Absolute silence in the vast glowing expanse. Livette instinctively noticed that the horse's dark shadow, clearly marked upon the ground, was already elongated, indicating that it was four o'clock.

She continued to question herself as to Renaud's attitude—what was he doing there, standing still like that?—when suddenly the sound of a woman's voice singing floated up to her ears.

In the perfect silence, that voice, clear as a bell, poured forth outlandish words that neither Renaud nor Livette could understand.

The zingara sang:

"Allow the romichâl, the tzigane, to pass. He is the spectre of a true king. Kingly is his tattered cloak. A saddle is his throne. Is the whole earth thy kingdom, Romichâl?

"At Bœrenthal they speak the language of the Zend. Oh! the Çoudra would become pope! Thinkst thou it was the evil-doer who invented evil? Nay, nay; put not thy trust in God, and remain free, Romichâl!

"The Rhine, too, is a Nile. And the Rhône likewise. But thy mare prefers to drink in the river of Châl! The Nile alone can make thy hope neigh aloud, O Romichâl!"

With her eye, like a migratory bird's, Zinzara had long before spied Livette perched up aloft between the crenelles of the church-roof, and, seeing Renaud riding toward her, she, in joyous mood as always, had begun to sing, from mere caprice and bravado, within the circle of the echo of the lofty walls.

Like the serpents at the sound of her flute, Renaud was fascinated. The gipsy suspected as much.

And when she had finished her song she showed herself.

"Surely thou hast killed thy foe, romi?" she said. "But how is it that I do not see his heart at the point of thy spear? Thy maiden whose blood is like snow will ask thee for it ere long. Ah! that was a kiss well avenged—for a Christian! For if thy foe still sat in his saddle, thou wouldst not be in thine, I suppose? Listen, then, my beauty—although it be, in very truth, a crime for us zingari women to deem a Christian fair to look upon, I must tell thee, none the less: On the honor of a queen, romi, thou art handsome as a son of my own race, brave as a highwayman, as fine a horseman as the best of us, proud as a free man! I regret neither my anger of the other day, nor my song of a moment ago, nor the compliment I pay thee now: for I never do aught save that which pleases me! and my very anger does me better service than reflection! Adieu, romi, may thy God guard thee, if He knows me!"

Livette had heard nothing but the sharp, incisive tone in which the gipsy spoke; she could not distinguish her words.

But as Zinzara went away, she took good care, before she disappeared at the corner of the square, to send a kiss to the drover with her finger-tips—a kiss which seemed to him, because he could see her smile, a bit of raillery, but which was in Livette's eyes a token of requited love. Renaud thereupon admitted to himself that he had returned to Saintes-Maries in quest of nothing else than this compliment from the gipsy—something that drew him nearer to the seductive creature!

Chapter XVI

From embrasure to embrasure she ran, to follow him with her eyes; and in a few seconds he rode out into the square in front of the church, at the foot of the Calvary erected there.

She leaned over and watched him. Where was he going? He had stopped.

Now he had no choice but to turn back. He preferred not to see Livette at once! He preferred to return to the free air of the desert, to set his thoughts in order, discover his real feelings, reckon up his chances, and, after that was done, to be left alone with the image of the gitana, from whom he parted willingly, however, for he was very glad to be at a distance from her, with unrestrained freedom of movement, the better to think of her.

Before leaving the roof of the church, Livette cast a glance upon the broad expanse of Camargue at her feet. Ah! how empty was that immense space! The few scattered houses which would have delighted her eyes in the plain, were hidden by the clumps of umbrella-like pines beneath which they stood. Nothing human replied to the cry of distress uttered by her poor heart, which longed to follow the bewitched drover into the desert, and which seemed to her to flutter down from the summit of the tower to the ground, where it was crushed by the fall like a bird fallen from its nest.

XVII

THE OLD WOMAN

Renaud rode at a foot-pace to the *Ménage*, one of the farms belonging to the Château d'Avignon. He had ordered Bernard to bring Blanchet to him there, intending to take him back to the château. It was but a short distance from one to the other.

He was exceedingly astonished to find that the more he reflected upon what had happened to him—and it was really what he had hoped for—the more dissatisfied he was.

He believed that he had finally formed, in spite of everything, a fairly accurate estimate of the gipsy's character—a fact that pleased him. He had simply said to himself that she was an uncivilized creature, since she could forget all shame of her nakedness in her haste to punish as best she could a man she deemed overbold. From her very immodesty, from the arrogance and malignity she had exhibited at their first meeting, he had, strangely enough, evolved a proof of chastity so sure of itself, so disdainful of peril, that the shameless creature seemed to him only the more desirable.

He knew that the gipsy women esteem thieves, but not prostitutes, and he had enjoyed seeing in Zinzara a sort of savage virgin, ferocious as a wild beast of the Orient, over whom he, the tamer of beasts, would be the first to enjoy the pride of triumph. And, lo! she suddenly aroused in him a feeling of repulsion which he could not explain. Simply because he had heard her pronounce a few words, of obscure meaning, like all gipsy words, and threatening in tone as he ought to expect,—more amiable, in point of fact, than he had any right to hope,—he believed her, as if it had been revealed to him in a dream, capable of anything, a *wicked woman*! He felt that the devil was in her.

He had no precise knowledge as to her age. Was she seventeen or twenty-five? The swarthy tint of her impassive yet smiling face told nothing, hid blushes and pallor alike.

Her face was extremely young, and its expression was of no age. Renaud had undergone the inexplicable fascination of that face, whereon the malignity born of a woman's experience of the world, false for the sake of omnipotence, was mingled with something child-like.

Stronger men than he would have been caught in the snare. Neither king nor priest could have escaped the evil fascination of the gitana! She would have had but to will. The very things that repelled one were attractive!

So Renaud was caught, and his manner showed it. Sitting upon his tired horse, upon the stallion whose fiery nature was subdued by so much hard riding in all directions, and who carried his head less high, the drover, supporting the head of his spear upon his stirrup while the handle rested against his arm, seemed like a vanquished king, humiliated by the feeling that he was a prisoner in the free air.

He found Bernard at the *Ménage*, in the huge room on the lower floor, like those in all the farm-houses of the province, with the high mantelpiece, the long massive table in the centre, the kneading-trough of well-waxed walnut, the carved bread-cupboard with little columns, fastened to the wall like a cage, and the shining copper pans. Upon the whitewashed wall a few colored pictures were hanging: the Saintes-Maries in their boat; Napoléon I. on the Bridge of Arcola, and Geneviève de Brabant, with the roe, in the depths of a forest.

An old shepherd was seated at the table, beside Bernard, slowly eating his slice of bread.

"Is it you, king?" said he as Renaud entered. "I have seen you hold your head higher! What's the matter with you? you look downhearted. Aren't you still a cattle-herder, my boy? A shepherd's virtue, young man, is patience, remember that. What you can't find in a day you may find in a hundred years."

"Ah! there you are, Sigaud, eh?" Renaud replied, without answering his questions. "When do you start for the Alps?"

"Right away, my son. We are behindhand this year. I am just getting ready."

Nothing more was said. When they had eaten in silence their bread and sheep's-milk cheese, and drunk a cup of sour wine made from the wild grape, they rose.

The shepherd threw his cloak over his arm, took his staff from a corner, and having doffed his broad-brimmed hat before an old image of the Nativity, that hung on the wall, embellished with a branch laden with cocoons, and beneath which, on a carved oak stand, stood a little lamp, long unlighted, he went slowly from the room.

When Renaud, mounted upon Prince and leading Blanchet, left the *Ménage*, he rode some time with the shepherds, by the side of the enormous flock on their way to the Alps, where they were to pass the summer season.

Two thousand sheep, led by the rams, and arranged in battalions and companies, under the care of several shepherds of whom old Sigaud was the chief, were trotting along the road with hanging heads, making with their eight thousand feet a dull, smothered pattering, as of falling hailstones, in the dense clouds of dust. The Labry dogs ran to and fro along the edges of the flock, full of business, but frequently turning their eyes toward their master.

A few asses scattered among the different companies bore upon their backs, jolting about in double wicker-baskets, the sleepy, bleating lambs.

Old Sigaud was in high feather, thinking of the cool, fresh air of the Alps, where the grass is green and the water pure, and where he could gaze in peace every night at Cassiopeia's Chair and the Three Kings and the Pleiades in the heavens studded with myriads of stars.

"Adieu, Sigaud," said Renaud, drawing rein when the time came for him to part from the flock and its guardians.

Sigaud also stopped in front of him.

"Adieu, Renaud," said he gravely. "There must be a woman at the bottom of your trouble. You are too sad. But we called you *King* to do honor to your courage, you mustn't forget that. Remember, too, that everything is of some use, my boy, and that good may come out of evil. It takes all kinds to make the world!"

Renaud found Livette sitting on the stone bench in front of the door of the château. He had not leaped down from Prince before she was covering Blanchet with kisses. Audiffret was very glad to learn that the stolen horse had returned to the drove, but when Renaud explained that he had come, on this occasion, to return Blanchet, Livette showed some feeling.

"So you are not satisfied with what he has done for you?" said she. "Such a pretty horse! and so clever!—or perhaps you are tired of teaching him for me, of preventing him from learning bad tricks in the stable, of training him so that I can have the pleasure of seeing him return a winner from the races at Béziers, where my father is anxious to send him next month?"

"Certainly, Renaud," said Audiffret, "you ought to keep him. He gets rusty here in the stable. But I am surprised at what Livette says. Why, would you believe that she was regretting him this very morning, saying that she proposed to ask you to bring him back to-day. And now she doesn't want him!—It takes a very shrewd man to understand these girls!"

But what Audiffret could not understand, Renaud, for his part, understood very well. The lovelorn damsel said to herself that, by returning the horse, her fiancé would rid himself of a reminder of her, which was a cause of remorse to him perhaps—whereas, he ought, like a jealous lover, to have wanted to look after Blanchet, and take care of him for her, as long as possible.

Renaud resisted as best he could. He would have a deal of hard riding to do at the time of the fêtes, he said, and he did not want to overwork Blanchet or to leave him with the drove to become wild again.

Thereupon, Audiffret, easily influenced by the last who spoke, agreed with Renaud.

While the discussion was in progress, Renaud had put up both horses in the stable. That done, he went slowly up to the hay-loft, whence he threw down an armful of hay into the racks through the openings in the floor.

When he went down again, Blanchet was standing alone in front of the mangers, nibbling at the hay.—Renaud ran to the door. Livette, having removed Prince's halter, was shouting at him and waving her pretty arms to drive him away, naked and free. Honest Audiffret, delighted at his daughter's cunning, laughed and laughed. And Prince, overjoyed to return to the desert after these few days of slavery, thinking no more of the oats to be had at the château, stood erect like a goat, neighed shrilly with delight, shook his luxuriant mane, flung up his tail and thrashed the air, alive with the flies he had driven from his flanks—and darted away toward the horizon through the lane between the trees in the park.

Renaud had no choice but to submit with an affectation of gratitude, and to laugh with the rest;—but it was more distasteful to him than ever to ride a horse that belonged to him less than any other in the drove, a horse that was his fiancée's.

Thereupon, Audiffret went about his various tasks; and, two hours later, when they were all assembled in the lower room of the farm-house, Renaud, being suddenly seized with *ennui* at the thought that he was likely at any moment to have to endure an embarrassing tête-à-tête with this same Livette whose company he had so ardently desired a few days before, spoke of taking his leave. Audiffret remonstrated, and invited him to supper. They would drink a glass in honor of his victory. Renaud refused awkwardly, conscious how lacking in courtesy such an utterly motiveless refusal was.

But when the grandmother, who hardly ever spoke, urged him to stay, he stayed.

The old woman rarely spoke, for her thoughts were always with the dead and gone grandfather, who had been the faithful companion of her toilsome life. She was slowly drying up, like wood that is sound in all its fibres, but has lost its sap. Hers was a lovely old age, such as are seen in the land of the grasshopper, where people live sober lives, preserved by the light. Already advanced in years when she came to Camargue, she had never suffered from the malevolence of the swamps. It was too late. The cypress-tree does not allow the worms to draw their lines upon its surface.

She was patiently awaiting death, sometimes mumbling *paters* upon her rosary of olive-nuts, gazing fearlessly, with her dimmed eyes, straight before her at the vague shadow wherein her departed old man, her good, faithful Tiennet, was waiting for her;—Tiennet, who had never, in forty years, caused her a pang, and whom she had never wronged by a smile, even in the days of her gayest youth. Tiennet, from the depths of the shadow, sometimes called to her softly, and then the old woman would be heard to murmur, in a dreamy voice: "I am coming, good man! I am coming!"

Being left alone for a moment with Livette, just before supper, Renaud did not know what to say. Nor did she. He did not dare to lie, and she hoped that he would open his heart and confess. At one moment, she felt that the very fact of his silence was sufficient proof of his treachery, and the next moment, on the contrary, she said to herself: "If there was an understanding between them, he would not be here! I was mad! He loves me."

At supper, he was very talkative, told about his battles and his hunting exploits; how, the year before, with that rascal of a Rampal, he had beaten up two coveys of partridges, on horseback, in a single morning. They had taken twenty-eight, more than twenty being killed on the wing at a single casting of their staves, Arab-fashion.

Audiffret, overjoyed at the recovery of a horse he had thought lost forever, drew from under the woodpile an old-fashioned bottle, a gift from the masters, those masters who are always absent—like all the landowners of Camargue, who prefer to dwell in cities,—Paris, Marseilles, or Montpellier,— leaving the desert to their *bailiffs*.

"Ah! the masters in old times!" said Audiffret, "they had more courage and were better served and better loved!" Renaud, becoming more and more animated, stood up for the times we live in. The grandmother, grave and serious as always, said once to Audiffret at table, speaking of Renaud: "Wait upon your son, my son." Well, well, he was decidedly one of the family.

And that certainty, which it behooved him to retain at any price, instead of moving his heart to gratitude, led him on to play the hypocrite. He was ready to betray Livette, without renouncing her, for he loved her so dearly, so sincerely, that he felt that he was ready, on the other hand, to renounce the gitana, without too great a pang, if circumstances should make it necessary. He laughed a great deal, raising his glass with great frequency, and winking involuntarily at Audiffret, as if to say: "We are sly fellows!" But honest Audiffret could not detect his excitement. He had never interested himself in anything except the farm accounts. He had never divined anything in all his life, not he!—As far as the gipsy was concerned, she certainly would not leave Saintes-Maries before the fête, that is to say, for a week or more. After that, she could go where she chose! it would make little difference to him. What could he hope for from a wandering creature like that? An hour's meeting at the cross-roads on the way to Arles! Nothing more!

As to Zinzara, he had hopes; as to Livette, he had certainty. And he was very light of heart.

So it was, that, when the time came for him to take his leave, he indulged in an outburst of affection toward his new family, quite contrary to his usual habit, and to the habit of all drovers, who are rough-mannered by profession.

You must know that the peasants, in general, do not kiss except on great occasions—weddings or baptisms. Only the mothers kiss their young children. The man of the soil is of stern mould.

"Audiffret," the grandmother suddenly said to her son, laying her knitting on the table and her spectacles on her knitting;—"Audiffret, every day brings me a little nearer the end, and I would like to see this marriage take place before I die. You must hurry it as much as possible, now that it's decided on. And if I can't be present on the wedding-day, don't forget, my children, that the old woman blessed you from the bottom of her heart to-night."

And, without another word, she calmly took up the stockings and needles.

She had spoken almost without inflection, in a grave, calm tone, moving her lips only.

Every one was deeply moved. Livette looked at Renaud. He, carried away by his emotion, forgot everything except this new family that offered itself to him, the orphan. Livette saw it and was grateful to him for it. She felt that he was won back, like the stolen horse, and she sprang to her feet in a burst of enthusiasm.

"Kiss me, my betrothed!" said she proudly.

He kissed her with heartfelt sincerity.

The father and the grandmother looked on with eyes that gradually became dim with tears.

When he had pressed the father's hand, Renaud turned to the grandmother, as she stuck her knitting-needle into the white hair that fluttered about her temples.

"Kiss me, grandmother!" he said, with a smile.

The old woman gave a leap, then stood erect, recoiling a little as if in fear:

"Since my husband died, no man has ever kissed me," she said, "not even my son there! Let young people kiss. Life is before them. I," she added, "am already with the dead."

And with that, the old peasant-woman, straight and stiff and withered,—the image of a by-gone time, when it was deemed a praiseworthy thing to remain true to a single sentiment,—sought the bed of her old age, which was soon to see her lying dead, with the tranquillity of a simple, loving, faithful heart upon her parchment-like face.

XVIII

THE BLESSED RELICS

The great day has arrived. From all parts of Languedoc and Provence, pilgrims, rich and poor, have come to Saintes-Maries. There are fully ten thousand strangers in the town.

For three days past they have been arriving in vehicles of all shapes and of all ages.

Many of these pilgrims lodge with the villagers at extraordinary, princely rates. A bunch of straw on the floor brings twenty francs. The villager himself sleeps on a chair, or passes the night in the open air on the warm sand of the dunes. If the bulls arrive during the night for the sports of the following day, he assists the drovers to drive them into the compound, in the wake of the *dondaïre*, the enormous ox with a bell.

The houses are soon filled to overflowing. New-comers are obliged to camp. Tents are pitched. People live in carts and wagons, in breaks, tilburys, calèches, omnibuses, as far away as possible, be it understood, from the gipsy encampment.

Around the little town, the hundreds of vehicles constitute a roving town of their own, resting there like a flock of birds of passage around a swamp.

And on all sides naught can be seen but tattered, crippled, hunchbacked, deformed, blind, or one-eyed creatures, broken in health, lame, maimed, scrofulous, and paralytic, dragging themselves along or dragged by others, carried in men's arms or on litters, some with bandages over their faces, others displaying unhealed wounds from which one turns aside in horror.

Here a poor fellow who has been bitten by a mad dog wanders about with gloomy brow, tormented by insane anxiety and hope, for a pilgrimage to Saintes-Maries is especially efficacious against hydrophobia.

All varieties of misfortune are represented. All the children of Job and Tobias have journeyed hither to find the healing angel and the miraculous fish.

A motley crowd swarms upon the public square in the bright sunlight, and in the narrow streets, under the luminous shadow of the awnings. From time to time, it parts, with loud shouts, before a drover, who rides proudly by, his sweetheart *en croupe* with her arms about his waist.

Here and there flat baskets laden with rosaries, sacred images, Catalan knives, and handkerchiefs of brilliant hue stand out like islets in the midst of the sea of promenaders, and all the merchandise displayed for sale takes on a pink or pale-blue tint through the great stationary umbrellas that shield it from the sun.

Amid the fantastic piercing notes of a *galoubet*, or high-pitched flute, tambourines can be heard humming in cadence in the interior of a wine-shop, where young girls of the province are dancing in Provençal costume, dark-skinned girls with white teeth beneath their sensuous lips; very like Moors they are, the descendants of some Saracen pirate who ravaged the Ligurian shore.

The town is flooded with joyous light. Everybody is in his Sunday dress. Upon the fever-haunted strand, whither a whole people flocks to pray to the Saintes Maries for bodily health, that joyous sun is dangerous. The whole scene has the appearance of a hospital ball, a fête given by dying men. The devil wields the bâton, it may be. One would think it, to see the faces of the gipsies, whose expression, notwithstanding certain cunning leers, is and remains undecipherable.

In the church with the black, dirt-begrimed walls, filled with a fetid odor by such an accumulation of misery, diseased flesh, and perspiring humanity, the people crowd about the iron balustrade of the little well, as if it were the Fountain of Youth. The poor, green, dilapidated pitcher humbly descends at the end of its cord to bring up from the sand below brackish water that to-day seems sweet.

Keep faith with them, O saints!—Faith gives what one wishes.

They are waiting for four o'clock, the hour at which the relics descend.

At four o'clock precisely, the shutter of the high window up yonder, under the ogive arch of the nave, will open. The relics will come down toward the outstretched arms. The little children will be lifted up toward them. The dead arms of the paralytics will be raised toward them. The blind will turn toward them their sightless eyes, or their empty, blood-stained orbits.

Meanwhile, Livette, who is standing there in the centre of the crowd, directly in front of the altar, facing the grated door through which you go down into the crypt, is preparing to sing the solo of invocation. Her fresh, pure voice is to be the voice of all these wretched creatures, crushed under the weight of impurity and disease.

Just below the high altar, which is studded with tapers, the gipsies are huddled together in their crypt, with tapers in their hands, invoking Saint Sara. The vault is dark. The gipsies are black. The little glass shrine of Saint Sara has become black under the accumulated filth of years. From the centre of the church you can see through the grated opening, which resembles an air-hole of hell, the innumerable twinkling lights of the tapers below, waving to and fro in the hands that hold them. A muffled sound of praying comes up through the opening.

In the church, every hand now has its taper, and they are rapidly lighted one from another. The lights dance about in the air. But the interior of the nave is dark. The high walls, pierced by narrow windows, are grimy with age. And all this obscurity, where suffering and misery crawl and cower, is studded with stars like heaven. To the gipsies in the crypt, who will not see the blessed relics descend, the body of the church, which they can see from below through the air-hole, is a heaven beyond their reach, the world of the elect.

But the elect, alas! are damned. Their heaven is the chapel up yonder, in which the power they invoke lies sleeping, beneath the stained wood of the boxes, like to a double coffin—the power that may remain deaf, the all-powerful power that will never perhaps awaken for any one, the marvellous power upon which cures depend and which withholds happiness!

Such was the interior of the three-storied church of Saintes-Maries on that day. And above the lofty chapel, there was the bell-tower overlooking the whole country-side. Surrounded by endless numbers of swallows and sea-gulls, for centuries past it has looked upon the glistening desert, the dazzling sea, the dumb infinitude of space, which could explain things if it would, but only beams and laughs.

The hour drew near. The crowd was panting with heat and hope and fear.

Renaud was not there.

"Remember—we promised to burn three tapers each before the relics," Livette had said to him.

"I will come to-night," was his reply. "There's the branding to-day. I have to look after my bulls."

So Livette was a little distraught. She was thinking of joining Renaud, of being present at the branding, of keeping an eye on her betrothed. Where was he?

But Monsieur le curé made a sign: Livette began to sing. Alas! why was not her lover there? Her voice, which she knew was pleasant to the ear, might have some effect on him. How eagerly he listened to the gipsy's singing the other day!—Livette sang, and the buzzing of prayers and litanies and invocations of all sorts, that every one was indulging in on his or her own account, subsided as her clear, pure voice arose. O God! what is this humanity of ours? It is vile and abject, but it has some sense of shame. The basest know how to pray that they may be cured of their baseness. And, however much they may have rolled in the mire of their natural inclinations, a time comes when they set the flame alight, when they burn incense, and when all keep silent to listen to the voice ascending to Heaven, imploring for them a grace that no one knows, that perhaps does not exist, but that every one imagines and desires!

"Eat your excrement, dog!" say the gipsies; "what care I? There is a light in the dog's eye that is not often seen in the eyes of kings."

Livette sang. The curé said to himself:

"O my God, mayhap this child of Thine will obtain favor in Thy sight!"

Livette's voice was as fresh as the water of salvation for which the assembled multitude thirsted. And how intently they listened! But, at the end of each stanza, weary of restraining their tumultuous ejaculations of hope, they sent up from thousands of throats an inarticulate roar in which only the two words: *Saintes Maries!* could be distinguished.

Livette sang:

> "Quand vous étiez sur la grande eau,
> Sans rames à votre bateau,
>   Saintes Maries!
> Rien que la mer, rien que les cieux——
> Vous appeliez de tous vos yeux
> La douceur des plages fleuries."[9]

"*Saintes Maries!*" roared the people; uttered at the same moment by a thousand voices acting upon a common impulse, the frenzied appeal was like an explosion.

Every one shouted with all his strength, for the saints must be made to hear! Every one shouted with all his lungs, with all his heart, with all his body, one might say. Heaven is so far away! Open-mouthed, their faces twitching convulsively, they gazed upward. The veins in their necks were swollen to the bursting-point. The muscles swelled and thickened in faces to which the blood rushed in torrents. The brothers, lovers, husbands, mothers, fathers, of the sufferers, availed themselves of their own strength to call for help, howling like wounded wild beasts turned toward the dawn. All this suffering multitude, all this swarming heap of tainted, diseased flesh, uttered the terrifying roar of a monster in pain—and still the preternaturally shrill shriek of some doting mother would soar above the horrid uproar. And all around the church, filled with the nameless appeals of these damned of earth, lay the calm, silent desert, the blue, foam-flecked sea, the brilliant sunlight, insensible to everything.

> "Sous le soleil, sous les étoiles,
> De vos robes faisant des voiles
> (Vogue, bateau!)
> Sept jours, sept nuits vous naviguâtes,
> Sans voir ni trois-ponts ni frégates——
> Rien que la mer et la grande eau!"[10]

"*Saintes Maries!*" roared the people, and each time the shout burst forth from thousands of throats, suddenly and at the same instant, with the effect of a strange kind of explosion.

> "Dieu qui fait son fouet d'un éclair,
> Pour fouetter le ciel et la mer,
> Saintes Maries!
> Amena la barque à bon port——
> Un ange, qui parut à bord,
> Vous montra des plages fleuries!"[11]

"*Saintes Maries!*" the people roared again. And the appealing cry, made up of so many cries, burst forth with a sound like that made by a great wave that breaks against a cliff and is instantly scattered about in foam! And again the young girl's voice arose above all the vociferating, grinning creatures. Might not one fancy that he saw a sea-swallow, white as the dove of the Ark, soaring over a bottomless abyss?

> "Vous pour qui Dieu fit ce miracle,
> Voyez, devant son tabernacle,
> Tous à genoux,
> Souillés du péché de naissance,
> Nous invoquons votre puissance,——
> Saintes femmes, protégez-nous!"[12]

And for the last time, the deafening, harsh cry arose:

"*Saintes Maries!*"

Oh! the thousand, two thousand ejaculations of insane longing that flew upward, at a single flight, flapping all their wings at once, to fall back, dead, upon themselves.

It is very certain that there was in that frenzied appeal all the madness of suffering, all the wrath of unsatisfied longing, and rage as of unchained beasts, against the very beings they implored.

Meanwhile, the double shutter up above had not yet been thrown open. And Livette, in accordance with the curé's instructions, was to repeat the last verse.

So she began again:

"Vous pour qui Dieu fit ce miracle———"

But these first words had hardly passed her lips when her voice faltered and died away. For a few seconds there was a silence as of utter amazement in the church. Of what was Livette thinking? Of what?—For the last minute, just God! her eyes had been obstinately fixed upon the black opening leading to the crypt. In that opening, on a level with the floor of the church, she had seen a head: it was the gipsy queen, who had come up from the crypt, in mischievous mood, curious to see Livette singing. Immediately below the great altar she emerged from the dark depths of the cellar amid the ascending smoke of the tapers. She came from her kingdom below, and with her copper crown and gleaming ear-rings, her swarthy skin and her fiery black eyes, she seemed to Livette a genuine devil from hell.

Zinzara ascended two steps more and her bust appeared. She darted a keen, penetrating glance at Livette. That is why Livette was confused, and why she called with all her strength upon the women of compassion, the holy women above, for help against this woman from the chapel below.

But the shutters that concealed the shrines were opened at last. And slowly, very slowly, they descended, swinging from side to side, with a slight jerky movement, at the ends of the two ropes, embellished here and there with little bunches of flowers.

Is not this the image of every life? Is there aught else in the world? Something descends from heaven, something ascends from hell; and we suffer with hope and fear.

"Saintes Maries!"

Amid the vociferations of the crowd, Livette lost her head, she forgot to sing, and, carried away by the prevailing excitement, hope, and terror, she began to cry aloud with all the rest, like a lost soul, while Zinzara, from below, continued to gaze fixedly at her.

What would you say, Monsieur le curé, to Livette's thoughts, who,—poor creature of the world we live in!—between the holy women and the woman devil, no longer knew which way to turn? Had she not reason to tremble? For the shrines descend to no purpose, they bring us naught but dead relics—while the sorceress is a creature of flesh and blood, whose feet walk, whose eyes see!

Far away from us, in the land of dreams, of supernatural hopes, above the sky and the stars, are the sainted souls that have pity for mankind; as far from man as Paradise itself are the chaste women who embalm the crucified ones in herbs and spices, while *she* is close at hand, always ready, always armed against the repose of Christian souls, she, queen of diabolic love, who, seeking only to gratify her caprice, makes sport of everything!

Livette became more and more confused beneath Zinzara's steadfast glance, and she tried in vain, after silence had at last been restored, to resume the invocation. She faltered and stopped again.

Thereupon there was great confusion among the waiting multitude. All those men and women who were holding their peace in order to listen to the outpouring of their own souls in the maiden's voice, to the pure, unspoken prayer which was in their hearts, but which they could not put in words, had been thrown back once more, and more despairingly than ever, upon themselves, upon their own helplessness, when Livette's voice died away. Just at the decisive moment, their interpreter failed them! They were afraid of their profound silence, so contrary to the impulses of their hearts. In order to be heard on high, their prayer must be offered; and, seized by the same thought, every one began to shout or sing on his own account, some beginning again at the very beginning, others taking the stanza they knew by heart or had before them in a book, others repeating at random bits of the litanies, one the *credo*, another the *pater*, and never did prayers offered up to God create such a hellish uproar, since the discordant cries of all the sorrows of mankind ascended to Heaven.

Stronger women than Livette would have been disturbed as she was, would have felt their powers failing. She put her hand to her forehead to detain her mind that seemed to be making its escape. Was not she the cause of all this trouble? What would become of her, in this state? She was afraid and ashamed at once.

Instead of looking up, instead of watching the blessed relics that had now accomplished half of their descent, she could not refrain from returning the fixed stare of the gipsy woman below, whose eyes seemed to pierce her soul.

Livette suffered keenly. The gipsy's gaze entered into her very being, and she felt that she could do nothing. It seemed to her as if a sharp-toothed beast were gnawing at her heart. Instead of praying, she listened to the terrible thoughts within her. She fancied that she could feel the hatred go out from her with the glances that shot from her eyes! She tried to stab to the heart with it that creature who was defying her down there. Would not somebody kill the witch, who was the cause of everything? Ah! Saintes Maries! what thoughts for such a place! at such a time!

The relics slowly descended, and, amid the roars that greeted them, Livette, in her overwrought imagination, fancied that she saw herself clinging to Renaud, beseeching him to be faithful and kind to her, and not to go to that other woman; and when he refused and left her, she leaped at the gipsy's face and scratched her and clawed at her like a cat.

Thus the sorceress's soul passed into Livette. Already, without suspecting it, she had begun to resemble her enemy, the gitana who leaped at the nostrils of Renaud's horse the other day. And yet this little fair-haired girl was not one of the dark-skinned maidens of Arles, who have African and Asian blood in their veins! No matter; she, too, has a wild beast's fits of passion. Love and jealousy are at work making a woman's soul.

The relics were still descending; and Livette feverishly told off *paters* and *aves* on her rosary.—Patience! on the day after the fête, the gipsies, she knows, will leave the town! Two more days and her agony will be at an end.

Meanwhile—she makes this vow in presence of the relics—she will not gratify Renaud by showing that she is jealous, as she is, and not until later— when Zinzara is far away, and there is no chance of her coming back—will she, perhaps, tell her promised husband that he lied to her, that he is a traitor, because, instead of avenging her upon the gipsy, he was false to his fiancée with her—for of course he is false to her, as he is not there!—She will tell him, then, not in a passion, but to punish him. It will be no more than justice.

By dint of uncoiling themselves by little jerks, the ropes have lowered the relics almost within reach of the hands stretched up to meet them. Thereupon the rabble of poor devils could contain itself no longer. Every one was determined to be the first to touch them. Those who were already in the choir, directly below the hanging relics, lost their footing, crowded as they were by those who were pressing in from the body of the church, jostling and crushing one another with a constant pressure. Livette was borne along on the wave, seeing nothing, and with but one thought in her mind—to touch the consecrated relics herself!—That she felt she must do, so that she might escape the influence of the glance the black woman had cast at her. She would seek to turn aside the fatal spell that had been upon her ever since her first meeting with the sorceress! But would she reach the shrines?—Livette felt that she was seized by two strong arms. She turned: it was Renaud! He had just entered the church with two other drovers, his friends. These three young men, glowing with the outside sunlight, healthy and strong, amid the lame and halt and blind, had the insolent bearing—cruel without meaning to be—of manly beauty, of life itself. They extricated the girl and made a ring about her. She was able to breathe.

"Would you like to touch the relics, demoisellette?"

Forcing their way before her, without great effort, but pitilessly, through the crowd of cripples, they cleared a passage for her. Livette walked quickly, she drew near the spot, and Renaud, seizing her around the waist, lifted her up like a child so that she touched the consecrated relics first of all!

Still with the three youths as a body-guard, before whom all were fain to stand aside, and without further thought—poor you! it is the law of the world —of the innumerable, nameless perils by which she was encompassed, she left the church content. Peace had found its way into her heart once more. Her Renaud was there by her side. Was all that she had dreaded a dream and nothing more?

"Ah! it is good to be outside!" he said, filling his lungs with the fresh air.

"Yes, but when will you light the tapers, Renaud, that you are to burn in the church as I promised for you?"

"Oh! I have a whole day before me," he replied. "Now let us go to the races."

———————————————————

XIX

THE BRANDING

The relics having descended, the majority of those present left the dark church and returned to the dazzling outside world.

As the crowd poured out through the narrow side-doors, another crowd was forcing its way in through the main entrance, making but slow progress,—two or three steps in a quarter of an hour,—all hot and perspiring, in a cloud of luminous dust.

Many young men were there, for the pleasure of being pressed by the crowd against the pretty girls, their sweethearts, whose sinuous bodies they could feel against their own, and who could not escape them there. How many hands and waists were squeezed which the mothers could not see!

And in undertones they said:

"I love you, Lionnette."

"Fie, François!"

"Let me go, Tiennet!——"

Thus, beside the infirm and incurable, who know naught of the good things of life, love saucily sports and laughs, feels its own force, and seeks return. The incense in the church serves only to inflame its desire, and more than one youth offers his beloved a rosary, whose boxwood cross he has ardently kissed before her eyes, so that she may find the kiss with her lips.

All day long, the pilgrims and invalids enter the church. Many will pass the night there, keeping vigil with the tapers, on their knees or prostrate before the relics; and more than one, each in his turn, will lie down upon them, on cushions brought expressly for the purpose.

For the moment—it is the first day of the fête—nothing is talked about in the streets of the town save the bulls and the sports.

"Are you going to the races?"

"Yes."

"Does Prince run? He's the best horse in all the droves."

"No, he won't run; Renaud, who usually handles him, told me that he was too tired."

"Pshaw! what a pity!"

"What about the bulls? Shall we have any that are a bit ugly?"

"There's *Sirous* and *Dogue* and *Mâchicoulis*. I cut them out myself with Bernard and Renaud. They gave us a lot of trouble! They refused to leave the herd. As soon as we got them out, back they would go again. But we set *Martin* and *Commetoi* at them, two bull-dogs that can't be matched anywhere; and even *Mâchicoulis* obeyed at last!"

"*Martin* and *Commetoi?*—Those are curious names for dogs!"

"It's a joke. When any one asks: 'How is your dog called?'[13] The dog's master replies: '*Commetoi!*' [Like yourself.] The other man gets angry, and it raises a laugh."

"And what about the full-blooded Spanish bull, with the horns twisted like a lyre; shall we see him?"

"*Angel Pastor?* He is sick. I like our straight-horned bulls better. The important thing is that the horns should be far enough apart for a man's body to go between them."

"Are there any heifers?"

"One, a wicked one—*Serpentine.*"

"And *bioulets?*"

"Young bulls, do you mean? Renaud has kept six of them, expressly to give the strangers a chance to see a branding."

"When will the branding come off?"

"In a moment. Suppose we go to see it."

The gipsy was present at the branding.

The arena was against the church, at the end opposite the main entrance.

The many-sided irregular enclosure was formed on one side by the high wall of the church; on another, by a house standing by itself, against which was a series of roughly made benches, one above another; on still another side by three or four small houses, each of whose windows formed a frame for a dozen or more heads of young men and women, crowded together and all laughing gaily. At the base of one of these houses was a café with a glass door opening on the arena and barricaded by tables and overturned chairs. On each side of the door was drawn, in deepest black, a silhouette of a bull of the Camargue type, that is to say, with straight horns of ample proportions.

On all sides of the enclosure where there were no stone walls, their place was supplied by wagons bound firmly together by their shafts.

At the corner of the wall of the church, there were three great iron rings one above another, and through them were thrust three wooden bars, which could be moved back and forth at will.

These bars were to be let down for the young bulls which were to be turned out of the arena, one by one, after they had been branded, to find their way alone to the desert. Outside the bars, a system of barricades closed the streets of the town to them, and—by compelling them to go behind the few houses facing the arena—guided them, whether they would or not, to the margin of the open plain in less than a hundred steps.

Zinzara was present, as we have said, standing in a wagon. She followed with impassive glance all the happenings within the arena, grotesque and heroic alike.

These duels between man and beast are grand or disgusting according to the character of the adversaries. It sometimes happens that the man attacks in a cowardly fashion, or that the beast, from astonishment it may be, or fatigue, turns about and tries to return to the stable. Fine contests are rare.

Sometimes a sharp stone is thrown from a safe distance by a disloyal foe. The surprised beast receives it full in the face; the blood flows in long streams from his nostrils to the ground. He looks straight before him, his great eyes filled with mirage, and does not budge, as if he were at once saddened and contemptuous.

Sometimes a mischievous rascal has the happy thought of coming very close to him and throwing sand in his eyes by the handful. Another, more mischievous than he, covers the bull with filth collected from the gutter! But the sand-thrower, being spattered thereby, himself picks up a handful, and the two heroes engage in a fierce battle with dung picked up smoking from the ground under the bull's very tail, amid the laughter and applause of a whole population, until the champions, reeking with filth, are abruptly separated by the bull, who bestirs himself at last and charges them.

"This way! this way, Livette!"

Livette had just come into the arena. Her young friends called her and gladly moved closer together to make room for her on the benches.

A stable just beside the café had been transformed into a *toril*. Just above the door of the stable was the long window of the hay-loft, level with the floor. Two herdsmen, sitting in the window with their legs hanging outside, rose from time to time, and could be seen pricking the *dondaïre*, the beloved leader of the herd, through the holes in the floor above the hay-racks. The *dondaïre* would thereupon go out and lead the tired bull back to the stable. Every time that a new beast left the *toril*, or one that was tired out returned, a dexterous hand swiftly closed the door.

All these things, which were probably by no means new to the gipsy, who was doubtless familiar with the tragic entertainments of Madrid and Seville, left her unmoved. Her eye did not kindle; it was as dull and vague as a heifer's.

The "amateurs" played with a few bulls. They were not ill-tempered. Somebody seized one of them by the tail. A whole party clung to his skirts, dancing the farandole—but were soon scattered. The performance thus far was not inspiriting, but it was amusing.

Behind the glass door of the café, which opened on the arena, some congenial spirits were emptying a bottle and smoking while they enjoyed the spectacle. The door was barricaded by a rampart of overturned tables, with their legs in the air and passed through a net-work of broken chairs.

Suddenly the bull, overturning tables and chairs, put the drinkers to flight: he had thrust his bulky head through a square of glass. The café rang with shouts of alarm mingled with amusement. The wagons in the arena shook with the joyous stamping of their occupants; the planks were torn off by excited hands; the people at the windows of the little houses rattled the shutters noisily in their delight. To see the crowds on the roofs laugh made one fear that they would fall in. Thus was the frolicsome bull applauded. The gipsy alone did not smile.

A great oat-bin stood in a corner of the arena, placed there purposely perhaps. A very old man,—not too old to play the merry-andrew,—armed with an old red umbrella, raised the lid, climbed into the bin, and opened his umbrella, which was of the most brilliant shade of red. The bull rushed at him—the old man let the lid fall. Bin and umbrella closed at the same moment upon the laughing bald head. The hilarity of the public was at its height. The gipsy did not seem amused by the old man's drollery.—Nor did she laugh when a manikin was set up in the centre of the arena and the bull carried him off on his horns and hurled him into the midst of the spectators; and she did not even smile when, a window on the ground-floor of one of the houses being thrown open, a little child was seen in his mother's arms, behind the iron bars, teasing the furious animal. Laughing with glee, he held a plaything out through the bars, a little pasteboard windmill, whose pink and blue wings were made to turn by the monster's breath.

Then came a tragic episode. A man—an *amateur*—struck by the sharp horns; his thigh pierced from side to side; the first cowardly movement of flight on the part of the other contestants; the return of the valiant fellows, who diverted the bull's attention and drew him off while the wounded man was removed, accompanied by the piercing shrieks of his wife and daughter.

At last, the serious business of the day began. It was announced that the branding was about to take place. Immediately thereafter would come the game of the "cockades," which consists in snatching a cockade suspended between the bull's horns by a thread. With his hand or with a hooked stick the rider breaks the thread, snatches the cockade—*Crac!* a quick recovery, and the victor has won the scarf!

The branding is hard work turned into a game; it consists in branding young bulls with a red-hot iron, with their owner's cipher.

A young bull having been turned into the arena, Renaud walked up to him, and, as the beast made a rush, cleverly avoided him by turning upon his heel. The bull having, thereupon, stopped short, Renaud seized him by the horns.

Clinging to him with his hands, closed like knots of steel about the horns, the man was dragged for a moment, standing, over the ground, in which his thick soles dug ribbon-like furrows. The spectators clapped their hands. The bull lowered his head and stood still. Renaud, with his legs apart and bent a little, and his feet firmly planted in the ground, threw all his weight to the left. All the muscles of his chest and arms stood out beneath his shirt, which was glued to his skin by perspiration. The bull, with all his sluggish strength, tried to throw himself in the opposite direction. Suddenly Renaud gave way, and the bull, losing the support of his resistance, fell heavily before a sudden contrary effort. And there he lay at full length on the ground, gasping for breath.

The man, who had not released his hold, forced his head to the ground by sitting on it.

"Bravo, king! bravo, king!" cried the crowd.

Bernard took the red-hot iron from a brazier and carried it to Renaud, who, thereupon, let go one horn, and kneeling heavily upon the beast's withers, seized the iron with his right hand and pressed it against his shoulder. The hair and flesh smoked and crackled. Renaud rose quickly, and the bull, springing suddenly to his feet, shook himself all over, lashed his sides with his tail, bellowed with anger, pawed the ground with his foot, and, amid the shouts of the crowd, darted through the barrier, which was opened at that moment. A moment later, he could be seen far away on the plain, galloping at full speed. He soon rejoined the drove which he or any of his fellows can readily find for themselves, even if it be on the other side of the Rhône, which they often swim.

Six bulls, one after another, were thus thrown down by Renaud.

The sport enlivened him, he was intoxicated by the consciousness of his great strength. Excited even more by the applause of the people, he trembled from head to foot. From time to time, he wiped the great beads of perspiration from his forehead with the back of his hand.

A sunbeam fell across one side of the arena, which lay in the dark shadow of the high church-wall. Renaud ran thither, hatless, in shirt-sleeves and close-fitting red breechcloth, shaking the short curly locks of his thick, jet-black hair.

The girls applauded, I promise you, more loudly than the young men, who were somewhat jealous. Zinzara's eye—her wagon was standing in the ray of sunlight—kindled at last.—And Livette, blushing deeply, was proud of her king.

When the sixth bull he had thrown was still under his knee, Renaud made a sign to Bernard. Bernard ran to him, knelt beside him, and seized the bull by the horns in his stead. Another drover came to help Bernard hold the beast, and Renaud rose.

He walked across the arena, and when he came to where Livette sat, beckoned to her. Everybody understood and applauded.

She walked forward to the edge of the platform on which the benches were built, and lightly placed her foot on the strong cross-bar that served as a support to the spectators in the front row; from there she jumped confidently into Renaud's arms, who caught her about the waist and set her down as if she had been a little child.

He took her hand and led her toward the bull.

If Renaud had looked at Zinzara at that moment, he would have surprised in her eyes a gleam which she did her best to hide behind her half-closed lids. The smile vanished from her mocking lips.

But Livette and Renaud, the pair of comely lovers, were thinking of naught but the fête, of themselves, of this strange betrothal at which all their people were present, and the like of which not even princes could give, for it required rare strength and address on the part of the fiancé. It was, in very truth, the triumph of a manly king.

"Bravo, king! bravo, queen!"

As they passed the brazier in the centre of the arena, he stooped quickly, and seized with his free hand—without stopping or releasing Livette's hand—the red-hot iron, which he handed to her as soon as they were beside the bull. She took it, and, leaning forward, branded the bull on the shoulder, and when they saw the flesh smoking under the iron she held in her strong little hand, when the bull began to quiver with wrath, the enthusiasm of the people burst forth. Hats and hands and scarfs were waved in the air.

"Bravo, king! bravo, queen!"

And Renaud, envied by all, escorted the maiden back to her place, while the bull, set free, rushed from the arena in his turn and out upon the plain. No, Zinzara no longer laughed.

The game of the "cockades" was next on the programme.

The first two or three were easily carried off—one from the head of Angel Pastor himself, the Spanish bull—by the young men of Saintes-Maries, and it had not occurred to Renaud to take part in the sport.

At last, Serpentine, a nervous little heifer, was let loose in the arena. Every one realized instantly that she was in a bad temper and would defend herself.

Several tried their fortune against her, but, just as they put out their hand to the cockade, Serpentine would turn about so quickly, and with such agility for a heifer, that they fled. Ah! the hussy! Zinzara suddenly became interested in the game. Renaud had gone down into the arena.

"The king! the king! bravo! king!" shouted the crowd.

And Renaud performed prodigies of skill.

Three times he placed his foot upon Serpentine's lowered head, and allowed himself to be hurled into space, to fall again upon his elastic legs. And as soon as he reached the ground the third time, he turned like a flash, ran straight to the heifer, snatched away the cockade,—avoiding the blow she aimed at him with her horns in her rage,—and was calmly walking away, when the agile creature returned to the charge.

Renaud ran, as chance guided him, closely pursued by the beast, and when he had leaped upon the nearest wagon, he found himself beside the gipsy, whom he had instinctively seized around the waist.

The heifer had already turned her attention to some of the other contestants, and very fortunately, too,—for the gipsy, who was standing on the edge of her wagon, leaning against the insecure boarding, lost her balance, and leaped down, perforce, into the arena, carrying Renaud with her.

Livette turned pale as death.

The heifer came galloping back at full speed toward Renaud and Zinzara, the latter of whom, being entangled in the folds of her ragged finery, thought that she was lost.—Boldly she turned and faced the danger, too proud to fly, at least when to fly would be useless. But Renaud had already stepped in front of her to protect her, and, seized with some insane idea or other,—the bravado of a horse-breaker, or of a lover, if you choose,—instead of entering into a contest with the heifer, instead of seizing her by the horns or the legs, stopped, and, without taking his eyes from the beast's face, quickly knelt upon one knee, squatted upon his heel, folded his arms, and, with his head thrown back, defied her. Like an experienced "trapper," he counted upon the beast's astonishment, and she did, in fact, stop short, and scrutinize him suspiciously. The gipsy, her lips pressed tightly together, having regained her place upon the wagon, looked back and saw her protector still in that singularly foolhardy attitude. As may be imagined, everybody was shouting: "Vive Renaud!" It seemed as if they would never weary of it.

When he rose, he was again charged by Serpentine, and had barely time to regain his place of refuge beside the gitana; and the furious beast attacked the flooring of the wagon just at their feet with such a fierce blow of her powerfully armed head, that it was caught there for a moment by the horns, so that Renaud had to force them out by stamping upon them with the heel of his iron-shod boot.

Then the gipsy smiled, and, bending over toward the drover's ear, whispered a word or two that made the handsome horse-breaker smile with her.

Livette—who was a long distance away, at the other end of the arena, but almost opposite them, and so placed that she could see them in the bright light —had not lost a single gesture, not a single glance.

What jealousy does not see, it divines, and that is not surprising, for it sees what does not exist.

XX

THE SNARE

The relics were exposed twenty-four hours in the church.

The second day, they reascended to their chapel, amid the howling of the same poor wretches whose hopes they carried with them.

At the moment when the relics take their departure, the spectacle becomes terrifying. What! all is over! what! they leave us in our misery, our woes sharpened by the disappointment! And it is all over! over, for a whole year! And yet the power that can heal is here, shut up in this box, so near us! among us! They rush at the shrines and cling to them!—Nails are broken and bleeding against the iron-bound corners!—And the inexorable capstan up above turns and turns, tearing from the writhing crowd at the bottom of the well the strange coffin, that goes up, up, at the end of the straining ropes. Standing on tiptoe, jostling, overturning, crushing one another without pity, the poor devils struggle for the last touch—the last, supreme touch that may, perhaps, because it is the last, secure the coveted grace.—And all in vain. Amid the sobbing prayers, the mysterious closed vessel goes up toward the lofty chapel, carrying the water of salvation of which so many feverish lips long to drink. And when the shrines pass out of sight, near the arch, behind the lowered shutters,—then veritable shrieks of agony go up from the frenzied crowd who cannot endure the death of hope.

Then the uproar becomes truly frightful; then selfishness breaks forth unbridled, each one uttering for his own behoof the bestial cry that should bring down on him alone the saints' compassion; then the lamentation is wild, the supplication horrible to hear, the prayers are prayers of rage! And in this deep moat, whose walls tremble with the noise, there is a great uproar as of unclean beasts, thirsting for their God as for a physical blessing, as for a vainly awaited promised land! And, nailed against one of the bare walls of the fortress-church, a great crucifix, with open arms and upturned face, above all those distorted faces, all those raised and writhing arms, seems to mingle with the fierce lamentations of the human brutes its divine but no less fruitless and much more despairing cry!

And yet, it is almost always at the last moment, at the precise second when the shrines disappear, that the miracle takes place, and a paralytic walks or a blind girl sees. One cries out: "Miracle!"

Lucky girl! She is surrounded, almost suffocated.

"Can you see?"—"I did see."—"Can you see now?"—"Wait— yes!"—
"What?"—"A bright red lily! a flash! an angel!"—"Miracle! miracle!"

A man, a villager, immediately takes the child in his arms. Ah! he has seen miracles before! See how he hurries to take the child away on his shoulders, on the shield! He carries her thus so that all may see the miraculously-cured; so that no one shall forget that genuine miracles are done at Saintes-Maries, and come again! And the crowd follows, giving thanks. They hurry to the parsonage; the miracle is recorded in the presence of several assembled priests.

"Did you see?"—"Yes, I saw!"

And the procession moves on.

Ah! Christophore, the old pirate!—How he hurries along, with his lie on his shoulders!—He is a poor inhabitant of Saintes-Maries to whom the presence of so many strangers every year brings in something, as it does to all the rest, and he trots joyously off with his living decoy.

The next day, the child of the miracle is found alone at the foot of the Calvary, on the beach, left there for a moment by the woman or child who acts as her guide.

"Well, can you see?"—"No."—"What about the miracle, then?"

Poor child! In her plaintive voice, she replies: "It has gone again!"—"But you did see, yesterday?"—"Yes."—"If you could see, why did they carry you?"—"Oh! monsieur, I couldn't see anything but flowers, bright red lilies; but as to walking—oh! no, I couldn't see to do that! And now it is all dark. I can't see anything at all any more; yes, the miracle—has gone away!"

As soon as the relics had disappeared, everybody left the church in procession, to go to bless the sea—the sea that bore the saints to Camargue—the sea whereon the brave fishermen risk their lives every day.

The curé walked at the head of the procession. He held a relic in his hand; it was the Silver Arm, a hollow object in which some relics of the saints can be seen through a little square of glass.

The crowd followed in order. There were hundreds, yes, thousands of them. Great numbers of pilgrims, sitting on the dunes, watched the procession winding its way along the sandy beach where a few flat-boats lay high and dry.

Behind Monsieur le curé, six men bore on their shoulders a carved and painted wooden image, of considerable size, representing the two saints in the boat. There was so much jostling, by so many of the crowd, to secure the honor of replacing the bearers, that the boat pitched and rolled on their shoulders as if it were at sea in a high wind.

Saint Sara, the black saint, came next, borne by dark-haired, swarthy-faced gipsies, with eyes that glistened like jet. Their little ones meanwhile glided through the crowd like rats, creeping between people's legs and stealing handkerchiefs and purses.

And in the wake of the saints came young men and maidens, carrying lilies, sweet-smelling lilies, collected in sheaves every year for the procession of the faithful.

Others held tapers whose light could not be detected in the bright sunlight, but the lilies filled the air with perfume. These lilies were Livette's delight.

Monsieur le curé reached the water's edge. He held out the Silver Arm. Thereupon, the sea, for an instant, recoiled—only a little. The poor fishermen's wives quickly crossed themselves.

And all those who were standing on the dunes, watching the procession pass, saw the bearers marching at the head loom taller and taller at every step by reason of the mirage. And the saints on the bearers' shoulders gradually increased in size with them, and seemed to rise heavenward, of prodigious size, as in a vision.

"Protect us, great saints! May the sea be kind to us of Saintes-Maries this year!"

Poor people, poor souls! Wait till next year.

Every year it is the same thing. All this returns and will return, like the seasons.

On the day following that on which the relics returned to their retreat, the majority of the pilgrims left the village. All the camps were struck at almost the same hour.

The carriages of all sorts, the cabriolets, dog-carts, *chars-à-bancs, jardinières*, break-necks, the rich farmers' breaks, and the peasants' wagons, covered with canvas stretched over hoops, carried away seven, eight, ten thousand travellers of all ages, sick or well, and the long line crawled like a serpent over the flat road between two deserts. Here and there, at the left of the line, mounted men, many of whom carried a girl *en croupe*, rode back and forth, looking for one another, now waiting, now riding on at a gallop to take the lead of the caravan.

This departure of the pilgrims was another spectacle for the good people of

Saintes-Maries, who stood around in noisy groups on the outskirts of the village, waving a last adieu to the guests whose presence they had taken advantage of to the utmost.

Those who had been compelled to give shelter to friends and had consequently been unable to put so high a price on their hospitality, good-humoredly repeated the amusing sentiment, that certainly smacks less of Arabia than do the horses of the district: *Friends who come to visit us always afford us pleasure; if not when they arrive, at all events when they depart.*

On the second day following that on which the gipsy had smiled upon the drover, when the party of zingari passed in their place at the tail of the procession, some mounted on sorry nags, others jolting about in their wretched wagons,—some of the women on foot, the better to beg, carrying their children slung bandoleer-wise over their backs,—it was observed that the queen's wagon was not among them.

Zinzara had remained at Saintes-Maries.

She proposed to give herself the pleasure of administering a rebuff to the drover, with whom she had made an assignation for that very evening.

This is what had taken place.

During the branding, Renaud had whispered in Zinzara's ear:

"Ah! now I have you, gipsy! what a pity that it is before all these people!"

"On my word, I have the same thought *at this moment*," she replied, deeply touched by the grand presence of mind he had just shown in defending her.

"All right," he said, "I'll come and speak to you very soon. These are lovely nights."

"No, to-morrow," said she, "to-morrow, do you understand? after the wagons have gone."

But at the close of the performance, when he saw Livette coming toward him with pale cheeks, so pale that she looked like a corpse, he was seized with poignant remorse.

"She saw me," he said to himself, "and she is suffering from jealousy."

And so great was his pity for the poor little girl that he felt capable of sacrificing to her, once for all, at the very moment when it had become more difficult than ever, his insane passion for the other. All the chaste affection he had felt for Livette from the very first, so different from passion and so pleasant to the senses, came back to him like the puff of fresh air that awakens one from a bad dream.

Furthermore, he was surprised, almost disconcerted, to find that the gipsy's formal promise did not afford him the pleasure he had expected when he had dreamed of it in anticipation.

Livette left him to join her father, who was not to take her back to the château until the evening of the following day, two or three hours after the departure of the pilgrims, in order to remain until the end of the fête, and to avoid the thick dust and the enforced slowness of the long procession.

And that day—in the afternoon—Renaud fell in with Monsieur le curé.

"Good-day, drover. What is the matter, my boy? You seem preoccupied."

"Oh! curé," said Renaud, "sometimes it is difficult to do what is right!"

With that he was about to pass on, but the curé seized his arm and detained him.

"Eh! curé," said Renaud, "you have still a powerful grasp!"

"Beware, Renaud," said the curé very slowly, "lest you become a great sinner. I know what I know. Your betrothed wife is weeping. She is jealous. Already rumors are in circulation concerning you. And for whom, just God! would you betray that virtuous girl, who, wealthy as she is, gives herself to you, a poor orphan? You would ruin a whole family, poor you! and your honor and the repose of your heart, forever! The devil is crafty, you are right, and to do right is difficult, but those whom the devil inspires, when you follow their momentary caprice and your own fancy, lead you on to abysses deeper than the *lorons* of the *paluns*. You are walking at this moment on the moving crust! If it bursts, adieu, my man! You will be engulfed body and soul. As for yourself, that is a small matter! but by what right do you compel the little one to run the risk of your downfall? You are dealing with an accursed creature, a woman who does not know herself, who is submissive to nobody, and who cares nothing for the misfortunes of others. Whatever she does is for her own amusement. I have seen her and watched her. The saints have taught me many things. Beware! The little one is brave. Some day there may be innocent blood on your hands, if you keep on in the road I forbid you to follow, for the devil is in the affair, I tell you, and all sorts of monsters are awaiting you at the turning in the evil road. A betrothed lover's infidelity, like a husband's, lays an egg filled with ghastly creatures, which sometimes hatches. If you have a heart, show it, Renaud, take my advice, and go back to your horses and cattle in the solitude of your plains, where the malignant fever is less to be feared than the disease you are taking here!"

Renaud, the tall, strong, dashing blade, listened to these wise words, hanging his head, poor fellow, like a child scolded for not knowing his catechism.

"If you are a man, make up your mind at once, and give me your word as a true-hearted drover."

"Take my hand, Monsieur le curé. I give you my word. I was in a fair way to go wrong. A spell was on me."

The two men exchanged a grasp of the hand.

The curé walked away with an anxious heart. He knew that Renaud was sincere, but he knew the strength of man's passion and his ingenuity in lying.

So the curé had been asking questions?—In that case, to consort with the gipsy was to risk a rupture with Livette.

Renaud was about to leave the village,—or, if you please, the town,—with his mind firmly made up to renounce the gitana. Yes, he would sacrifice her to Livette, to his earnest desire to have a peaceful, happy home and a family, he, the wandering cowherd, the orphan, the foundling of the desert. That was happiness;—a roof to shelter one, a roof whose smoke one can see from afar on the horizon, thinking: the wife and little ones are there.

He would renounce the gitana; yes, but he proposed to make known his resolution to her himself. At the thought of leaving Saintes-Maries without *seeing her again*, for the purpose of telling her that he would not *see her again*, a weary feeling came over him; it seemed to him that he was suddenly shut up in a narrow space, and left there without air, without horizon.—But he would see her again—he must. It would be better so. Must he not soothe her anger first of all? She would be angry enough in any event. Why exasperate her?—In very truth, if he did see her again, it was—he reached this conclusion after much thought—it was principally in order to protect poor Livette against her! Yes, yes, it was for her sake that he would see her again. See her again! At those words, which he repeated softly to himself, a joy in living, in moving, in breathing, took possession of him.

Meanwhile, Zinzara, for her part, was vowing inwardly that she would enjoy a hearty laugh at the drover when he should presently seek her out!

Why, in that case, had she answered *yes* to his amorous questions? Oh! because at the moment when he whispered them in her ear, if she had been able, upon the spot, to give herself to this savage, all aglow from his conflict with bulls and heifers, doubtless she would have done it. He had awakened desire in her, as heat awakens thirst, as a summer evening awakens longing for a bath.—And then it had given her pleasure to say to herself that, over at the other end of the arena, the woman to whom he had paid queenly honor by giving her the smoking, red-hot iron, like the sceptre of a magician or a wicked zingaro king,—that that woman was suffering torments.

But he came too late. The desire had passed away. And the acme of delight to her now lay in the thought of refusing the promised favor to the Christian she detested, while giving Livette to believe that he had been false to her.

Sitting upon a stone, alone, at some distance from her wagon, she awaited the drover. Her resolution to take vengeance by refusing was written upon her compressed lips, whose smile became more malicious than ever when she saw him riding toward her.

A few steps away he stopped. As he looked at her, he felt a sudden rushing of the blood in all his veins, a strange, delicious pressure at the pit of the stomach. He recognized the characteristic agitation of love; but he made an effort, and said, in a voice which he felt to be unsteady: "I expected to be free to-night, but I am not. The master has sent for me, and I must be far away from here by night-fall. So I must go at once. Adieu, gipsy!"

Zinzara understood instantly that he was running away from her, and why!
—— She rose, like the serpent that rises on its tail and hisses with anger. All her harsh resolutions vanished in a twinkling; and, in a short, sharp, jerky voice, entirely different from her natural voice, she said: "I want you, do you hear? No one else shall give you orders when I have orders for you. What I want done is done. Are you going to act like a coward, pray—you, who have taken my fancy because, when you are on your horse, you resemble a zingaro who knows neither master nor God? Come, go on!"

Thus, the same motive of passionate hatred,—as pleasant to her taste as love,—that a moment before induced her determination not to go with Renaud, now threw her into his arms. And to him the love or hatred of such a woman, at the moment when she gave herself to him, was one and the same thing; were there not still her passion, her animated features, her gleaming eyes, her lips that, as they moved, disclosed two rows of pearly, sparkling teeth? Was there not her flexible, ballet-dancer's body, significantly held out toward him to whom she laid claim?

A thrill of savage joy shook Renaud from head to foot; and, as his rider shuddered, as if he had been touched by a cramp-fish, the horse seemed to experience a similar sensation, and pawed the ground an instant, between the knees that involuntarily pressed closer to his sides.

What was he to do? Ah! blessed saints! His betrothal had kept him virtuous for a long while, you know; had held him aloof from the frail damsels with whom he formerly consorted, and his youth was speaking now. The sea-bull must have the wild heifer. Lions that have loved gazelles, so says the Arabian legend, have died of it. Living creatures, by the law of nature, crave paroxysms of passion; so long as they have them not, they seek them; and pay for them, if need be, with their own and others' blood. Who of us will blame them for becoming delirious sometimes, if we remember that life longs to live, and that that longing overshadows the fear of death?

"Come, go on!"

The queen uttered love's command. And with one bound she jumped to the saddle behind him. In a twinkling she had wound her right arm about the horseman's waist: "Go on!" she said again; and then, in an undertone, in a voice that was no more than a warm, speaking breath upon the man's neck, and made him shudder to the very roots of his hair, she added: "I want you, do you understand? I want you! So go on, go on! The man who goes on, arrives!"

He was caught, fast bound. The sorceress's arm was about his loins. He felt it against him, living, trembling, stronger than aught else.

The stupefied Renaud tried to regain his self-control,—to shake off the spell. He sat there, dazed, unable to disentangle his thoughts, to determine what he should do, trying to collect his ideas of a moment before, the good curé's advice, his word of honor, none of which could he remember or repeat to himself in his mind, intelligibly. It had all gone from him, out of reach of the effort of his memory. When an intense amorous passion guides our movements, it is as legitimate as physical force,—honor is not betrayed: it has ceased to exist!

Those few seconds of hesitation afforded Zinzara perfect comprehension of what was taking place within him. His desire was no longer ardent enough to satisfy her pride, since it was possible for him to waver ever so little!

"Where are we going?" said she, resuming her sharp, jerky tone, in which there was a suspicion of a hiss. "Where are we going? You must know of a hiding-place somewhere, some deserted cabin in the midst of your swamps here,—a perfectly safe place, all your own, where you have taken other women—what do I care? *Pardi!* I don't suppose that you waited for me, to *learn!* I will go wherever you take me. Remember this—it must be somewhere where nobody can find me, for my race doesn't mix with yours: the zingara who gives herself to a Christian is the only despised one among us, and if one of our people should see me, there would be knives in the air, you may be sure, for you and for me!"

He still hesitated, remembering that he had reasons for hesitation, but unable to remember what they were. Mechanically he held back his horse (it was Blanchet!), who was acting badly.

At last, in the hurly-burly of his thoughts, he seized, at random, upon one thing he had entirely forgotten, the tapers promised by Livette to the Saintes Maries. He was to have lighted them devoutly in the church, during the night before or that morning. Yesterday his fiancée had reminded him again of the promise. Doubtless, Livette had lighted them for him, but that was not the same thing. And so the devil had him, do what he would. He lost his head. He felt that he was sliding down an inclined plane, and finding his struggles of no avail, he abandoned himself to his fate and hastened his fall.

"I know where we will go," he said; "to the Conscript's Hut, in the swamp."

It seemed to him that he was forced to reply, but he no longer felt any internal revolt against that obligation—far otherwise.

"Is it far?"

"Yes, in Crau, on the other side of the Rhône, near the Icard farm. The devil couldn't find me there. Rampal might come there, no one else——"

"Wait," said she at that name, with a sudden gleam in her cat-like eyes.

She whistled.

He said to himself that some one from Saintes-Maries would certainly see them, and that Livette would learn the whole story—that it would be better now to start at once.—Or perhaps—who knows?—the delay was a good thing! Livette might pass, herself, and all would be changed. He would hasten to her side. They would be saved. Who would be saved? and from what? from a vague, terrible thing that was before him. He could not have told what it was; but it was simply the renunciation of his own will.

The gitana's clear, shrill whistle summoned a little zingaro of some ten years, a veritable wild cat, who came running to the horse's side.

From the saddle she said a few words in the gipsy language to him, in a short, imperative tone of command. The gipsy language is composed of German, Coptic, Egyptian, and Sanscrit. Renaud listened without the slightest suspicion of the meaning of the words.

In a fit of amorous hatred, the swarthy queen said to the little fellow:

"You know Rampal, the drover? go and find him. He is in the village; I saw him not long ago. Go at once and tell him this: he will find me to-night, with his enemy, whom you see here, in the Conscript's Hut, which he knows! And I will join you and the wagon to-morrow evening, in the town of Arles, by the old tombs."

She thought of everything. The wild cat disappeared.

"What did you say to him?" Renaud inquired.

She began to laugh, an insolent laugh.

He felt that he abhorred her, that he would delight to see her conquered, under his heel, absolutely in his power, gipsy queen and sorceress that she was, like an ordinary woman.

Each desired the other in hatred.

She laughed as she thought that the man about whom her arms were thrown like a lover she was luring to his destruction. That very night—before or after the joys of love; what cared she for that?—there would be between him and that other a struggle as of wild beasts, which she longed to see; a witches' carnival of love, to rejoice the souls of the dead; and she laughed.

"Queens," said she, "cannot leave their kingdoms without issuing secret orders. Come, my beast!"

Was she speaking to the man or the horse?—To the man, doubtless, in whom she had awakened an animal like herself.

She pressed him tighter, and again she whispered:

"Come, come!"

He felt the vampire's breath playing in the short hair on his neck and descending in hot flushes to his feet, which were nervously tapping his horse's flanks. Renaud trembled. His passion had taken possession of him once more in all its intensity. It seemed as if a hurricane were raging in man and horse alike. They started off at full speed.

Renaud believed that he had a victim in his grasp, but he was himself the victim, and he rode away with the witch clinging fast to him—as the kite sometimes flies away with the serpent, thinking that he has mastered it, only to be strangled in its folds at last.

XXI

HERODIAS

They galloped across the plain. At every step, Renaud felt the gentle pressure of the woman's arm. Zinzara and Renaud galloped away upon Livette's horse!

Of what was the drover thinking? Was she girl or woman? His pride made him persist, in spite of himself, in wishing that she might be the former, although it seemed hardly probable, heathen females mature so early!

A breath of air blew in their faces. It brought to their nostrils the pungent smell of tamarisk blossoms. He slackened his horse's pace.

"Go on, go on!" said she, "press on! We will talk later—by ourselves, romi, where nobody can see us."

The horse darted forward afresh.

Renaud was conscious of a vague yet overmastering feeling of pride in being there, in trampling the grass of the plain with four feet, in knowing no obstacles, in having that woman close beside him—and, over yonder, another!

One would run risks and be false to the traditions of her race for his sake. The other, if she should know, might die of the knowledge. And, although he loved her, the thought caused a thrill of savage joy, but he promptly repressed it. Luckily, however, she would know nothing of it. And he became intoxicated with the rapid movement and with pride, man and beast combined, fairly launched upon his mad career.

Magnificent was the sky, studded with more stars than the dunes have grains of sand and the desert waving flowers clinging to the twigs of the *saladelles*. The Milky-Way was as white as the pyramids of salt seen through the morning mist. One would have said that a vast bridal veil, torn in strips, was floating above the whole plain, alive with murmurs of love.

Innumerable little snails were perched, like blossoms, upon the stalks of the reeds, and swung to and fro.

A very gentle breeze was blowing and raising a slight, uncertain ripple along the edges of the marsh, with the sound of a furtive kiss among the flowering rushes. At times, a lark or a flamingo, asleep among the reeds or in the shallow water, would awaken ever so little and chirp to let his mate know that he was there, not far away.

June is no hotter. Sometimes the smell of roses filled their nostrils, coming in long puffs from far-off gardens. Yonder, in the park of the Château d'Avignon, the Syrian tree was sending forth its pollen.

Renaud, after skirting the sea for some distance, rode due northeast, beyond the pond of La Dame.

He was bound for Grand-Pâtis. The people at Sambuc had some boats that he knew of.

For a moment, they rode beside a drove. Bulls, standing in water up to their thighs, hardly noticed, were feeding on the flowering reeds. White mares fled at their approach, followed faithfully by stallions anxious not to lose sight of them. The sap of May was flowing in the reeds and rushes, in the sambucus and tamarisk. The very water exhaled a saline odor, stronger than usual, and more heavily laden with desires. The wild vine called to its mate, that came borne upon the heavy breath of the blooming desert.

Again Renaud stopped, seized with a mild, pleasurable vertigo.

The fresh, love-compelling breeze in which they were bathed laid an imperious command upon him.

"Get down," said he, "get down at once! This is a good place to rest."

But she remembered the order she had given.

"We must go where we were going," said she. "I will not get down until we are there. We must cross the Rhône, you say? Press on, press on!—Gallop! The gipsy loves the horse."

She would have none of his caresses except at the place appointed. She would not submit to him until they should be where he was, by her agency, in danger of death or suffering. A kiss under other circumstances would be a triumph for him, and she gave herself to him for her own pleasure alone. She desired to feel, in the interchange of caresses, that the moisture of her lips was poison, that her bite would cause death or madness.

Firmly seated *en croupe*, still clinging fast to the drover—her victim—with her arm wound about him, her bare legs hanging in the folds of her skirt which the wind raised as they sped along, with her head thrown proudly back, she swayed gracefully with the rocking motion of the gallop; and her face, which had a sallow look in the moonlight against the neck of the man whom she was leading astray, albeit she seemed to be carried away by him—her face was wreathed in smiles.

When Herodias had obtained the head of John the Baptist, she lifted it by the hair from the gold charger, whereon it lay with a circle of blood around the neck, raised it to the level of her face, and after gazing upon it with deep interest, examining the closed eyelids and long lashes and the transparent pallor of the cheeks, she suddenly placed her mouth upon that lifeless mouth and sought to force her tongue between the lips to the cold teeth too tightly closed in death, esteeming that kiss, inflicted on her dead foe, more delicious than the incestuous caresses for which he had reproved her.

What was left of Renaud's suspicions of Zinzara, while she was smiling in the darkness, and the warm breath from her lips was playing upon his neck? He had ceased to reflect; he rode on. He willingly postponed the longed-for hour, now that he was forced to go on. He thought no more of violence. His happiness was secure. He could wait. In the midst of the deserted plains, still warm from the sunlight though refreshed by the night air, love came without calling, but he enjoyed the anticipation more than anything he had known.— And then she might escape him even now. He must be careful not to startle her. When they reached the nest yonder, he would keep her there some time. And so he rode on, inhaling the saline air of the desert, which was his—with his stallion's four shoeless feet trampling through the sand and water, which were his also—bound for the horizon, which would soon be his.

Once, however, in the midst of a swamp, where the water was above his horse's knees, he stopped again.

"What is it?" said she.

Renaud turned his head, and throwing himself back, called her with a smacking of his lips.

"When I am ready!" said Zinzara in a mocking tone.

As she spoke, Blanchet leaped forward, with all four feet in the air, and made a tremendous splashing in the water, which fell about their heads in a heavy shower.

And, unseen by Renaud, the gipsy smiled against his neck, as she replaced in her hair the long gold pin she had plunged into the beast's flank.

Suddenly there was a shout of *Qui vive?* directly in front of them, so unexpected in the solitude, that Blanchet jumped again.

"*Qui vive?*" the voice repeated.

"The king!" Renaud replied gaily.

"Ah! is it you, Renaud?"

It was the revenue officers; but Renaud hurried by, at a safe distance, so that they might not recognize the gitana.

They were near the salt spring of Badon. The rectangular heaps of salt seemed like so many long, low houses, with sharp roofs. In its shroud-like whiteness the spot resembled a little town, geometrically laid out, asleep under dead snow.

They reached the shore of the main stream of the Rhône.

Zinzara was on the ground before Renaud had stopped his horse.

He alighted in his turn, and handed the rein to the gipsy. She held Blanchet while he was drinking in the river.

"Now for some oats!" said Renaud.

He took a small sack that was fastened across his saddle-bow, from holster to holster, and at Zinzara's suggestion emptied it into her dress which she held up with both hands.

Poor, poor Blanchet! there was only a handful of grain.

"Wait for me; I'll go to find the boat."

Renaud disappeared in the darkness behind the reeds and willows that grew along the bank, drowned in the mist, floating like pallid spectres in the darkness.

Zinzara heard nothing save the plashing of the water, and the crunching of the oats between Blanchet's teeth, as he swept them up with his long lip from the hollow of the dress.—Oh! if Livette could have seen that!

"Here I am, come!" said Renaud's voice.

He approached, raising the oars. She walked to the water's edge.

"Hold the reins fast. The horse will follow us."

She stepped into the boat and stood in the stern. Blanchet followed, in the wake.

Renaud knew the current at that spot. He rowed diagonally across and reached the other shore more than a hundred yards farther down.

He tied the boat to the trunk of a willow and tightened the girths, and they were off again.

It was necessary to ascend the stream a long distance to find a place to ford the canal that runs from Arles to Port-le-Bouc. When they had crossed the canal, he said:

"We are almost there."

They had ridden nearly five hours.

His desires were approaching fruition. He was seized with the impatience that comes with the last half-hour. He had a vision of what was to come.

"It is in the *gargate*," he said. And he explained: "The *gargate* is like thickened water. It is about the same as mud. The cabin we are going to is in the midst of one of these patches of mud. Ah! we shall be well protected there, gitana, I promise you. A man once lived there for a long while; a conscript who wanted to evade the draft. And later, an escaped convict, a native of the neighborhood, who knew about the place. No one could dislodge him there. Others know the spot; but never fear, I have a way to fool them. Trust me, gitana, we shall be well guarded there, by death hidden in the water around us!"

They reached their destination.

Renaud tied his horse to a tree, and took Zinzara's hand.

"Follow me," he said.

The moon was rising. With the end of a stick, he pointed out to her, just above the surface of the water, the heads of the stakes, looming black among the stalks of thorn-broom and reeds and the broad, spreading leaves of the water-lily.

"Always step to the left of the stakes," he said; "they mark the right-hand edge of the solid path just below the surface of the water."

Renaud had taken off his shoes and stockings. She lifted her skirts and walked with bare legs, and he held her hand. They walked thus for some time. Her interest was aroused by her surroundings. The place pleased her.

The water was disturbed a little here and there. She stopped and watched.

"Turtles," said he; and added: "Here is the cabin."

The cabin stood in the midst of the bog, built on piles, as was the path leading to it. Reeds and a few tamarisks surrounded it, and made it invisible from almost every direction. On the gray, thatched roof, shaped like a hay-stack, the little cross gleamed in the moonlight, bent back as if the wind had tried to blow it down.

The back of the cabin was turned to the *mistral*. They entered. Renaud took a candle from his wallet and struck a match. The light danced upon the walls.

The low walls were of grayish mud, set in a rough frame-work. The floor was covered with a bed of reeds. A cotton cloth, to keep out the gnats, hung before the door. There was a stationary table against the wall at the right, near the head of the bed; it was a flat stone supported by four pieces of timber fastened to the floor.

Renaud set his candle down on the stone. The gitana, already seated on the rough bed, watched him with a savage look in her eyes. She began to feel that she was a little too much in his power, that it was a little too much like being under his roof.

The cabin was like all the cabins in the district. From the ceiling bunches of reed blossoms hung like waving silver plumes. The big cross-timbers of the ceiling were pinned together with wooden pegs, the large ends of which projected, and some few scraps of worn-out clothes were still hanging from them. There was a fire-place in one corner, made of large stones placed side by side, and in the roof, directly above it, was a hole for the smoke.

Renaud hung his wallet on one of the pegs.

"Now, wait for me," he said, with a loud laugh, "I'm going out to attend to the horse."

She was surprised, but after she had glanced at him, she could think of nothing but Rampal.

He went out to Blanchet, removed the saddle and laid it on the ground, then mounted him, bareback, and rode him to a pasture some distance away, where he hobbled him and left him.

A quarter of an hour later, Renaud returned, with his saddle across his shoulders, to the cabin where Zinzara was awaiting him. But, as he walked along the solid path, a black ribbon covered by a sheet of shallow water, he took up the stakes that marked one edge of the path, and moved them from the right side to the left;—so that, if that beggarly Rampal, the only man likely to follow him to that lair, chose to come there, he certainly would not go far, but would remain there, buried up to his neck at least!

When he had changed the position of the first twenty stakes, the only ones visible from the shore of the bog, Renaud stood up and walked swiftly toward the cabin. His heart at that moment was sad, and more filled with slime and noxious things than the waters of the swamp, which, though they glistened in the moonlight, were black beneath the surface.

XXII

IN THE NEST

In the contracted cage, whose thatched roof, with its peak of red tiles, shone in the moonlight amid the marsh plants, the two beasts of the same species, Zinzara and Renaud, were shut up together.

"I am hungry," said she, in a hostile tone.

He took a tin box from his wallet and raised the cover; it contained the wherewithal to support life; he cut the bread and uncorked the bottle.

She ate silently, still with the savage look in her eyes. He waited upon her, partaking also of the dry bread himself, and putting his lips to the flat bottle, filled with the strong wine of the wild grape.

When they had eaten, he handed her a small flask of brandy. She drank from it, joyfully, and soon her eyes began to sparkle. He looked at her, ready to embrace her. She answered him with a glance so mocking and unfathomable, that he hesitated, waiting for he knew not what, weary besides, and feeling that his brain was confused.

He saw her thereupon take her tambourine, which she wore fastened to her belt by a small cord, under her dress; and she began to play upon it. She was sitting on the bed. She struck regular, monotonous blows upon the vibrating skin, and at every blow the charms depending from the tambourine jangled noisily.

Then she began to sing outlandish words, in slow measure, beating time with the tambourine. And this proceeding at length fascinated the drover, who gazed at her, as completely under the spell as the lizard listening to the locust in the sunshine on a summer's day.

This lasted an hour. He watched her, enchanted, proud, thinking of nothing but her, and he felt his heart leap and quiver in his breast at every touch upon the tambourine.

But one would have said that she had drawn about herself a circle that he could not cross. He waited until the circle should be broken. He was like one of the great dogs trained to guard droves of bulls; that are so fearless of blows from the horns of their charges, but sit obediently by watching their master at his meals, waiting for the crumb he tosses them, slaves of the king, of their god, who is man.

She had now the effect upon him of a genuine queen, a queen in some fairy tale, with her studied attitudes accompanied by the monotonous music, which was accentuated by the ceaseless motion of the sequins of her crown of copper against her swarthy brow and the dead black of her hair.

Suddenly she laid her tambourine aside. He started toward her. She held him back with a stern glance, and snatching away the silk handkerchief that covered her shoulders, appeared before him in a rich waist of many colors; and he saw upon her breast necklaces of gold pieces—her fortune.

"Await my pleasure," said she. "Leave me in peace a moment."

She covered her head with the ample handkerchief she had taken off and remained hidden behind that veil for a moment. Renaud heard her muttering unfamiliar words—*mormô, gorgô*—words of sorcery, without doubt.

When she threw back her veil, she was laughing.

What vision had the sorceress evoked? what had the seer seen?

"It will be better than I hoped!" said she. "Now, look!"

She rose, and to the accompaniment of the jangling of the sequins in her diadem and the gold pieces of her necklace, set in motion by her slow dance, in the course of which she did not move from where she stood, she removed her garments, one by one.

By the flickering light of the candle, that waved back and forth as a breath of air came in through the door, Renaud watched the familiar vision reappear.

Zinzara swayed this way and that as she unfastened, one after another, her waist, her skirts—and took them off, bending gracefully forward and backward, raising her arms above her head or lowering them to her ankles. And now you would have said it was a bronze statue, glistening in the half-darkness. Renaud knew that figure well, from having seen it one day in the bright sunlight, and so many, many times since then, in his imagination.

The necklace tinkled upon her swelling breasts; several large rings were around her ankles, and upon her brow, the crown from which the trinkets hung.

She turned and twisted gracefully about, her dark skin gleaming like a mirror.

"You see," said she, "Zinzara gives herself, no man takes her, romi. The wild girl belongs to no one but herself. And even now I could, if I chose, nail you where you stand, forever!"

As she spoke, she threw down upon her clothes a keen-edged stiletto that had gleamed for an instant in her hand.

"Come!" said she.

They lay, side by side, on the floor of that hovel, upon the crackling reeds.

At that moment, he looked into the depths of her eyes, and he saw there vague things by which he had already on several occasions been profoundly alarmed. The gitana's hidden purpose, as to which she herself had no clear idea, flickered uncertainly in her glance, making its presence felt, but giving no hint by which it could be divined.

Her smile, which was ordinarily visible only at the corner of her mouth, had spread, more unfathomable than ever, over her whole face, which wore an expression of triumphant mockery. More mysterious she appeared and more desirable. If Renaud had been familiar with the carved stone animals that lie sleeping in the Egyptian desert, he would have recognized their expression, an expression that words cannot describe, upon the speaking face that gazed at him and called him.

And, lo! the hatred he had once before felt for that face, for that glance, returned swiftly, imperiously, to his mind; an irresistible desire to seize the woman by the neck and choke her with cruel, unyielding hands.

Even that feeling was love, for otherwise it would have occurred to him to part abruptly from the sorceress, to fly from her; that thought would have come to him, once at least, and it did not come. On the contrary, he felt that he could not really possess her except by some violence of that sort. Is it not true that mares look upon bites as caresses?—She saw the thought in his eyes, and began to laugh.

Again she recognized distinctly, and with delight, the brute like herself that she had aroused in him. And she did it to demonstrate her power to subdue the brute, with a look.

"Oh! you may!" she said, with a smile.

As she spoke, he caught a rapid glimpse of the part she was to play in his destiny: the pollution of his life, the loss of real happiness, of all repose, and the false love—the strongest of all passions.

Their glances, laden with amorous hate, met and struck fire like knife-blades.

He seized her around the neck and was very near choking her in good earnest; he thought that he would strangle her. "Come, come!" she said in a languishing voice; but, suddenly feeling the pressure of the hand that was really squeezing her throat, she leaped up at him, and, with a strangled laugh, hurled her mouth at his and bit his lips. They could hear their teeth clash. He uttered a cry which was at once stifled, for their angry lips had no sooner met than they were appeased.

She gazed at him for a long while, looking always into his eyes. She saw them more than once grow dim and sightless, and then, exulting in the thought of this wild bull's weakness in her hands, she laughed silently; but no emotion dimmed the brightness of her eyes. Suddenly, when he had grown calmer, a profound sigh caused him to look with more attention at the savage creature he had conquered at last. A pallor as of the other world overspread her swarthy face; her features were distended. She was no longer smiling. The wrinkle that ordinarily raised one corner of her lips and gave her an air of mockery had vanished. The corners of her mouth, on the other hand, drooped a little, imparting a sad expression to her face. One would have said she was a different being. There was no trace of animation upon her features. She no longer belonged to herself. An attack of vertigo had taken away her power of thought. She was like a drowned woman drifting with the tide. Something as everlasting as death had proved stronger than she.

As if from the midst of one of those dreams which, in a second, open eternity to our gaze, she returned to herself with amazement.

The snake-charmer realized that she had been defeated in a way she was unaccustomed to; she experienced a curious sensation of shame, a sort of proud regret that she had forgotten herself as never before.—And was he, without even suspecting the trap she had set for him, tranquilly to carry off the gratification of his passion with which she had baited the trap? In that case she would have betrayed herself! She would be the victim of her detested lover! of Livette's betrothed!—The mere thought was intolerable to her. And in a frenzy of rage and humiliation she put out her hand and felt among her clothes that lay in a pile near by, for the stiletto she had insolently thrown upon them just before.

Renaud understood only one thing; the beast was becoming ugly again! He seized her wrists and held her arms to the ground, crossed above her head, and then he began to laugh in his turn.

Her insane rage came to the surface; she writhed about and tried to bite, but could not. She felt that her power was gone, that she was in the hands of one stronger than herself. Without understanding her, he felt that she was dangerous and he mastered her. The Christian had her in his power! It was too much. She felt her eyes bursting with the tears that were ready to gush forth, but she forced them back. A little foam appeared at the corner of her mouth.

"Dog!" she exclaimed.

At that, the man whose face she saw above her own, bending over and rising again quickly, touched her lips with his. And he had the feeling that the hand that grasped the stiletto relaxed its hold.

At that moment, a wailing cry rent the air above the cabin, then ceased abruptly, before it had died away in the distance, as if the bird that uttered that signal of distress had lighted among the reeds near at hand, and had at once become mute.

Renaud took his eyes from the gitana's face.

"What is that?" said he.

"A curlew flying over!" she replied, without moving.—"The curlew goes south in winter."

Renaud was on his feet, pale as death.

"King," said she, "do you love your queen? Then look at her!"

And, as she lay upon her back, she began to make her snake-like body undulate and gleam like a mirror, keeping time with her tambourine, which she held above her head.

The bursts of laughter with which she punctuated the outlandish music displayed her glistening teeth from end to end.

"Come back here," she said, "are you afraid?"

He was ashamed, and, returning to the straw pallet, resumed his rôle of subjugated watch-dog in love with a she-wolf.

In that one night, the young man felt the whole power of his youth, learned more of life and realized more dreams than many real kings.

The pleasures of love are no greater to the prince than to the charcoal-burner.

The day was breaking. Bands of violet along the horizon changed to pink and then to yellow. An awakening breeze passed like a shiver over the desert of sand and water, entered the cabin, and blew out the flickering light on the stone table.

A cock in the distance welcomed the dawn.

Thereupon, Renaud started to go to find his horse. The wallet was empty, too.

"At the Icard farm," said he, "I can get what I need."

"Do you suppose," said she, "that I intend to stay here all day like a captive goose?"

"Is it all over, then?" said he, "and are you going away, too?"

"To return may be a pleasure," said she, "but to remain is always a bore."

She hummed in the gipsy language:

"God gave thy mare no rein, Romichâl."

"If you choose," she continued, "we will ride together till night. My horse has wings."

"Very good," said Renaud. "Do you cross over to solid ground first. We will go together and get my horse. It will be a fine day."

"And a good one! be sure of that!" said she, in her jerky voice, her voice which resembled *another's*.

He went with her as far as the first of the stakes he had displaced, to point out the safe road to her, and when he saw her reach the edge of the swamp sixty feet beyond, he stooped and began to put the stakes in place one by one as he walked toward the firm ground.

When he reached the last, he sprang to his feet with haggard eyes.

Livette, with head thrown back, face turned toward the sky, eyes closed, mouth open, and grass mingled with her straying hair, was lying among the water-lilies, as if asleep, and in the throes of a bad dream. He also saw her two little clenched hands, above the water, clinging to the reeds.

Transformed for a moment to a statue, Renaud soon aroused himself, and, bending over Livette, put his hands under her armpits. The poor body, buried in the thick, black ooze, came slowly forth, torn from its bed like the smooth stalk of a lily.

When he had the poor body in his arms, inert and cold, perhaps dead,—the body of the poor, dear child, whose skirts, entangled in a net-work of long grasses, clung tightly to her dangling legs,—Renaud suddenly uttered a roar as of an enraged wild beast, and ran like a madman at the top of his speed to the nearest farm-house.

XXIII

THE PURSUIT

One forgives only those whom one loves; only those who love forgive. Love at its apogee is naught but the power of inspiring forgiveness and bestowing it; and the social laws, which are of the mechanism of human justice, seem to have realized that fact, since they ignore the testimony of all those who would naturally be expected to love the culprit.

Sympathy is simply a laying aside—in favor of those we love—of the implacable severity which we use but little in dealing with ourselves, and which attributes to those who pass judgment an unerring wisdom which is not human, or a self-confidence which is too much so.

Livette, as she lay sick upon the best bed in the Icard farm-house, already had, in her sorrowing heart, an adorable feeling of indulgence for Renaud, which would have made the blessed maidens who laid the Crucified One in his shroud, smile with joy in the mystic heaven of the lofty chapel. She believed that she would die by her fiancé's fault, and she pitied him. Forgiveness sooner or later redeems him who receives, and consoles him who accords it. In the sentiment of compassion is hidden the divine future of mankind.

Renaud was still ignorant of Livette's indulgence. Indeed, he could not deserve it until he had come to look upon himself as forever unworthy.

For the moment, he had not gone to the bottom of the hell of evil thoughts.

When he found Livette half drowned in the *gargate*, his first impulse, born of true love and pity for her, in absolute forgetfulness of himself, lasted but an instant—but it had existed. Renaud at first suffered for her and for her alone.

His second impulse, almost immediate, and praiseworthy still, although there was a touch of selfishness in it, was to condemn himself, through fear of moral responsibility. Had he not with his own hand displaced the stakes that marked the path, with the idea, indefensible at best, that Rampal would be misled by that treacherous method of defence? Yes, almost immediately after he uttered his cry of agony, he shuddered with terror at the thought of the remorse that was in store for him, as soon as he felt that Livette was like a dead woman in his arms.

When he had given her in charge of the women at the main farm-house of the Icard farm, where there was great excitement over such an adventure at that time of day, he questioned two old peasant-women who knew more than all the doctors in the province. After doing what was necessary for Livette, they cheerfully declared that the poor girl would not die of it; they even said that it was "nothing at all." He did not even try to understand how she had come so far to fall into the trap!

She would not die! That was the essential thing at that moment. What a relief *to him*, for he was already accusing himself of his little sweetheart's death! He had been so afraid! And it turned out to be only a warning! God be praised, and blessed be the mighty saints who had performed such a miracle!

But the devil rejoiced when he looked into Renaud's conscience, for he saw the course his ideas were about to take, a course that would lead him from bad to worse.

Reassured as to Livette,—and as to himself,—he flew into a passion with the accursed gitana, the indirect cause, at least, of all this misery.

"Ah! the beggar! I will kill her!—it will be easy to find her again. She can't be far away—I will kill her!"

His wrath took full possession of him—he ran for his horse. Kill her!—kill her! Nothing could be more righteous.—And he went about it.

Poor Renaud! the victim of all the involuntary falsehoods which, starting from ourselves, one engendering another, sometimes render the best of us irresponsible and drive us on to disaster when passion makes us mad.

This chain, often undiscoverable, of false but specious reasons with which men deceive themselves, each fitting into the last without violence, each explaining and justifying the one that follows it—leads insensibly to acts incomprehensible to him who is not able to follow it back, link by link. It is the chain of FATALITY, in which the links, consisting of trifling but suggestive facts, of decisive circumstances, unknown sometimes to the culprit, alternate with the fictitious good motives he has invented for his own benefit in the reflex movements of his mind. To re-establish the logical sequence of facts, of sensations suddenly transformed into ideas, is the work of equity which reasons, or of love which divines. In default of tracing back the chain of insensible, imperious transitions, we find between the criminal who has long been an honest man and his crime, the abyss at sight of which fools and unthinking folk, filled with the pride of implacable sinners, never fail to exclaim: "It is monstrous!" But if God, infinite Love, does exist, everything is forgiven, because everything is understood; there are, mayhap, simply the miserable wretches on one side, and divine pity on the other.

Yes, Renaud would have killed the sorceress, with savage joy, to avenge

Livette. But was not that desire, which he deemed a praiseworthy one, simply a pretext for seeking her out again that same day, for seeing her once more?— That, at all events, is what the devil himself thought as he crouched on the floor of the crypt in the church of Saintes-Maries-de-la-Mer, on the spot occupied the day before by the dark-browed gipsies, beneath the shrine of Saint Sara.

And so, mounted upon Blanchet, Renaud galloped furiously away upon his tracks of the night, intending to kill Zinzara.

Livette would not die!—That idea caused him great joy, so great that he was no sooner out-of-doors, away from the painful, wearisome spectacle of the poor unconscious child, than he yielded, alas! to the influence of the bright sunlight, and breathed at ease. He had already ceased to think of Livette's sufferings. His satisfaction had already ceased to be anything more than selfishness: not only would he not have to reproach himself for her death, but, more than that, now that she knew everything, was he not absolved, as it were? There was nothing more for him to fear. The worst that could happen had happened! And he actually felt as if a weight had been taken from his shoulders, as if he were once more sincere in his dealings with Livette, a better man, in short, thanks to what had happened. Although he did not reason this out, the thought went through his mind. It was what he felt. For everything serves the passion of love; it turns to its own profit the very things that would naturally tend most to thwart it. Moreover, he need feel no qualms of conscience, as he was going to chastise the malignant creature, to kill her, in fact:—a vile race!

No, she could not be far away. Doubtless, if she had planned the catastrophe, she had concealed herself near at hand to see the result.

He rode back toward the bridge over the canal. No one had seen the gipsy there. He descended the Rhône to the spot where they had left the boat the night before. The boat was in the same place, fastened by the same knot.

He began to fear that he might not find her. But when, after searching two hours, he was certain of it, he was much surprised to find that he did not feel the righteous wrath of the officer of justice at the thought of a culprit eluding the vengeance of the law, but the sudden distress of a betrayed lover. He did not cry to himself: "I shall not have the pleasure of punishing her!" but: "I shall never see her again!" And that cry burst forth in his heart as a fierce revelation of unpardonable, pitiless love. What! he loved her! he loved her! and he learned it for the first time at that moment! he admitted it to himself for the first time!—yes, beyond cavil he loved her—*now*! His heart failed him. He was bewildered. He felt a vague sense of well-being, due to the mere joy of loving, marred by a feeling of intense chagrin at the thought of the certain misery that lay before him. He was horrified at himself, and, at the same moment, decided upon his future course in a frenzy of excitement.

The physical power of love is superb and appalling. It stops at nothing. And the man who is watching beside the dying or the dead, even though it be some one who is dear to him, feels a thrill of joy rush to his heart, if the being he loves with all the force of his youth passes by.

Renaud had just held Livette almost dying in his arms, and already he had no regret save for the other, for the woman he should have trampled under his feet!

Thereupon, all the events of the night returned to his mind, and finished the work of poisoning. He could not be reconciled to the thought that he should never again see what he had had for so short a time. No, it could not be at an end. If she were a criminal, why then he would love her in her crime, that was all! The black bull was loose.—But Livette? aha! Livette? a swan's feather, or a red flamingo's, under his horse's hoof.

What was the placid affection the young maid had inspired in his heart compared to the frenzy of sorrow and joy the other caused him to feel? Sorrow and joy combined, that is what love is; and the love men prefer is not that which contains the greater joy as compared to the keener sorrow—it is that in which those emotions are most intense. It was that law of passion to whose operation Renaud was now being subjected. He realized that he had definitely chosen the other, the gipsy, despite the cry of his outraged sense of honor.

That cry of his honest heart, to which he no longer lent a willing ear, he still heard, do what he would, and he suffered half consciously, for many reasons which he did not distinguish one from another, but which resulted in producing a confused feeling in his own mind that he was a monster.

A monster! for now that he considered the matter more carefully, it became his settled conviction that the gitana had intended to kill Livette—and yet it was that same gitana that he loved!

Ah! the witch!—She had certainly seen Livette, her poor little head, like a dead woman's, lying on the water among the grass, her mouth open for the last cry for help, her teeth glistening with water in the sunlight! She could not have helped seeing her.—And she had passed her by without a word!—It was because she was determined to be her ruin. She had evidently led her into the trap. How? What did it matter! but it was no longer possible to doubt that it was the fact.

But in that case—if she was really guilty—there could be no doubt, either, that having seen her desire accomplished, she had fled. She would appear no more! he would have no opportunity to kill her! he would never see her again! And the thing that moved him most deeply in connection with Livette's misfortune was the thought that it involved Zinzara's flight. He tried in vain to put away the abominable regret; it returned upon him like a wave. What! he should never see her again!

Oh! those caresses of the night before in the cabin of the swamp were clinging to his arms and legs like serpents. They twined about his body as creeping plants about the branches of the tamarisk, or as one eel about another: biting at his heart. And he shivered from head to foot.

"Ah! the witch!" he repeated. "Ah! the witch! What! never again!"

Never again!—Why, did he not think that night that he should be able to keep her on his island; that it would last a year at least, until the next year's fêtes; that he would have the wild beast to himself in the desert, in his wild beast's lair—all to himself, with her lithe, graceful body, her ankle-rings and bracelets, and her beggar queen's crown?

But did she not love him? Had it all been mere trickery and craft on her part?

The horse's blood flowed freely under the drover's spurs; but the horseman's heart was bleeding within him a thousand times more cruelly.

All mere trickery and craft! He repeated it again and again to himself, and would not believe it.

That she was false to the core, he firmly believed, and, by dint of thinking about it, soon ceased to believe it. That would have been too horrible, really! His self-pity and the feeling that he must be proud of her forced back the thought, which, driven away for a moment, returned again at once with more force as a sure, proven, established fact. It returned like a flash of light which hurt his eyes. Yes, yes, she was false to the core! yes, from pure wantonness the woman had deceived him again and again since the day of the bath, when she exhibited her naked body to him with the deliberate purpose of leading him astray, of leaving him, some day, stranded in the desert, without his fiancée, without his love—alone.

And he struggled desperately to see her again—in his memory at least—in order to question her crafty features, but, try as he would, his mind was unable to restore the picture, drowned as it was beneath a wavering, irritating mist. He opened his eyes to their fullest extent, as if, by causing them to express a fixed determination to see her again, he could compel her to appear before him in flesh and blood. And he no longer saw the trees or the moor that lay before him, or the sky or the horizon, but neither did he see her whose image he sought to evoke. Then he suddenly closed his eyes, and for a brief second—in the darkness—he caught a glimpse of her. Was it really she? He had not time to recognize her. Once, however, the image became clearer, and he *saw* her; but still it was only a shadowy face, still veiled with falsehood and impenetrable to him.

Chapter XXIII

She went to the farther end of the Allée des Alyscamps, between the rows of tall poplars, amid the stone monuments, and lighted a fire of twigs, to give her light enough to look about and select a spot where she could sleep comfortably.

What he was seeking was her real face, WHICH DID NOT EXIST, for a face is the expression of a soul, and she had no soul. Had she ever loved him? that is what he would have liked to ascertain, if nothing more. Had she smiled on Rampal? Perhaps—God! could it be possible? Who knows? Of what was she not capable to consummate her crime?—And yet he secretly admired her for the extraordinary perfidy he attributed to her. The Saracen blood, the blood of heathen pirates, did not flow in his veins for nothing.

Yes, indeed, if, in her hate-inspired work, she had had need of Rampal, with whom he had several times seen her talking, was it not possible that she had given herself to him in order to make him absolutely submissive to her will? What was he thinking of? Given herself to him? No, not that!—Not in its fullest meaning, at all events—but she might have let him steal a kiss—a long kiss, perhaps—from her lips. And the herdsman felt the keen point of the spear of jealousy pierce his heart.

He thought and thought, feverish with passion, excited by his excessive exertions for several days past, and he rode through the fields and swamps, amid the grass and stones of Crau, surrounded by buzzing insects maddened by the heat, which was terrible.

Great God! only the night before, he had believed that she had a veritable woman's passion for him, a passion like those he had often aroused in women, with his strength, his courage, and his prowess as horse-breaker and cavalier. And as she was the daughter of a free race, and queen of her tribe, he had been proud of his conquest. He had straightened himself up in his saddle, like a crowned king, conqueror in many battles. He had handled his spear with a firmer hand. He had glanced proudly at the other drovers, his comrades, with a distinct feeling that he was "better than they," since this savage queen, who, in her travels, had doubtless seen so many brave and comely men, had chosen him—even though he were not the first!—that she, whom the laws of her people forbade to love a European dog, the slave of cities, had chosen him, the drover of Camargue!

Now that that happiness was gone from him, he suddenly realized its value. An immense void lay before him. For the first time, the desert seemed a melancholy place to him, too vast, too bare. He realized that henceforth his whole life would lie in the past. He was no longer the king! He would never be the king again! She had never loved him! And she had pretended that she did!

But when she had cried out and turned pale in his arms, had she not forgotten that she was acting a lie? If that were so, she must be very sure of finding elsewhere such ardent caresses as his, from another. Otherwise she would not have fled, for he scouted the idea that she was afraid. Such a one as she could have no fear! And if, as he thought the night before, he had really taken her fancy, would she not have remained, guilty or not, to enjoy his caresses anew, even though she were to die of them?

But she would not have died of them! She, sorceress as she was, must have known that he would have forgiven everything. Therefore she had *wanted* to go. She cared nothing for him. If, on the other hand, it had pleased her to keep him with her, to continue their liaison, she would have found a way to do it, in spite of everything. She had only to desire to do it. She did not *desire*!—Even so, he desired her!

He rode away at headlong speed. He must find her again. Then they would see! And he circled round the cabin in the swamp like a hawk, examining all the clumps of thorn-broom, all the tamarisks and reeds. Oh! he would find her!

He had been riding for several hours, and he began to feel that his quest was useless. If she were outside the limits of the last greater circle that he had described in his search for her, it was all over! he was too late.

At last, convinced of his discomfiture, he leaped from his horse and seated himself on the sloping bank of a ditch. It was near midday. He was neither hungry nor thirsty, but the sun told him that it was midday.

The gnats were humming about his ears, devouring him, riddling the hide of his horse, who hung his head and sniffed at a tuft of salt grass without eating it, pulling a little upon the rein which Renaud, still seated, held loosely in his hand.

Renaud was looking straight before him, and now that he was assured of his misfortune, now that he had neither betrothed nor mistress, neither present nor future, he felt that he was becoming cold and hard, and was astonished to find it so. It seemed to him as if his misfortune had happened to a piece of wood or stone. The wood and the stone were himself. How could he have had such dread of the certainty that had come to him at last? While he had that dread, he still hoped and suffered. Now that all was said, he found that he was insensible to it all—dead, in a measure. And that gratified him.

He who had wept so bitterly the night that he tried to put aside his nascent passion, now, in this final catastrophe, which should have called forth all the tears in his body, felt as if the springs had run dry. Instead of being more deeply moved than ever, he found that he was strangely composed, as if armed against fate.—He received the blow like a soldier, like a drover. His tranquillity became more pronounced and more extraordinary as the excessive severity of the disaster became more certain.

Tranquillity for an hour, perhaps! But what did that matter? He had no suspicion of it. He found that he was strong in the face of disaster. Ah! she could make up her mind to go? She was laughing at me? Very good! I have no need of her, the vagabond! I have seen through the sorceress! I know her, I know her! Good-evening!

He rose, to return home. As he raised his head, he saw the gitana—five hundred yards ahead of him.—Her back was turned to him, and she was walking tranquilly along.

In a twinkling, he was in the saddle. "Stop!" Blanchet, smarting under a blow from the stirrup-leather, flew over the ground, making the sand and stones fly, snorting with wrath as the spur tore his flank. In four minutes they made half a league. The gipsy, still in front, with her back turned to them, walked quietly along. It was her orange handkerchief, her copper crown, her undulating gait. It was certainly she!

Suddenly, when she reached the shore of a pond, she walked out, with the same tranquil step, upon the surface of the water, which bore her weight as if it were covered with ice; while, not far away, a large brig, decked out with flags, was bearing down upon him, with all sail set, through the furze-bushes and prickly oaks of Crau, across the arid fields.

Renaud sadly hung his head. The brig explained it all. It was all a spectre due to the mirage! Discouragement came upon the man and crushed him.

Thus, all the strength he had expended, his shameful acceptance of such a love, his toilsome day of fruitless search, after the mad ride of the preceding night, the exhaustion of horse and rider, all came to an end in the endless trickery of the mirage!

The sorceress must be far away! And in what direction? There was nothing for him to do but abandon the pursuit. He retraced his steps to the Icard farm. The fruitlessness of the effort affected him more keenly than the effort itself.

He no longer looked about, he no longer thought, he no longer loved or hated. Weariness had suddenly fallen upon his shoulders and his loins like a weight too heavy to be borne. He rode on, bent almost double, swaying like an inert thing, with the motion of his horse. He felt as if he were falling from a great height in a sort of sick man's dream. His eyes, worn out with gazing over the fields and scrutinizing every bush, closed in spite of him. His nerveless hand knew not where the reins were; nor did his brain know what had become of his ideas.

Blanchet went forward mechanically, with his head almost touching the ground. He, too, was without will-power, overdone, exhausted, his eyes injected with blood; his breath was short and quick, and his flanks beat the charge.

At another time, the careful horseman, who loved his beasts, would very quickly have noticed that his horse's wind was broken, when he felt his sides rise and fall with that short, hard, jerky breath; but Renaud was conscious of nothing. There was nothing in his head but a burning void. He did not even long for shade or rest. He was suffering from the utter dejection that follows terrible crises, from the great sorrow caused by death, from hopeless despair. Overwhelmed as he was by his selfish weariness, if he had been capable of recognizing any sentiment in his mind, he would have found there a vague, cowardly feeling of annoyance at having to enter a sick-chamber, at having to witness the spectacle of Livette's suffering. He would have liked—but he had not the strength to do it—to dismount from his horse, to lie down in the fresh air, under a tamarisk, and sleep there a long, long time; to forget himself, to cease to see or speak or hear or listen or exist!—He was like one walking in his sleep.

Suddenly Blanchet stopped, and began to tremble in every limb, and, before his rider had come to his senses, his four legs, planted stiffly like stakes, seemed to be broken by a single blow, and he fell in a heap.

Renaud awoke, standing on his feet beside his fallen horse. Blanchet was dying. It was soon over. The honest creature opened, to an unnatural width, his great glazed eyes, green as the stagnant water in the swamps, and filled with that wondering expression which the infinite mystery of living or of having lived imparts to the gaze of little children, animals, and dying men; he straightened out his four legs, trembling like the reeds in the marshes. A shiver ran over his whole body, riddled with the stings of a myriad of gnats and great flies, some of which flew up into the air and settled down again in the corners of the dim, wide-open eyes. Then the poor creature became motionless, with an indefinable something that was alarming and terrible in his immobility, something that put joy to flight, that seemed to imply finality. It was death. Blanchet had ended his humble Camarguese life in the open desert, in the bright sunlight. Livette's horse was dead in the service of Renaud's passion for Zinzara!

The faithful beast did not know what had happened; he did not know the reason of the forced journeys, the multiplied wounds inflicted by Renaud's spurs, by the stings of the gadflies, and by Zinzara's pin, buried in his flesh; he had submitted, without a murmur, to the destiny that bade him suffer at the hands of those who might have made life pleasanter for him, and, as he lay dead, his eyes still expressed his endless amazement at his failure to understand what was expected of him.

It was all over. He was dead. The affectionate creature had fallen a victim to the violence and malignity of human passions. Man had betrayed him for a woman's sake. And now his graceful form, made for swift movement, was infinitely sad to see, because the eye could see clearly all that there was in its immobility contrary to the purpose for which it was designed—and irreparable.

Renaud gazed stupidly at him.—He saw again, like so many reproachful words, Blanchet's last look, his short, rapid breath, the shudder that ran over his bleeding skin. And, restored to his senses by this unforeseen catastrophe which awoke a thousand salutary thoughts in his mind, he felt his heart grow soft. He burst into tears.

Thus Blanchet served his mistress still by his death. "Everything is of some use," said Sigaud.

Renaud stooped and returned, upon his still warm nostrils, the kiss he had received from him on the day of his first despair; then, having removed the saddle and bridle and concealed them in a safe place, he returned on foot to the Icard farm, with an intense, affectionate desire to do his utmost to care for and comfort poor Livette, for the death of her horse brought him back to her more quickly than anything else could have done.

He promised himself that he would return and bury Blanchet, but he did not have time. The good horse belonged to the vulture and the eagle.

In the evening of that same day, while Livette, sleeping soundly, seemed to everybody to be out of danger,—while Renaud lay, like a dog, in front of her door, determined to defend and save her,—Zinzara arrived at the Alyscamps at Arles.

There, thinking that Renaud might, with the devil's assistance, succeed in overtaking her,—although she may have had her reasons for thinking that his horse was not in condition for service at that time,—she left her house on wheels, in order that she might not be taken by surprise therein like a wild beast in its lair,—not from fear, but because she was desirous, before all else, not to see him again. She went to the farther end of the Allée des Alyscamps, between the rows of tall poplars, amid the stone monuments, and lighted a fire of twigs, to give her light enough to look about and select a spot where she could sleep comfortably.

She went there late, when the lovers who congregate there on May evenings, to make love upon the tombs, had returned to the sleeping city.

Along the whole length of the avenue, between the tall, straight poplars, run two rows of sarcophagi, some very high, with massive lids, others low and without lids, with a few scattered blossoms, sown by the wind, at the bottom. The dead who once slept there were sent down to Arles in sealed urns, abandoned to the current of the Rhône by the cities farther up the river. Now flowers are springing from their dust; and their open tombs are nothing more than beds for vagabonds and lovers.

By the bright light of her fire, which cast her shadow, enormously exaggerated, upon the wall of the ruined chapel, Zinzara selected her couch. She tossed an armful of grass and leaves upon the bottom of a sarcophagus; and, while the nightingale, who builds his nest there every year, was singing for dear life, the strange creature slept peacefully, with her face to the sky, trusting in her destiny; and, as a ray of moonlight fell upon her calm face with its closed eyelids, the sorceress resembled her black mummy, which concealed and idealized corruption—embalmed beneath a golden mask.

XXIV

IN THE GARGATE

When he received Zinzara's message from the gipsy child, Rampal, who was still suffering from his fall of a few days before, did not think of going in person to surprise Renaud. He did better than that. He went at once to Livette, and told her of the rendezvous at the cabin.

"Your lover, Livette, who defends you so fiercely against a harmless kiss, is with a woman to-night—you ought to be able to guess who she is—in the Conscript's Hut, near the Icard farm."

As Livette stood aghast, with pale cheeks, he continued:

"Your father has good horses; if you want to see for yourself, you can. It will be worth your while."

"Thanks, Rampal," said Livette.

Not for an instant did she doubt the truth of what he told her, and she said to her father:

"Go with me to the Icard farm, father, as you know the people there. Let us go to the Icard farm at once; my happiness depends on it. There is something there that I want to see to-morrow morning."

The poor man did not understand, but he always yielded to her caprice. They set out at once for the Château d'Avignon.

They left the wagon at the château; they harnessed the best pair of horses to the cabriolet, and made seven or eight leagues without stopping.

"Thanks, father. I must be here to-morrow morning. I will tell you why——"

It was eleven o'clock at night.

When all were in bed, Livette, being familiar with "the place," which her father had pointed out to her anew at her request,—Livette furtively left the house to prowl about the spot where disaster awaited her, for love knows no obstacles, and we follow our destiny through everything, and rush on to death in pursuit of our last sorrow.

And then?—Ah! throughout the visions of her sick-bed Livette constantly lived over that terrible moment when she was prowling around the swamp. In truth, she was still there, in agony of mind.

About the swamp, in the darkness, Livette hovered like a sea-gull in distress. Like a lost soul from hell she flitted about the edges of the bog, trying to pierce with her gaze the dark clumps of reeds and tamarisks.

From time to time, according to the spot from which she looked, she could see the gray roof of the cabin, silvered by the moonlight.

Was any one there? Had Rampal told her the truth? Ought she to lose this opportunity of convincing herself with her own eyes of Renaud's treachery?

Should she give her life to a traitor without endeavoring to unmask him, although warned? With her widely dilated eyes, she imagined that she saw lights that did not exist; or—if she did really see a feeble gleam through the chinks in the door—she refused to believe her eyes.

The blood was tingling in her ears, and she thought she could hear voices. It seemed to her at times as if her head were bursting. She could see, inside her head, beneath her skull, a great white light, and in the centre of the light Renaud and the gipsy together. Oh! to think of not finding out!

And, if it should be so, what should she do?

The essential thing was to find out. Afterward, she would see. If she were strong enough, if she could do it—she would certainly kill the woman.— How? Livette did not know. Simply with a look, perhaps.—Madness rises from the swamps with the miasmatic exhalations at night. Livette felt that she was going mad.

"How do you get to the cabin?" she had asked her father.

Ah! yes, the path is marked by stakes, is it not? To the left of the stakes is the path. She cannot see the tops of the stakes in the dark water. Frogs were sitting on them, perhaps, to look at the moon; or turtles on those that were just level with the surface. But no, it was grass that covered them all. And Livette's eyes ached with her endeavors to open them wider in the darkness, and find some sign upon the indistinct objects about her.

But suppose Rampal had deceived her?

At one time, it seemed to her that she could hear something resembling the gipsy music that made the snakes dance—but so weak! Surely it was in her poor, tired head,—for if it had been the real music, all the reptiles in the swamp would have come out to dance, all at once, in the moonlight.

Bah! Why should she be afraid? As if there were so very many of the creatures in the country! They are not fond of the salt in the bogs, nor the high winds.

She hovered about the swamp like a sea-gull lost at sea!

"Yes, yes, this is the way, here is the path under the water and the stakes that mark it! I must keep the stakes at my right as I walk along."

She starts to take the first step, and dares not—but suddenly the sound of voices comes to her ears. She distinguishes two voices—two!—beyond any question. And now it is surely the metallic sound of the tambourine that floats through the reeds in the moonlight, bringing to her heart the frightful vision of the other's joy!

She will go. After all, since her unhappiness is certain, what matter if she die of it! Ah! how bitter would be his punishment if, on coming out, at daybreak, he should find her there, drowned!

She makes a step; she sinks! but she does not cry out. No, she will extricate herself unaided—she must. She clings to the long grass, to the reeds which break in her hands. She is sinking! Ah! God! is she to die there? They would be too well pleased, aye, both of them, to have caused her death! Therefore she must not die! She will not! She struggles, and sinks deeper. As she lifts one foot, she rests her weight on the other, which goes down, down, and the ooze gains upon her. It rises to her waist; and still she cannot refrain from raising her feet, one after the other, as if to climb an imaginary stairway, the solid ladder that she dreams of but cannot find!

With every upward effort she sinks lower; it is horrible. Her hands are so small that she does not grasp enough grass, enough reeds, at once! Everything about her yields, everything fails to give support. How the reeds break between her fingers! like grass threads! It seems to her that clammy creatures are rubbing against her legs, her hands—ah! yes, the snakes—the bloodsuckers! She will be eaten alive by the bloodsuckers.—But where is the stake, near the edge of the swamp, that she thought she saw a moment ago? She lets go the grass to which she is clinging, with the result that she sinks deeper, still deeper. Now the cold water submerges her bosom, surrounds her neck, crawls up toward her mouth. Will she be compelled in a moment to drink that filthy water? At that thought, she makes one final effort. Her dishevelled locks cling about her neck, as if to strangle her, all drenched and cold and slimy, like veritable snakes!—She struggles, tosses her hands about this way and that—until one of them comes in contact with the wooden stake, firmly planted in the ground.—Saintes Maries!—She seizes it, twines her fingers about it, digs her nails into it, and does not relax her hold. Nor will she, even when she is dead! But her arm no longer has the strength to raise her, and her head falls heavily back—her eyes close. Is this death?—It was at that moment, just as she lost consciousness, that the brave-hearted maid cried out,—not until then. And her cry rang out over the swamps, like the call of the birds of passage, which ceaselessly, over all the waters upon earth, seek the repose that can never be found.

That ghastly vision recurred again and again to Livette, while the women of the Icard farm were busying themselves, a little too noisily, around her bed. At last, there was silence in her room. She saw her father come in, but she did not choose to explain anything to him. She sent word to the grandmother not to be anxious, that she would return home in three days. Livette asked to see Renaud. Her father went to find him. She closed her eyes.

She fancied that she could remember, now, certain things that happened to her during her sleep of death in the *gargate*, but were not reproduced in her dream. She felt Renaud's arms lifting her out of the mire, and that, after all, is the one thing to be desired, more than life itself—the protection of the man she loved, her lover's mourning for her, thinking that she was dead.—But before that, a moment before, had she not felt the weight of a fixed gaze upon her?—She had looked dimly forth between her drooping eyelids, through her long lashes which seemed to her like a thick grating; and she fancied that she saw the gipsy, the ill-omened gitana, standing before her. "Yes, it is she, it is really she. She is standing here beside me. She looks very, very tall. Her head touches the sky. She is on the path leading to the cabin. She is just coming from the rendezvous. She has been kissing Renaud! When will he come? Will the witch's black shadow, standing so straight there, never go? What more do you want, witch? Don't you see that I am dead? I must make you think I am dead. Then you will leave me, at last!—The wicked woman is always smiling. Ah! there she goes.—How heavy her glance was! And how tall she was! She kept all the light from me. Now I can see the sky again. Is it you, Renaud, is it you, Jacques, who take me in your arms as if I were dead?—It is you, at last!"

Thus cried poor Livette, delirious once more. But Renaud was sitting beside her bed with his face in his hands, listening to her.

"It is you," she went on; "you think me dead, and I can feel you take me in your arms and quickly carry me away. But why do you not weep, when you see me so? It is you, at last! I am dead, and still I feel you. You have me in your arms. Your heart beats fast. Mine has ceased to beat. Where were you, bad boy? What did you say to her? But that is past and gone!—Is that woman very dear to your heart?—Why do you come no more to my father's house in the evening? He is very fond of you. Grandma is a dear old soul. Do you see how faithful she is to her dead husband? People knew how to love one another better in her day, she says. Is it true? Do you believe it, Jacques? And if I die, won't you keep my memory sacred, as she keeps grandpa's?—Why do you make me suffer so?—Are we two never to walk under the great elm again? Our pretty stone bench under the rose-bushes is very sad now, and lonely like a tombstone. Ah! if you had chosen! I was pretty, yes, pretty,

pretty! And now I shall be ugly. For I have done with life, even if I am not dead. My life is at an end, at an end!"

XXV

THE PHANTOM

Livette, who had been carried back to the Château d'Avignon many days before, had not left her bed. The fever clung to her obstinately. Nothing could be done.

Was it really true, O God, that she was doomed to die, and he to see it? Was he to lose the future he had dreamed of, a future of unruffled happiness, of love and peace, as her husband; the joy he had known for such a brief space, of having a woman, sweet and dear and helpless as a child, to cherish and protect?—Was he condemned never to know the pleasure of having a family —a pleasure that had been denied to him, an orphan, and of which he had often dreamed as of one of the joys of Paradise—was he condemned never to know it, because he had forgotten his longing for a single day? The picture, dear to country-folk, of the chimney with the smoke curling upward, that seems to say to them, as far as it can be seen: "The soup is hot, the wife is waiting, the children are calling," recurred sometimes to his mind, and he sighed profoundly.

The punishment that he saw coming upon him did not seem to him proportionate to the offence. There was no justice in it!

What is the meaning of that most terrible of all mysteries: that the love of the senses is more powerful than the love of the heart when separated from its object, even though the last be recognized as the more certain and the sweeter?

Between the lofty chapel and the subterranean crypt of the church of Saintes-Maries-de-la-Mer, on the level of human life, does the miracle come always from below? And if it be so, is it any less a miracle? Which of you has fathomed the meaning of life? Who can say: "It is unjust," or: "It is useless," or: "What I do not see does not exist"? Who can say if Livette's sufferings and Renaud's, their troubles and their heart-burnings, all the invisible and inexplicable movements within themselves,—of which they knew nothing,— were not preparing the way for realities inconceivable to our minds? The *ideal*, the dream of what is best, is the essential condition of the *material* development of mankind. No force is wasted; everything is transformed. "Everything is of some use," said the old shepherd Sigaud. "It takes all kinds to make a world."

Livette had forgiven Renaud, Renaud had not forgiven himself.

Sometimes he gazed at her, deeply moved, and he suffered with her for hours at a time. Sometimes he had sudden fits of rage against her—paroxysms of wickedness, as it were. Was she not an obstacle in his path? At such times, he believed that he was possessed by a devil, and he would kneel by Livette's bed and pray to the saints, the women of compassion.

Ah! how thin she was! Her eyes seemed to have grown larger, and to have changed from blue to black, because the pupils were still dilated. Her long, fair hair no longer shone. It seemed as if the muddy water of the swamp had taken away its gloss forever.

She often started at noises that she imagined she heard.

She, who in the old days used to talk but little, was constantly telling of the things she had dreamed, and she would be vexed if they were not remembered.

The doctors of Arles tried everything. Nothing was of any avail.

"I want no more of their medicine," she said one day to Renaud. "They might do very well for swamp fever, but there is something else the matter with me. It was my heart that you drowned. I never could believe you again; it is much better that I should die."

She had explained nothing to her father or grandmother.

"They would have turned you out of the house," she said, "and I wanted to see you to the end."

Her journey to the Icard farm, her nocturnal flight, her accident, all were attributed to an attack of fever, which was supposed to have been responsible for her actions, whereas, on the contrary, her illness was the result of them all.

Renaud, by a desperate effort, mastered his passion at last. Was it forever? He chose to think so, because it was necessary that it should be so, in order to keep her alive.

He tried not to think of the other. He tried to repent. Every moment he tore from his mind by an exertion of his will—as he would tear up grass with his hand—some one of his memories. He told amusing stories, pretending to laugh loudest at them.

His heart was filled with a great pity for Livette, but, for all that, you would not have had to lift a very large stone to find there, in a spot that he knew well, the sleeping viper.

"I shall die, I shall die!"—Livette often said, "but I want to see the fête of

Saintes-Maries once more. I want to live till then. You must carry me there and lay me on the relics; that is where I want to die. And at my burial, I want the drovers, your comrades, to follow on horseback—promise me this—with their spears reversed, like the soldiers I saw at Avignon one day, marching to the cemetery, holding their guns that way."

With a sort of gaiety, she often recurred to the subject of her burial, and embellished it with other details, saying, with the air of a playful child:

"There must be lilies, as there are in the procession at Saintes-Maries when they go to bless the sea; I want lots of lilies! Lilies are so pretty and white! they are so proud on their stalks, and they smell so sweet!"

Meanwhile, the season was hastening away; the months came and went, like the same months in years past for centuries.

Summer set the sky and land and sea ablaze, drawing the last drop of moisture from the swamps, sowing the venomous seeds of miasma in the heavy air that people breathed. The crops ripened; then came the harvest. It was autumn. The redbreast sang in the park of the Château d'Avignon. The nights grew long once more. The leaves fell. The sad days of the year began.

The buttercups had disappeared. The Vaccarès, which had been dry all summer, no longer exposed to the sun its lovely mouse-gray bed; it was once more a sea. The light golden tint of the September sky was long since hidden from sight behind the rising mists.

The birds of passage began anew their flight over the mirror-like island which promised them abundant prey. The eagle hurried from the Alps to make war upon the fish-hawks. And at night, when the wind howled and the rain fell in torrents, the storks and cranes and geese passed over in triangular flocks, at a great height in the drenched atmosphere, uttering cries like cries of alarm.

Livette's suffering became more intense. She passed whole days sitting at her window.

One evening, Renaud was sitting beside her, in silence, while the grandmother and Père Audiffret were dining in the room below. The room was dimly lighted by a lamp. Suddenly Livette sprang to her feet, then fell back, crying:

"There she is! there she is! No! no! don't go with her! I don't want you to! no, no, Jacques!"

Renaud also had risen, and was staring vacantly at Livette; following the direction of her gaze, he began to tremble. Outside the window stood a pale, uncertain, but very recognizable spectre, the gipsy herself! He had no sooner recognized her than she disappeared, after making a significant sign to him, that said: "Come!"

It was not a vision of the sick girl's imagination, for he, too, had seen it!

Perhaps the fever-laden island had sown its poison in the blood of both. The germs of fever were taking root and flourishing in them. The blight of the *paluns* implanted in their brains, as in a cloudy mirror, the image everlastingly repeated of the familiar plaintive objects of the desert, with which the current of their thoughts was mingled.

"Don't go! don't go! my Jacques!"

She dragged herself along the floor on her knees, shaken with sobs, imploring the drover, as she clung with both hands to his jacket.

The father and grandmother had hastened to the room.

The father, too, was sobbing, and knew not what to do. The grandmother slowly seated herself by the bed on which Renaud had gently laid Livette.

Calm and silent, the old woman gazed long and with a beautiful expression of perfect trust upon the copper crucifix and the images of the saints that hung on the wall of the recess.

And, on the bed, Livette, uttering cries like a lost bird, twining her fingers about her as if clinging to life, to the reeds in the swamp wherein she still fancied that she was drowning—Livette breathed her last.

Livette was dead.

The drovers, on horseback, with spears reversed, attended her body to the cemetery. Her favorite dog followed her thither.

Renaud placed lilies on her grave. She sleeps in the cemetery of Saintes-Maries, at the foot of the dunes, under the cultivated lilies, among the wild asphodels, on the sea-shore.

Renaud returned to the desert, too much like the bull that, when wounded in the arena, returns to the solitude of the swamps, where he can lick his wounds, give free vent to his rage, bellow at the clouds, and to no purpose, but to his heart's content tear at the steel left in the wound.

One day they found, on the shore of the Vaccarès, Rampal's bleeding body, pierced by horns in two places. Bernard alone saw his duel with Renaud one evening, when the sky was red with the afterglow. They fought hand to hand, in the midst of the drove, and Renaud, lifting his enemy from the ground in his arms, laid him face upward, dead, on the horns of a heifer that came rushing at them and, with one motion of her bulky head, tossed a corpse into the air.

Rampal died without a cry. He lay three days where he fell. The black bulls, that mourn nine days when one of their kind falls dead in the pasture, bellowed for three days around Rampal's body, at a respectful distance.

Bernard alone saw the duel and said nothing; but the people of the desert knew; they guessed the truth.

Since that, Renaud has become like a phantom himself.

In all weathers, summer or winter, rain or shine, he can be seen here and there, in the Camargue desert, sitting erect and melancholy on his horse, spear in hand.

He regrets Livette. He loves Zinzara. He weeps only for himself, the wretched creature! He has lost the paradise of affection he had dreamed of, and the appetizing hell of savage love he had tasted. He has nothing. It seems to him that Livette's death, for which he blames himself, has left him free to abandon himself to his passion for the other; but the other is absent—and, though absent, she tortures him as relentlessly as on the day when, clinging to his horse's mane, she defied him with insulting words, and aroused his passions, while he dared not shake her off, trample upon her, or seize her.

The memory of her is upon him like the gadfly that persists in following back the bloody track of its sting. Vainly does he shake himself; he cannot rid himself of it. Renaud loves Zinzara; he longs for her without hope, and, ruled by that single desire, he feels no other, so that the unexpended power of his youth accumulates within him and drives him mad.

The friends' houses, the fêtes he used formerly to visit, have no further interest for him, because the only being he seeks cannot be found. The desert, once peopled with hopes in his eyes, has become an empty void. The roads that traverse it no longer lead anywhere.

He surprises himself sometimes, at night, bellowing with the bulls, against the wind that annoys them, toward the distant horizon. He is like one possessed. A devil dwells within him.

When he is weary of wandering about and of being in the saddle, and chooses to lie down and sleep for a day, he repairs to the cabin of his love, in the *gargate*, and there, full sure of being undisturbed, raves like a wild beast, in his frenzy at being alone. In the morning, he emerges from his retreat, more depressed, more miserable, more haunted with visions than ever.

At times, he fancies that he sees Livette under his horse's feet, imploring wildly, with hands outstretched—but he digs his spurs into his horse and rides on. A terrible shriek constantly rings in his ears.

He rides toward another spectre that calls him from the farthest point of the horizon.—He says, to any one who cares to listen, that he has come from Egypt, where he was a king, and that he will return there some day, King of Camargue.

His disordered mind seems the very incarnation of the wild moor. He fancies that he is flying about in circles with the birds of the swamps that weep in the drizzling rain. The *mistral* lashes his wings. When the wind blows through his hair, he pities the poor grass of the plains because the *mistral* is torturing it.

All the lamentations of the reeds and swamps, of the river and the sea, are but the ringing in his ears, and their loud wailing is constantly punctuated by a shriek—oh! so heart-rending it is!—the shriek of Livette!

As the bell-tower of the church of Saintes-Maries is filled with owls, so his heart is full of the remorse of a Christian; and the curé's kindness to him does not drive it away.

When he stands upon the sea-shore, many times he feels an overpowering desire to urge his horse, bleeding beneath the spur, far out to sea, farther and farther, until he vanishes in the direction of the country, vaguely seen in dreams, from which the saints and gipsies come—but something stops him; his destiny holds him back; he belongs to his kingdom.

If he has known one hour's peace of mind, it was on a certain morning when, among the usual hideous nightmares inspired by the memory of Zinzara, he had a pleasant dream, in which he saw Livette, dressed in white, with lilies in her hands like the saints in church pictures, smiling and saying to him: "I have forgiven you. FORGIVE YOURSELF."

The respite was of brief duration, for the herdsman did not know that excessive repentance is a crime, when it goes so far as to dry up the springs of will-power in a man, when it renders sterile his field of activity, when it bars the way to doing better in the future.

Self-pardon, at the proper time, after due penance has been done, is one of the secrets of the wise among men; for, without it, the first misstep would lead to never-ending despair, and would render all courage useless forever.

Such was the curé's opinion, which Renaud listened to, in the confessional, without paying heed to it.

He suffers, therefore, incessantly, awaiting the hour when his suffering shall be allayed. He is like the camping-grounds abandoned by shepherds and flocks, the *jasses* of the desert, still black from an old conflagration, and surrounded by briers where rose-bushes once flourished. He is like the aloes that wither instantly in desolation, after the stalk their love has caused to bloom has risen high into the air.

The dream in which Renaud saw Livette was explained to him several times by Monsieur le curé, but always to no purpose.

How, indeed, could his remorse cease, when his passion still endured, and when he was constantly committing anew, in desire, the sin that caused all the misery?

My friends, there is but one wise course to pursue: "Plant a tree, build a house, rear a child. Be patient—everything comes in due time. The thing that does not happen in a hundred years, may happen in six thousand. The future is still yours!"

When Renaud, in the dreams of his unhealthy life, feels, as he sometimes does, that his love is stronger in him than his passion, it seems to him as if Livette were drawing him toward death, but truthful, kindly beings never inspire thoughts of self-destruction.

Of one thing, at least, he is certain. He feels that voluntary death would not remove him from the circle of the accursed. He would, on the contrary, descend still lower in the spiral pit of mortals damned by love.

They say that persons drowned in the Rhône, borne along without doubt by the irresistible current, which brings them all together at the mouth of the river, return, on certain evenings, to hold a carnival of despair on the surface of the water.

Happy are they since they are, on those occasions, united.

But they who are drowned in stagnant waters, and they who, to join them, die by their own hand, are never aught but solitary spectres. They seek each other all the time, but always unavailingly. They are the souls of the damned. They wander through the desert, calling to one another; but never even approach or see one another; and at night, in the deserts of Crau and Camargue, the traveller hears long-drawn, wailing cries, flying unavailingly hither and thither over the vast plains, forever and forever.

Even the clouds call and answer one another in their aerial flight.